Left Behind

a novel

EMMALINE HOFFMEISTER

"The world needs more boys with reputations like The Wilde Boys."

"A heartbreaking journey so profound it will change you."

"Hoffmeister's writing is heartfelt and heartbreaking."

"Hoffmeister has a gift for developing flawed characters and their emotionally wrenching dilemmas."

"A beautifully layered story."

"The emotional journey is made more engrossing by the descriptive language of Hoffmeister's lyrical writing."

"*Left Behind* will resonate with readers who love a tale full of heart and soul."

"I cried chapter after chapter. *Left Behind* broke my soul before piecing it back together in a whole new way. I will never be the same again."

"I absolutely could not put this fabulous book down. I treasured every word and was left yearning for more."

"I cherished every word of *Left Behind*—it should be on everyone's must-read list. Devastating, poignant, haunting, and tragically beautiful."

ISBNs
eBook: 978-1-936850-23-5
Paperback: 978-1-936850-24-2
Hardcover: 978-1-936850-32-7

Jacket, cover, and interior design by Emmaline Hoffmeister
Editing by PWA Editing Services
Cover image © Shyanni / Pixabay
Section break illustration © Giuseppe Ramos G @gstudioimagen / Canva
Recipe illustration © Elena Malgina / Adobe Stock
Fonts EB Garamond, Josefin Sans, and Slight
Author photo © MJ Hodges Photography

For permissions requests, write to the publisher at:
Rhemalda Publishing
c/o Author Emmaline Hoffmeister
101 Rainbow Dr. #9867, Livingston, TX 77399

For Aldrich and Darce
Having an author for a mom
isn't always the dreamy life it
sounds like—it's a lot tougher
than having a *normal* mom.

I believe in heaven, we have the
chance to choose our families.
And with all my heart, I
am eternally grateful that you
chose to journey through this
life of adventure and live/love
alongside dad and me.

And for the Cauayan
Philippines Mission
For embracing our Elder with
love and support during the
best two years FOR his life.

Contents

CHAPTER ONE 1

CHAPTER TWO 21

CHAPTER THREE 34

CHAPTER FOUR 46

CHATER FIVE 58

CHAPTER SIX 74

CHAPTER SEVEN 89

CHAPTER EIGHT 99

CHAPTER NINE 112

CHAPTER TEN 126

CHAPTER ELEVEN 139

CHAPTER TWELVE 150

CHAPTER THIRTEEN 160

CHAPTER FOURTEEN 177

CHAPTER FIFTEEN 192

CHAPTER SIXTEEN 210

CHAPTER SEVENTEEN 225

CHAPTER EIGHTEEN 242

CHAPTER NINETEEN 259

CHAPTER TWENTY 269

CHAPTER TWENTY-ONE 280

Apple Butter Recipe 302

Apricot Chipotle Sauce Recipe 305

Herbed Tomato Jam Recipe 308

Endnotes 311

Left Behind

a novel

CHAPTER ONE

WINTER HAD FIRMLY ENTRENCHED its presence in my tiny town in the foothills of the Cascade Mountains. Nestled between the mountains in the Wenatchee River Valley, it lay beneath a thick blanket of snow, transforming the landscape into a silent, pristine wonderland. The town, with its modest collection of homes, a few local shops, and the ever-present scent of pine, was bustling with tourists on their way to Leavenworth for the tree lighting. Like clockwork, the first Saturday in December, our little town transformed from its usual liveliness to extreme hecticness.

Riverbend Farmstand, the adorable farm-fresh mercantile my parents had been taking me to since birth, and where I now worked, was bursting at the seams with families all day. Half a dozen times, I found lost toddlers crying in corners and walked hand-in-hand with them around the shop, asking them if the statues of Santa gnomes or wooden reindeer were their parents. Their exasperated *"no's"* would dry their tears until, on cue, they flung themselves into the arms of their parents, some of whom hadn't even realized their little one was missing.

A win for today was when I kept my composure long enough to stop a pre-teen from squeezing copious amounts of marionberry-flavored honey into his mouth straight from the sample honey bear. Forget the tiny tester spoons we offered in little jars around the displays—he was full-on guzzling. To be fair, it was thoughtful of him to make sure his lips didn't touch the bear. Instead, he held the container high above his head, squeezing the honey bear's belly and letting a stream of honey land in his mouth. When his mom heard me ask him to stop and noticed what he was doing, she took control by shrieking, "Joseph Nathan Archer, what do you think you're doing?"

Everyone, and I mean everyone, turned to witness the spectacle. Joseph jerked his face towards his mother mid-stream, drizzling a trail of dark purple honey down the front of his shirt and onto the farmstand floor. She snatched the honey bear from his sticky hands and tossed it at me.

With a now humiliated Joseph under his mom's care, I retreated around the corner and down to the far end of the jam and jelly aisle. I bent over in laughter, holding my side. It hurt to keep it in. When I was ten, it had been my fondest wish to do the same thing. But since I'd grown up coming here, I knew my mom would box my ears if I tried it. Given the opportunity, I would've done the same thing, except I would've chosen the huckleberry flavor. It's the best flavor on Earth.

"Excuse me, do you work here?" I glanced up and locked eyes with a young woman my age. I straightened up, and said, "Yes, I do. How can I help you?"

She pointed to the top shelf where jars of Apple Butter were neatly displayed, just out of her reach. "Can you grab one for me? I can't find a stool."

"We don't keep stools out for safety reasons, but I'd be happy to help." I reached for a half-pint jar and handed it to her.

"Could I get the larger one instead?" she asked, and I swapped it for a pint.

In a hushed voice, I leaned closer and spoke in a secretive, spy-like manner, "This stuff is great, but just between us, my mom's recipe is *amazing*."

Curiously, she raised an eyebrow. "Is that so? Can you prove it?"

"I could, but you don't seem familiar. Are you just visiting the valley?"

With a teasing smile, she replied, "Maybe. But what difference does that make?"

"If you're a tourist, I don't have time to prove it. You're only here for a day or two, right?"

She seemed surprised and asked, "How do you know I'm a tourist?"

"There are only eleven girls in town over the age of fourteen. I know them all." She giggled, a sound as light as the scarf around her neck.

"Only eleven? Poor thing. Maybe I should move here with my two sisters and make it fourteen."

"A whole family of beautiful sisters? The town might tip off its axis with that kind of charm." Her cheeks flushed a soft pink, and she fell silent. I reached for another jar, holding it out to her. "Here, try this one, too. It's Herbed Tomato Jam."

"Herbed Tomato Jam? Sounds unusual," she said, eyeing the jar skeptically.

"Don't let the name fool you. Picture this: herb crackers, a thick layer of cream cheese, and a spoonful of this jam on top. Trust me, it'll change your life."

She hesitated, but took the jar, wrinkling her button nose. "I'm not convinced."

"Anna," a voice called from behind her, "did you find the Apple Butter?"

She turned toward the voice, holding up the pint. "I did. And Noah here," she said, glancing at my name tag, "was just convincing me to try jam made from tomatoes and herbs."

"Recommending, not convincing," I corrected, offering her mother a smile as I repeated the cracker suggestion.

Her mother nodded with approval. "That does sound lovely. A combo of sweet and savory, just the way I like it." She put the jam in the shopping basket draped over her arm. "Do you have any other recommendations?"

I thought for a moment, considering their tastes. "Actually, yes." I led them to the sauces and pointed to a small jar with bright orange contents. "Apricot Chipotle Sauce, perfect on white fish. Even if the fish is a bit off or muddy-tasting, as my dad sometimes complains. This sauce will make you the best cook in the Pacific Northwest."

"Chipotle? Isn't that hot?" Anna's mother asked, hesitating.

I grabbed a jar, twisted off the ring, and used the edge to pop the seal. I offered them both a taste with small tester spoons from my apron. "It's strong on its own, but over fish, it's just right."

They tasted it, their faces lighting up. "Oh, this is good," Anna exclaimed.

"We'll take it," her mother added.

I grabbed a sealed jar and handed it to them.

"We can buy the one you opened, so it doesn't go to waste," Anna's mother said.

I screwed the lid back on and dropped it in my apron pocket, then winked. "Don't worry about that. I'll take it home. My dad loves this stuff."

"And your mom doesn't have a better recipe for this one?" Anna bantered with a playful glint.

I twisted the jar so the label was visible. "Wilde Growers. I'm Noah Wilde. This *is* my mom's recipe."

Her mother laughed and added another jar to the basket. "In that case, better make it two."

I walked them to the front, where the rest of their family waited. Ruth, the farmstand owner, rang up their items and carried on a light conversation with Anna's mother. "You chose wonderful flavors. These will really dress up your holiday meals."

I excused myself. With no customers left in the shop, I made sure the floors got a thorough cleaning, paying extra attention to the sticky spots in the honey section and spreading out a full twenty feet in every direction. That sticky honey mess was everywhere. Finally, it was time to go home.

As I bundled into my coat and prepared to leave, Ruth called out, "Noah, those girls sure thought you were something."

I grinned. "Just doing my job, Ruth."

She chuckled, shaking her head. "You and your brother, Jacob, have every girl in the state under your spell."

"Not every girl in the state, just the girls in our county!" I called back.

That's when I heard Harvey outright laugh. Harvey was Ruth's husband and partner in crime for forty years. In the cozy corner of the room, next to a pot-bellied stove, he relaxed in an antique wooden rocker, whittling a small stick he'd picked from the nearby woodpile. Little wood shavings littered his belly and the floor.

"Humble too," Harvey added.

Ruth waved her hand to shush him while she packed a few items into a beautiful woven basket. "Don't listen to him. Are you heading straight home tonight?"

"Yeah, it's movie night. Dad is picking tonight. I think we're watching *Ghostbusters*."

"That sounds perfect. Harvey loves that one too," Ruth said, with a nod toward her husband, who was still whittling in the corner but now also wore a grumpy frown. "Can you do me a favor on your way home?"

"Of course. Anything for you."

"Can you drop this off at Mrs. Bean's?"

"Sure thing." I took the basket and peeked inside: triple chocolate scone mix, double chocolate brownie mix, hot fudge sundae sauce, a dozen hot cocoa packets, and chocolate hazelnut pirouettes. "Looks like Mrs. Bean is getting her chocolate fix."

"Speaking of chocolate fixes, does your mom need anything? I swear, no one in the valley eats as much chocolate as your mom," Ruth said with a grin.

I laughed. "True! Nah, not today. I picked her up some contraband yesterday, and I noticed an unopened Amazon box on the counter before coming to work. I'd bet my life she added some sort of chocolaty delight to the order."

"That's it then. See you next Tuesday."

"I'll be here," I called over my shoulder as I carried the basket out to my truck.

The cold bit at my fingers as I fumbled with the key in the lock. When the door creaked open, it groaned in protest against the chill. I slid onto the worn leather seat, my breath fogging up the windshield as I started the truck. The engine coughed, hesitated, then rumbled to life in a slow, uneven rhythm. The dashboard lights flickered. Despite it only being six in the evening, darkness had already settled in the valley.

Snow crusted over the windshield, too thick for the wipers to handle. With a sigh, I reached behind the seat for my heavy-duty ice scraper, bracing myself as I climbed back out into the cold. The first few swipes with the brush end hardly made a dent, just squeaked against the frost. After a few minutes of steady scraping, the windshield, windows, and mirrors were clear.

I knew better than to rush it. My old truck needed time to warm up. Cold seeped into everything up here in the mountains, making metal stiff and brittle. I pulled my coat tighter around me. The fabric crackled as it brushed against the seat. The heater, like the engine, took its time. Patience, I reminded myself, was part of living here.

I reached into my pocket for my phone, hands trembling from the cold as I connected it to the portable speaker lying in the passenger seat. The pickup's radio hadn't picked up a decent channel in over two decades. The speaker blared to life, filling the cab with Christmas music: cheerful, bright, and wrong for a teenage male who just worked a busy Saturday.

"What in the world?" I muttered, noticing that my rock playlist had a dozen holiday songs added to the top. "Mom!" I grumbled, but no one heard. She'd gone and added all our family's favorite Christmas songs to the top of every playlist on our shared Spotify account.

I deleted the festive tunes from my playlist. Then I scrolled through my songs until I found something that matched the night: gritty, powerful, with a beat strong enough to rattle the windows. Naturally, I cranked it up. That's Dad's influence for sure. Don't tell anyone, but I know Mom blasts her late '90s nostalgia when she's driving alone, Nirvana, Creed, Alanis Morissette, Ace of Base, and even Nickelback. Sure, Dad claims it's his kind of music, but I've caught her pretending to prefer Amy Grant, Faith Hill, Mariah Carey, and Shania Twain ballads, like it's motherlier or something. She can't fool me. I know better, but I let her pretend.

I leaned back, feeling the warmth spread from the vents as the music pulsed through the truck. The defiant roar chased away the lingering cold. At last, the engine smoothed out, signaling the old girl was ready to go.

I rubbed my hands together, breathing on them for warmth before shifting the truck into reverse. I backed out of my favorite spot in the far corner of the farmstand lot. Parking way out here kept the snowplow attached out of the path of the customer's shins.

Highway 2, heading north into Leavenworth, was at a standstill. Lucky for me, I was going south. The traffic flowed, but at about a quarter of its normal speed. A couple of miles later, it thinned out when I made the turn onto Highway 97, and most of the remaining travelers continued toward Wenatchee. As I picked up speed, the open road stretched ahead, clear of traffic, until I reached the old road paralleling the highway. I slowed to a stop, dropped the plow, and cleared the side road for Mrs. Bean and her neighbors. Despite being next to the main highway, the county was slow to plow this stretch. Mrs. Bean would need a clear path to go to church tomorrow, and if I didn't plow it now, Dad would send me over, nice and early, before church.

Once, when she couldn't get her car out, she threw on her late husband's snowsuit over her Sunday best and rode his snowmobile along the ditch all the way to church. Mom had been fit to be tied when she found out, but Grandma Bean, what Jacob and I affectionately called her, loved every second. She told the story, with animation, to anyone who would listen. Jacob, then sixteen, drove the snowmobile home for her, grinning like he'd enjoyed it almost as much as she had.

I banged on her back door, the one with the sign that read, *Back Door Guests Are Best.* Then, cracking it open, I called, "Grandma Bean, it's Noah. You here?"

Of course, she was here. Her car was nestled in the barn. Every light in the house was blazing, and Bing Crosby was crooning through her vintage surround sound loud enough to wake the dead.

"There's my favorite Noah in the whole wide world!" she exclaimed, dancing into the kitchen just as I was unloading the basket and tucking her chocolate treats into the cupboard. I wrapped her in a tight hug, then twirled her twice, her laughter filling the room.

"Ruth told me she'd have you drop this off. You've saved me a world of trouble, my boy," she said, beaming as she eyed the goodies.

"You and Mom both. She's always asking me to 'bring home a little chocolate something.'"

"You can't blame us ladies for needing a chocolate fix now and then. Some say a bit of dark chocolate is good for the heart."

"So, what, a lot of milk chocolate's your way of making up the difference?" I teased.

She snapped her towel at me. "When did you get so full of spit and vinegar?"

"Who, me?" I quipped, catching the towel and pretending to flick it back at her, just for fun.

She laughed and turned on the electric kettle. "How about some cocoa?"

"I'd love some, but it's movie night. I need to get home. Everyone's waiting for me. Plus, you know Mom. She'll have cocoa with our treats." I closed the cupboard after putting away the last item and gave her another hug. "After I grab you some more wood," I added, noticing her stock by the fireplace in the adjoining room was running low.

"Thanks, Noah. You're a good boy," she said as I swapped my coat for her late husband's old work coat and lined leather gloves. I hurried out to the wood stack by the barn, grabbing as many chunks as I could carry. After two more trips, I was positive she had enough wood to last until midweek, when I'd be back again.

She hugged me tight and sent me on my way. I plowed the rest of the old highway until it reconnected with the main road. Then I raised the plow and gunned it onto the highway, urging the old beast to pick up speed before the approaching headlights got too close.

Just a few more miles stood between me and Canyon Road, where the orchards gave way to the mountains and my cherished home, Wilde Growers. My home, perched not far up Pendleton Canyon, was the last orchard in the valley. Up here, the wind howled with a ferocity only mountain dwellers understood. The isolation was both comforting and profound, as if the rest of the world had fallen away, revealing nature's raw beauty.

The wind swirled through the leafless trees of the frozen landscape, its keening cry slicing through the barren orchards. I lowered the plow to plow the stretch of road from the highway to our home.

Just beyond our orchard, the Cascade Mountains loomed like ancient sentinels, silent witnesses to the frozen valley below. The wind roared through their passes, a wild, untamed force that reverberated through the valleys and canyons, its voice echoing off the sheer cliffs and rocky outcrops.

Ice crystals glittered like shards of broken glass in my headlights, scattering in a thousand directions as the plow threw the snow aside. Beneath their sparkle, the cold seeped into my bones. It seemed winter, with its relentless snow and biting wind, was trying to swallow me whole. I reached over and cranked the heater higher, hoping for a little more warmth.

With the last stretch plowed, I stopped and lifted the plow attachment before heading up our driveway. The slight upward slope, combined with the position of the orchards and the mountains behind us, always left us with snow piled two feet deeper there than anywhere else on the property. Dad's truck was the only one powerful enough to handle plowing it; my little pickup could only manage on the way out. Pushing snow uphill was too much for the old girl, even if the incline was scarcely noticeable.

I gunned the pickup through the unplowed driveway. The tires spun, kicking up a spray of gravel and snow before finding traction. The drifts were so deep I had to bust through the last stretch in the true Wilde way, just like Dad taught me last year when I officially learned to drive *Gun 'er. Don't lose control and hold on for dear life.* I had been operating vehicles and farm equipment since I was too small to reach the pedals, but it wasn't until I turned sixteen that I was deemed officially qualified, so Dad made sure I knew how to do it right.

Orchards flanked the driveway on either side, their leafless apple, cherry, and apricot branches a comforting reminder of the place I'd called home all my life. As I navigated the long drive, the familiar sights of home came into view. Snowdrifts buried the old wooden fences that lined the yard. A lone light shone from the peak of the farthest shop on the property, and at the edge of my headlights stood our house, nestled amidst the trees. Its warmly lit windows glowed like beacons, and chimney smoke curled upward into the evening sky, promising warmth after a long day's work in town.

I drove over to the nearby shop where we kept the kids' truck. As I opened the door, the cold winter wind hit me hard. Up here on the mountain, it can drop another ten degrees within the space of a mile. A chill ran up my spine as I hurried to get the shop door open. I braced both feet against the frame and pushed with all my strength. Slowly, the door moved as the drifts pressing against it gave way. Once I got it open wide enough, I rushed back to the truck and pulled it inside.

Tiny white flakes pelted my exposed skin like sharp slivers of ice as I crossed the distance from the shop to the house. My teeth chattered, protesting against the cold that seeped into every fiber of my being. It seemed to penetrate all the way to the marrow of my bones. Each inhalation hit my chest like a punch, and with each exhalation, a frozen mist escaped my lips. I slogged my way to the house, pushing against the relentless attack of the wind. My coat did little to shield me from the icy assault, and my boots crunched as they sank into the thick snow. I wished I had warmer gloves; my fingers stiffened as if on cue.

At the front door, I let out a long breath, watching it form a cloud of fog in the air. My freezing fingers curled around the doorknob, and I threw the door open. A welcoming rush of warmth hit me, dispelling the tension that had built up in my body.

"My land, what was that?" Mom cried, startled by my sudden entrance. "Hey Buddy, welcome home," Dad said simultaneously, his voice warm and welcoming. Normally, Mom would've heard my rattly old pickup coming up the drive, but not today. The wind had swallowed the sound completely.

"Noah, come in. Get out of the cold," she called from the kitchen, waving me in. When the wind caught the door behind me and slammed it open, she pointed over my shoulder. "My goodness, it's a howler out there. Did you have any trouble getting home?"

Before I could respond, she smiled down at the pot she was stirring, then glanced at a cup on the counter. I nodded, shedding my snow-covered layers, thankful to be home and embraced by the warmth.

"No trouble, but I'm late because I dropped off some chocolate delights to Grandma Bean on my way home. I plowed her road and stocked her wood so she wouldn't have to go out."

"What a good boy you are," Mom said, handing me a cup of hot cocoa, heated to perfection. She gave her usual double head jerk to the left, her familiar signal for me to lean down so she could kiss my cheek. Someone ought to tell her that her head jerk looked more like a nervous twitch, but it would not be me.

Honestly, it's a charming quirk, uniquely hers. Besides, if I mentioned it, I might hurt her feelings, and that was the last thing I wanted. Hurting Mom's feelings meant enduring one of Dad's twenty-minute lectures about respecting women, not just Mom, but every female I've ever or would ever meet. I knew precisely how it would unfold and didn't want to sit through that spiel again. Yes, you heard me right, again. I've had that lecture before.

At sixteen, I may look like my mom, but I'm all Wilde, like my dad. I tower over her five-foot-one-and-three-quarters-inch frame. Yet that never stopped her from getting the kiss she wanted. I bent low, careful not to spill my cocoa, and let her kiss my cheek. Then she turned her face toward me, and I kissed that perfectly round little age spot on her right cheek. It's my favorite spot to give *Tinker Bell Kisses*, as our family calls them.

Jacob, my big brother, was five years old when he christened the kisses with that name, and it has stuck ever since. Most little boys that age adored Lightning McQueen or Paw Patrol, but not Jacob. His heart belonged to Tinker Bell. I still remember our family trip to Disneyland when he was six and I was four. We stood in line for what seemed like an eternity, waiting excitedly to see Tinker Bell. Just as we reached the front, an announcement informed us that her workshop had closed. The tears Jacob shed were monumental, great big crocodile tears. So many tears, I thought he might flood the entire theme park. He kept crying no matter what Mom, or I said, and especially not what Dad said. Jacob was inconsolable. To him, it was all dad's fault. Dad had insisted we go on the Buzz Lightyear ride first. After all, it was on the way to Tinker Bell's Workshop, and Dad was adamant about not backtracking in the Disneyland mayhem. Had we gone straight to Tinker Bell's, Jacob wouldn't have missed her, and he could have asked her on a date!

I made it worse when, in my youthful innocence, I declared, "You couldn't ask her on a date, anyway. You're not sixteen." Those were the rules: no dating until you were sixteen, no dating the same girl twice in a row, and only double or group dates until your mission. They ingrained the rules in us since birth. Mom grew up with the same rules, and she turned out great, so we should too.

Jacob's heartbreak lingered as a bittersweet reminder of childhood innocence and the simple wishes of a little boy. Even now, years later, every *Tinker Bell Kiss* carried a touch of that magic—a nod to a beloved fairy and a brother's sweet crush.

Oh, the memories one silly little kiss on Mom's cheek invoked. Of course, that little age spot wasn't there when I was four. In truth, I can't remember when I first noticed it, but when I did, I remembered thinking, *aww, look, proof of all our Tinker Bell Kisses right there on Mom's cheek.*

It made me wonder if she had the same affection for the age spot as I did. I doubted it. I'd caught her trying to cover it with makeup. It was pointless. You could still see it, but don't tell her that.

I about died with silent, gut-wrenching laughter the day I caught Mom securing lemon juice-soaked cotton balls to her face with Band-Aids, trying to lighten the spot. I ran to my room, jumped on my bed, buried my head in my pillow, and gasped with a silent yet uncontrollable belly laugh. You know the kind, silent, but your stomach jumps, and your chest shakes as you gasp for air that only comes in short, quick breaths. If you didn't stop laughing soon, you'd pass out from lack of oxygen and die from suffocation because your head was under the pillow, all so Mom wouldn't hear you.

I loved trips down memory lane. Speaking of which, that's what I found when I walked into the living room carrying my steaming mug of cocoa.

In the heart of our home, amidst the gentle crackle of the fire, my middle-aged father found solace in his leather recliner, a sanctuary where time seemed to slow its relentless march. His once raven-black hair now bore the marks of wisdom, strands of silver woven like threads of moonlight amidst the darkness, a testament to the years of laughter and hard work etched upon his countenance. When anyone mentioned his graying hair, he would tilt his head to the side and swipe his hand first along one side and then the other as he declared, "This side is for Jacob, and this one for Noah. I didn't have a single gray hair before I had kids." He loved to make everyone laugh with his trademark dad joke. That one was his favorite.

Dad's recliner propped up his feet under his favorite plush blanket, its comforting weight a shield against the chill of the night. His voice, deep and resonant, carried the weight of years of experience and wisdom.

Beside him, Jacob, now eighteen, reclined on the sofa. The pair, engrossed in conversation, sipped mugs of their own creamy chocolaty delight.

Jacob stood at the precipice of adulthood, his vibrant energy a stark contrast to our father's quiet strength as he talked about his mission possibilities. His laughter was infectious, his eyes ablaze with the excitement of his unknown mission location. Yet, beneath his youthful exuberance lay a depth of emotion that belied his tender years, a sensitivity inherited from our father. Despite the difference in age, their connection transcended generations, bound by a bond that only a family could forge. I wondered if I had that same strength and wisdom. I doubted I had it yet, but I prayed fervently it would come with time.

As I came up frpm behind them, the world outside seemed to fade into insignificance. With a heart brimming with gratitude, I bore witness to the unique perfection that defined us, the Wilde family. We are a mosaic of imperfections held together by the unbreakable bonds of love and devotion. Each member, with their quirks and idiosyncrasies, contributed to our combined resilience and strength. These moments reminded me of life's inherent goodness, a truth that transcended the trials and tribulations that beset us. Every hardship, every setback paled compared to the profound richness of familial love. For in the embrace of my loved ones, I found the courage to face life's challenges head-on, fortified by the knowledge that, no matter how arduous the journey, the Wilde family stood as an unyielding bastion against the tempests of fate.

With unwavering resolve, we stood united, our backs pressed together, fists raised in defiance against the vicissitudes of the world. We were not simply individuals but a collective force to be reckoned with, an embodiment of the enduring power of family.

I listened to catch their conversation topic and then smiled, realizing Dad was telling his usual mission stories. I'd heard them before, lots of times. Jacob's upcoming mission made them the most common conversation topic of late. Discussing Dad's experiences in the field wasn't a novelty. In fact, these stories had accompanied me all sixteen years of my life. Trust me, any life event has the potential to relate to one of Dad's mission stories. Any event, and I mean any event.

"You wait and see. Soon, you will have your own stories to tell," Mom shouted from the kitchen.

Dad's tales brought comfort. But if I'm honest, tonight, though I longed to plop on the other couch and join them, I wanted distance. For the first time, the stories pained me instead of bringing me happiness. Jacob would soon leave us, which hurt. Although Mom and Dad accepted it, I wasn't ready to let go.

Jacob had been a constant presence all my life. We were inseparable, my older brother and I, bound by an unbreakable bond that defied time and circumstance. From the moment I came into this world, he took on the role of my protector, my confidant, and my everything. I'd been told countless times that the second he met me, he declared me *his baby*, and that was it, our lives intertwined and became one. We were rarely called by our names, Jacob and Noah. No, around these parts, everyone called us *The Wilde Boys*.

Jacob had always been by my side, every single day of my life. Not once had we stayed anywhere without each other. I wasn't sure anyone other than me realized this. I didn't dare say it aloud, but I was terrified Jacob wouldn't be with me anymore. The impending two-year gap hung heavy in the air. It cast a shadow over our parallel existence. Two years, an eternity in my young life. A period where the threads of our lives would diverge, leading us down different paths. Jacob would venture left, and I would tread right. Two separate journeys awaited us, brimming with uncertainty and uncharted territories.

A deep ache settled in my heart now, as the time had come. Duty and destiny beckoned, signaling the time for him to fulfill one of his eternal callings: to champion Israel and Let God Prevail. *Hurrah for Israel! Hurrah for Israel! Hurrah for Israel!*

Our tales would no longer intertwine as seamlessly as before. Instead, we would each forge our own stories, our own adventures. And while I knew that this separation was only temporary, it didn't ease the sting of impending loss. The bond between us, though strong, would be tested by time and distance; however, I knew deep down that this was how it was meant to be. It was part of growing up, of stepping into our own destinies. I acknowledged the bitter truth. While I remained behind to finish school and worked to save enough money to pay for my future mission, I would witness his triumphs from afar. I would be a champion for his success, but heaven help me, I would miss my big brother.

"Hey, Noah," Jacob's voice broke through my thoughts, pulling me back to the warmth of our living room. He grinned at me, a grin so familiar it tugged at my heartstrings. "Come join us. Dad's telling the one about the time he got lost in São Paulo and had to find his way back using a torn map he couldn't read and a few broken phrases in Portuguese."

I smiled back, the melancholy lifting somewhat. That story was one of Dad's classics, filled with suspense, humor, and a lesson wrapped in his signature style. The tale never lost its charm, no matter how many times I heard it.

"Sure," I replied, moving toward the couch. I settled in, holding my mug of cocoa close, the warmth seeping into my hands. As I sat there, surrounded by my family, listening to Dad's voice rise and fall with the rhythm of the story, I allowed myself to savor the moment. My heart still ached, but the knowledge that this, this togetherness, this love, was what mattered most tempered it.

Jacob leaned over, nudging me with his elbow. "You're going to be okay, little bro," he whispered, his voice full of quiet reassurance. "We both will be."

I nodded, not trusting myself to speak without my voice betraying the emotions churning inside me. He knew me. My perfect brother knew the imperfect me, and when he was the one heading into the unknown, he saw what I needed and offered me comfort. I took a deep breath, inhaling the familiar scents of home: Mom's cooking, the pinewood from the fireplace, the faint hint of

Dad's aftershave that lingered in the air. I let those scents ground me, anchoring me to this moment, to this place where I belonged.

Dad's story reached its climax, his hands gesturing vigorously as he recounted the moment he finally found his way back to his apartment, much to the relief of his mission companion, who spoke even less of the language than Dad. Jacob laughed, the sound bright and full of life, and I couldn't help but join in.

For tonight, I would set aside the worries of tomorrow. I would bask in the warmth of family, in the love that had carried us through every storm. Regardless of life's journey, I held onto the hope that the bond between the Wilde boys would endure. Like Dad's story, we'd always find our way back with a torn map of our life and faith.

The fire crackled in the hearth as the snow continued to fall outside, bringing a sense of peace over me. The journey ahead might be uncertain, but tonight, surrounded by those I loved, I knew I was ready to face it, whatever *it* might bring.

"Are we ready for a movie?" Jacob asked as Dad finished his story. He snatched up the remote and found the movie as we all declared a resounding "yes."

CHAPTER TWO

"Jacob, come check this out," I called as I rummaged through the closet.

This closet served as the place Mom stashed non-essential items like books and photo albums. It was supposed to be a linen closet, but not in our house. Mom always insisted that extra sheets and towels were superfluous because no one dared visit our nuthouse overnight, and it was easy enough to wash and reuse linens. This led to beach towels being used as bath towels whenever guests stayed overnight, which was rare. Those who dared to stay over at our crazy house had to make the most with what they got. With her linen logic, she had found an empty closet to store a minor part of her book overflow. The small closet had soon become a hub for all kinds of books. Unfortunately, it was now stuffed so full that closing the door was impossible. But Mom didn't seem to mind. Incessantly, she crammed books into the tight space, leaving no room for anything else. Then she just let the door hang open, constantly.

It had hung open for so many years that I didn't even stub my toes on it anymore.

The woman, you know, the one I called Mom, was a book-buying fiend. She visited used bookstores and library sales more often than the grocery store. That was saying something, considering two teen boys lived at home. She loved to scan the spines and squealed when she spotted something familiar. Mom brought home stacks of novels she had already read because she liked how the new covers looked. She bought unknown hardback books without their cover wraps from unknown authors, without knowing what the story was about. Then she told everyone she met they needed to read them. For goodness' sake, Mom bought books she thought the mailman's wife's cousin would want to read. She didn't even know the mailman's wife's cousin.

Good grief, she was obsessed with books. Fine, I confess, it proved impossible to be around her and not get excited about reading. So maybe I liked to read, a little, mind you. But I would deny it when asked. I justified my denial because only those who read as much as my mother could be proficient readers.

Don't even get me started about our road trip down the Pacific Coast Highway two years ago. Dad talked the trip up for months, saying how much fun we would have. How many beaches we would visit. How we would learn to body surf in the waves. Ultimately, we only visited two beaches, but one didn't count since it was adjacent to an old hotel with book-themed bedrooms. What did we do for a week and a half, if not beach hopping and body surfing? We visited over twenty-five mom-and-pop independent bookstores. Mom left every store with a stack of hardcovers teetering in her arms and the same warning on her lips. *If we didn't buy independent, the stores would go out of business, and we'd have to read eBooks.* Heaven forbid an eBook!

Mom didn't stuff her purchased books in the back of the SUV and forget about them. No, she propped them on the seat between Jacob and me. She claimed we were to protect them, so they didn't get jostled or have their corners damaged. Occasionally, Mom would turn, lean back, and caress the imperfect tomes. Her hand lingered until she was satisfied that the books remained safe. She checked on her books more often than a mother checked her infant in a car seat. At least, I assumed so, since Aunt Vee didn't check on my baby cousin half as much as Mom checked on her books.

I leaned my pillow against the stack and bent the corner of one. It was another copy of *Little Women*. Mom had at least four copies that I knew of already. Why she needed another, I would never understand. *Whoa Nelly,* I thought *Mom would either have a coronary or toss me out the car door over it.*

That was only the tip of the proverbial iceberg of books. Yesterday, as I walked by Mom in the kitchen on my way to the cupboard for a glass, she nodded for me to grab her phone off the counter and call Dad. She was in flour up to her elbows, making bread for a family who needed dinner. What do you think I found on her phone? An open book right there on her reading app: a dreaded eBook. I found something interesting when I backed up to her library screen. Want to know what I found? You guessed it, over a thousand more eBooks. As my great-granddaddy used to say, *How in the patooties does she read so many books?* And she lectured us about buying independent!

Anyway, back to the linen-book closet I was telling you about. A jumble of books, old and new, hardback and paperback, always filled the space. Opening the door after it was forced shut would risk the entire collection spilling onto the floor. These were the extra books. The books we treasured, our special books, had their own special place: a six-foot by three-foot, five-shelf bookcase of our very own. Mom had three of them!

My shelf held a curated collection of diverse comic books and fantasy novels, each complemented by stunning artwork. Other bookshelves housed Christian fiction, romance, mystery, suspense-thrillers, science fiction, self-help, and biographies. No matter our reading preference, Mom shared a chapter-by-chapter breakdown of her current book every night over dinner. *Romance novels are more than just the blissful wishes of lonely women. You can learn a lot about a woman's heart from reading a good love story.*

I digressed. I dug through the bottomless book pit of our linen closet to get to the good stuff. By that, I meant the family photo albums Mom kept stashed at the back on the bottom shelf.

Mom was not like those cutesy scrapbookers. Her talents were that she was a whiz with a three-ring binder, clear document covers, and color-coded tabs. Our entire lives, mine and Jacob's, unfolded right there for everyone to see, month by month, year by year.

"Report card! Dang, I remember that," Jacob guffawed. "Stupid. Wasn't it? I complained that homeschooling wasn't fair because the other kids got paid for their good grades. Mom made that dumb thing and gave it to me with a fiver."

"I remember." I laughed hard, a snort escaping. "You grabbed your bike and were determined to head straight to the store to spend your hard-earned cash. Mom gave you fifty more and a shopping list the length of your arm. Dude, we live forever away from town and on a mountain. Did you honestly think you could bike there and back in one day with groceries? I still can't believe you made it all the way to town *and* did the shopping *and* were on your way back before you called Mom. When we arrived to pick you up, the distance you had traveled shocked Mom. Then she realized you weren't still on your way to town; you'd already been there, done that, and had the grocery sacks knocking against your knees to prove it. She had never suspected you would make it half so far. You must have pedaled that old huffy at lightning speed."

"Darn right! As you aptly said, we live on a mountain. I pointed that thing towards town, peddled a few times to get started, then held my legs out to the side because the bike pedals were spinning faster than my legs. A couple of stretches I was keeping up with the cars and scared to death. I made great time going to town, it was the coming home where I had a problem. It's straight uphill and those flimsy plastic sacks kept ripping. I had to tie little knots everywhere to keep the contents in. I only called Mom because they were beyond salvageable, and it was impossible to carry her precious goods and ride the bike. Oh, and you can bet your bottom dollar I never asked for a report card again. Or rode my bike to town, for that matter."

"Stop, my sides hurt. Oh my gosh, my sides hurt." I bellowed as I pinched the right side of my stomach and took a deep breath to stop from laughing so hard. I thought that was one of my favorite Jacob stories. Right up there with the crocodile tears over Tinker Bell.

Jacob took hold of the report card I held out to him and gave it a look. He flicked it twice with his finger before handing it back to me. "Straight A's." His eyes sparkled as he took in the organized column of A's.

"It seems you were always destined for greatness," I teased.

After accepting the report card, I returned it to its rightful spot in its sheet protector. The stark white paper bearing the make-believe school's name, *The Internationally Acclaimed Wilde Academy: A School for Accomplished Young Men*, glared back at me, daring me to mock it.

"You know, Mom is one rock away from falling off her rocker. I swear, my friends' moms don't come up with half the crazy stuff she does."

"She has to. She homeschooled us, and it was hard to keep two Wilde boys entertained for longer than ten minutes."

"True that!"

"Turn to March of the following year. There should be a real certificate."

"I beg to differ, bro, that right there is a REAL report card," I teased as I tapped it just as he had.

"Whatever!"

I scanned the right side of the binder, looking for the March tab. Once I found it, I skipped a small stack of pages and flipped it open. An actual State Academic Award stared back at us, featuring a picture of Jacob standing on stage. Our parents beamed at him from the audience.

"I took that picture," I said, pointing to the perfectly focused and Jacob-centered image displayed next to the certificate.

"When I returned from my mission, that award came with a scholarship. I can use it at BYU. It will pay for an entire year of college."

Driven by the desire to excel in all aspects of his life, including his studies, Jacob said, "Hard work pays off." A small smile played on his lips as he plopped down on the floor beside me. "But there's more to life than just good grades."

"Like being the first assistant in the Priest Quorum at church?" I asked, recalling how he had led our congregation's young men with true leadership skills. From organizing service projects to offering encouragement, Jacob had been a textbook example of a quorum assistant.

"Exactly," he responded. "Being able to serve my friends and help them grow in their faith was important to me. Likewise, it was important to have good grades in school. Now, I work hard at my job and prepare to be a great missionary."

I admired Jacob's determination. From the age of twelve, he worked at the orchard. At sixteen, he began working at a retirement home and saved every penny. Despite foregoing luxuries, like new clothes and gaming consoles, Jacob had remained determined to save for his mission and college.

"Can you believe it? I saved twenty-five thousand dollars. It was tough, but well worth it in the end." His eyes held a determination that spoke volumes about his commitment to faith and family.

"Wow," I whispered, my chest swelling with pride for my older brother. "You've done it all, haven't you?"

"Hardly," he admitted. "There's still so much more to learn and experience."

"True," I mused, my thoughts drifting back to our father's stories of his mission in Brazil. "But I know you'll rise to whatever challenges come your way."

"Thanks, Noah," he said with genuine warmth, giving me a pat on the shoulder. "With God's help, I knew I could do it. And so can you."

Seated with our backs against the couch, sunlight cast rainbows on the floor through Mom's crystal rainbow makers. I looked at my brother, my admiration growing stronger. He consistently served others and strengthened his spiritual connection with God.

At eighteen years old, he had already become a man I admired. As a devout member of the church, he had spent his entire life preparing for this moment, serving a mission like our father had.

I too desired to serve a mission, but Jacob declared it to God and the world courageously. While part of me admired his courage and strength of belief, I knew I could never be so vocal about my faith. Mine was an introspective faith, one I kept hidden away from the noise of society. A gentle flame flickering in the solitude of my soul, illuminating the path of my existence. As strong as any outward proclamation, but more powerful for not capturing the notice of men.

My faith did not demand grand gestures or ostentatious displays. Instead, it found peace and solace in the whispered prayers escaping my lips, the silent conversations, and moments of stillness when I communed with Heavenly Father. In those sacred moments of reflection, my faith took shape and found its voice. Amid the chaos, faith offered refuge, a sanctuary from noise and distractions. And so, I embraced my faith, knowing it would illuminate my path and buoy my soul in times of weakness. My faith connected me with something greater than myself. Yet, as much as I believed in my faith, another part of me doubted it would ever measure up to Jacob's.

My older brother could move mountains with his faith. I had seen him do it. Well, not literal mountains, but I had seen him call forth miracles from God just by praying. Jacob didn't just ask for miracles; he expected them. God always delivered, too. He had to because Jacob's faith was so strong; he ripped the miracles straight out of God's hands. To me, that was tantamount to moving mountains.

"Jacob," I began, trying to smile around the bittersweet taste of the moment. But seriously, tonight, I was having difficulty keeping it together. "Remember when we visited Grandma during her third round of chemo? We weren't supposed to be there because we were too young to be in the cancer treatment facility. You sweet-talked the nurse, and she let us visit long enough to give Grandma *Tinker Bell Kisses*. Do you remember?" I asked, recalling one of the many moments showcasing his kindness. He had a gift for making the sick and elderly understand they were important, loved, and not forgotten. Their faces lit up whenever he entered a room, and it warmed my heart to witness it. Yet another thing I admired about my big brother.

"Yes, I remember. That was a good day," he recalled.

"Sure was," I lied.

The dread I experienced that day flooded over me in waves. The memory of the treatment facility filled my heart with an overwhelming sense of fear. Sterile corridors loomed like a forbidden labyrinth, lined with doors that held in the weight of suffering.

It wasn't the unknown cancer outcome that haunted my thoughts. It was the fear of witnessing Grandma in a state of fragility and pain. She was our beloved matriarch, my father's mother—a Wilde Woman, bearing her title with pride. Grandma Wilde had always been the vibrant anchor in every situation. She provided steadfast support and reliability while bringing energy and joy to every occasion. Her presence was both grounding and invigorating, making her indispensable in times of need and celebration. The mere remembrance of her illness pierced my heart with an ache that was difficult to bear. I longed for the days when her laughter had echoed through the walls of her home when I visited. I longed for her arms to wrap tight around me in an engulfing hug, like the ones that always brought comfort and solace when Mom and Dad went on vacation, leaving us with our grandparents. But seeing her frail and vulnerable was a devastating blow to my soul. No, it was not a good day when we visited Grandma. It was horrible.

In my apprehension, another fear surfaced. That my arrival as a young, healthy boy might disrupt the delicate emotional balance. I imagined the gazes of those battling their own health demons turned on me, their weary eyes filled with longing and resentment. Would they see my vigor as a reminder of what they had lost? Would my presence deepen their wounds, amplifying their pain? I yearned to shield them from more anguish, to spare them the burden of comparison. It was a product of my imagination, but it still existed.

Dad called these thoughts *"dragons"* and said, *"they should not hold space in your mind."* But that was easier said than done. Too often, dragons occupied the forefront of my mind, especially when Grandma was sick and then again when she died.

But amidst my internal turmoil, Jacob stood before me, unwavering in his faith and commitment to our family. His resolute spirit shone, casting a radiant light into the darkness. He navigated the labyrinth of fear and uncertainty with grace. An unyielding belief in the power of love and the resilience of the human spirit guided his steps. Jacob was my rock, my steadfast anchor in the storm, embodying strength in the face of adversity. His unwavering faith had a magnetic pull, drawing us closer to the core of our family. He strode into that cancer ward, head held high, an enormous smile plastered on his handsome face. I walked close behind, hovering in his shadow. His smile brightened the room. Everyone waved and yelled greetings, which Jacob accepted and multiplied, responding in kind. He wished for the health and happiness of all in return. They loved him, and as I hovered behind him and heard their words directed at me, I knew they loved me too. I had nothing to fear.

Grandma Wilde loved the extra attention she received when we came to visit. I could still remember her bragging as we left. "Aren't my Wilde Boys the greatest?" All the other patients declared her *The most beloved and best grandma any boy could ever have.* But, of course, they were right. She was.

"It's amazing how much you can learn from those who've lived so long? They have so much wisdom to share."

"Definitely," I nodded, knowing Jacob valued every opportunity to expand his wisdom and knowledge, no matter the source. It was an integral part of who he was, and he invoked inspiration by his dedication.

"Two years, huh?" I ventured, bracing myself for the conversation that lay ahead.

"Yep. I hope I can make a difference. Mom did some research. It seems like they send out mission assignments on Tuesdays. I should get my call via email in a few days. I can't wait to do my part in sharing the good news of Jesus Christ. Hurrah for Israel!" he shouted with combined solemnity and excitement. Only the prophet could inspire such enthusiasm in mission-age men and women worldwide.

"Hurrah for Israel," I repeated. My hurrah was a little less exuberant than his.

"Where do you think they will assign you?" I posed the million-dollar question, the query on everyone's lips, a looming question in the hearts of countless missionary families worldwide. The inquiry held tremendous weight for the prospective missionary. Every person who asked it did so with anticipation, curiosity, and genuine excitement.

In the hallowed halls of our faith, we understood the significance of submitting mission papers. The pivotal moment of submitting mission papers forever changed one's life. It signified a profound commitment, a dedication to a sacred mission ordained by God. Choosing to serve a mission was a decision requiring sacrifice, discernment, and personal revelation. It marked the culmination of countless prayers and was a testament to the individual's faith in the Savior and readiness to serve God. The decision to embark on a mission spreading the light of Jesus Christ was a sacrifice not taken casually.

The weight of Jacob's decision shone in his eyes and etched itself upon his countenance. He radiated joy, anticipation, and perhaps even a hint of trepidation. The million-dollar question carried with it the potential to reshape his life. It would set him on a path of service and spiritual growth. A mission would challenge him in ways he could not yet imagine, in ways I could not imagine.

"Wherever the Lord needs me. I know He will send me to people ready for me," Jacob responded with perfect faith.

"You're going to be the best missionary ever!" I reassured him, conviction swelling in my chest.

Emotion welled up in my throat, making it difficult to speak further. I turned my face away to avoid eye contact.

When I didn't hear him making any noise, I looked back. Our eyes met, and I could see it all. Jacob's boldness carried him through life. His love for our family. His unwavering faith shone like a lighthouse beacon on a foggy night. I knew our feelings were mutual. Yet, I saw a little sadness in his countenance as he said, "Thanks, Noah. I'll miss you. You know you're the best brother anyone could ever wish for."

"I'll miss you too, big brother," I replied. It made me happy to consider that he thought of me as the best brother, knowing full well he was, in fact, the best brother.

In the following days, I watched him gather mission essentials and pack them into his luggage. He was ready for his mission. Though I'd miss him, my pride in him was immeasurable.

CHAPTER THREE

"IT'S HERE! IT'S HERE! My mission call arrived." Jacob raced out of his bedroom mid-morning on Tuesday. He shouted and waved his phone like a madman. His face was flushed red, and I thought he was about to have a heart attack.

Mom rushed in from the laundry room, her hands full of folded kitchen towels. "Don't open it yet. Wait for Dad to get home from work so we can plan your party," she said, though she didn't need to. Jacob knew to wait. We all did.

Mom's been preparing for Jacob's mission call opening party for weeks. Honestly, she started planning it before he even submitted his mission application. Last week, she even set up an online game for people to guess where he will serve. She bought a world map made from fabric to use as a backdrop for his opening. After the party, she plans to quilt it and embellish the backdrop with a large red star marking his mission area. The finished piece will hang in her office with a mission flag, a tangible tribute to Jacob's service. Mom's enthusiasm doesn't stop there. She sourced missionary-themed fabrics to match the world map backdrop. I'll admit, the fabric is adorable. It features strips in various colors with little missionary companionships, temples, and the phrase *Called to Serve*. Complementing these, she added blue, green, purple, and black fabrics to make Jacob a handcrafted, one-of-a-kind mission blanket. Mom's sentiment shines like a beacon as she proclaims, *Each stitch is a hug. Whenever you face challenges, you can wrap yourself in it, and I'll be hugging you.*

Where does she find the time to be supermom? I'm a kid, and I don't have time to think about half the things she accomplishes daily. Jacob and I scored when heavenly families got assigned, and we came to Earth as her sons. No joke, Mom of the Century.

Jacob and I tease her for being over the top, but we love it. Jacob whips out the blanket whenever someone mentions mission supplies and shows it off. He has pictures of it on his phone and loves telling people every stitch is a hug. I wish I could be a fly on the wall the day he pulls the blanket out of his suitcase, and some macho missionary asks about it. My mama's boy brother risks savage teasing the way he moons over it.

I'll admit it, I want one made for me when I go on my mission. I hope my eccentric mom hasn't run out of steam by then. Once again, I'll deny it if asked.

Dad was taking his sweet time getting home from work today. It's a love-hate situation for me. On one hand, I'm happy he found work as a Field Service Technician for a fruit processor. On the other hand, I miss having him here at our family orchard, which has been in our family since the dawn of the 1900s. During my childhood, running outside during homeschool recess and jumping on the tractor with Dad was a nice reprieve from my boring lessons. We called it our *Man Time*. I miss it, but that's the breaks. It has become nearly impossible for a single-family operation to remain viable these days. The upper valley experienced a devastating loss of the entire apple crop because of mealworms one year, followed by a deadly spring frost that destroyed the cherries the next. Our orchard was part of both losses three years ago.

The thought of losing the orchard devastated Dad. For a month, he wracked his brain for ideas on how to save our heritage. He devised a plan to secure a job in town while also working in the orchard during off-hours and weekends. Dad was sure that with mine and Jacob's help, we could do it all. He went to his first interview and came home downtrodden and empty-handed. Although not the right fit, the line manager understood my father's plight and recommended our orchard to the crop manager. The crop manager called that night with a tempting proposal. Dad signed a lease with the conglomerate that would save our orchard. Two weeks later, he found a job inspecting fruit coming out of all the orchards in the valley. Dad had been working in the orchard industry for three years now, relishing his role on the front line. He dedicated himself to helping fellow growers maximize their crop yields. In the meantime, we kept ownership of the orchard, the land, and our family home.

The lease guaranteed payment, regardless of crop performance. The conglomerate covered all annual expenses and managed pickers' hiring and payment. Our family expenses had never been so flush, as my mother said.

It benefited us boys, too. If not for the lease, we'd be stuck doing hard labor in the orchard for low or no pay. You know, being the sons of the orchardist and all. Now, we could work in town with easier work, nicer conditions, and better pay. A win, win, win.

Despite being a difficult decision, one that made my tough-as-steel father cry, it wasn't too good to be true in the end. It turned out to be a godsend. A miracle right when we needed it most. God, beyond question, carried us through our rough patch.

I caught Jacob waiting at the window like an eager toddler, but I didn't razz him. I wanted to, but I understood his situation. He wanted to share his news with Dad. Dad will be so excited!

Dad's arrival was unmistakable. Jacob burst through the door, leaving it wide open and letting a blast of icy air in. He raced outside, waving his cell phone around like a madman. "Dad, Dad, it's here!" he called out the moment Dad opened his door and stepped out of his work truck.

"What's here?" Dad asked, as if he didn't already know. Jacob was too eager to notice Dad was teasing him. I knew Mom had already texted Dad and told him Jacob's call had arrived. Dad was enjoying making sport of Jacob, letting him have the spotlight.

"Let's open it," Dad declared.

Jacob hesitated, considering. "Do you think we should? I could open it now and then fake it when everyone comes for the party?"

"No!" our rule-following mom huffed.

"I couldn't care less," Dad said. He propped his briefcase against the wall next to the front door, walked over, and kissed Mom.

I loved that he carried a custom leather, very manly, monogrammed briefcase. It was extremely impressive, and I longed for one just like it. I have nothing to put in it now, but someday I will. Honestly, Dad's job doesn't warrant a briefcase either, but he looks super sophisticated carrying it, and Mom never fails to tell him so, which I can tell he loves.

"When I received my mission call, you know, back in the '90s when you filled out the paperwork by hand and waited months for it to arrive by snail mail, I had it opened before I hiked back up the driveway. No one watched me open it. But, of course, my mom didn't throw me a party, and we weren't live streaming it so half the nation could watch."

I love it when Dad joke-mocks. Today is a good one. I waited. I knew Mom would have a snappy comeback. She always does. Sass comes naturally to her.

"I don't care what they did 30 years ago, in the Stone Age, when you served," Mom declared. There it is! "I've watched all the videos and joined three missionary mom chat groups, and this is what everyone is doing now. I want Jacob to take advantage of everything. So, we're doing this my way."

We three Wilde men raised our hands and nodded our heads to my feisty Wilde mom, who clearly ruled the roost.

Instead of randomly choosing a date and time for the event, like today, and hoping people would free their schedules, Mom took the extra effort to ensure people were available. She called and consulted every family member about their schedules. She collected this information on a yellow notepad and scrutinized the responses to determine the optimal time. By the time she finally arranged everything, the bishop even threatened to open it on his end, claiming he was dying to know where Jacob was assigned to serve. Ultimately, Mom decided Saturday at noon would accommodate the most family and friends. She was going to make Jacob suffer for five whole days before finally opening his mission call email. Seriously! Five days! He's going to die, or peek, before Saturday rolls around. To notify everyone when Jacob would open his call, she designed an invitation featuring his official mission photo, embellished with balloons, streamers, and the phrase *Called to Serve,* and shared it on all her social media platforms. She also texted it to those people she thought were most important. And then, she embarked on a baking spree.

She baked more than just your typical cookies. An array of delectable treats filled our kitchen, each one more enticing than the last. From chewy chocolate chip cookies to gooey brownies with a fudgy center, she had mastered them all. But she didn't stop there. There were tangy lemon bars that melted in one's mouth, rich and decadent peanut butter and jelly thumbprint cookies, and whimsical unicorn sugar cookies decorated with vibrant icing. Her creativity knew no bounds as she experimented with unique flavors and textures. By the time Saturday at noon rolled around, she had enough goodies for a full-fledged stake activity.

Mom estimated twenty-five people would brave the roads and come to the house. I swear she baked for over one hundred. She claimed, "You can never be too prepared." She figured another fifty would join online if Jacob was lucky.

And show up, they did. After the fifty-third person squeezed into our humble abode, the sheer size of our gathering was staggering and stifling. The bishop suggested moving to the more spacious church. The logistics of transferring everyone miles away and setting up Mom's cutesy backdrop again, plus the video and computer equipment, seemed daunting. My father, ever the practical man, dismissed the idea with a wave. "No need, just squish in. We're all friends and family here." His voice resonated with resolute determination. "Let's get this show on the road."

Monday through Friday, he worked, and on Sunday, he had church obligations. But today was Saturday, a rare day when Dad had no obligations except relaxation. He relished staying home, savoring the comforts of family and familiar surroundings, taking a well-earned nap, watching nostalgic episodes of *Voyager*, and binging on his favorite vinegar chips. Today, all those people were cramping his style.

Dad called out to Jacob, beckoning him to step forward through the crowd and join him and Mom at the front.

Jacob wove his way through the crowd, his eyes meeting our parents' loving gazes. Dad's hand found its place on Jacob's shoulder, a silent symbol of pride and support. Mom enveloped him in a warm embrace around his waist. The air brimmed with anticipation as Dad prepared to share his heartfelt sentiments.

In a hushed tone, Dad expressed his profound pride for Jacob and then offered a heartfelt prayer, his voice laced with emotion. He sought divine guidance and blessings for Jacob's mission. As he concluded, Dad stepped aside, allowing Jacob to take center stage.

The room fell into a reverent silence as Jacob solemnly opened the email that held the key to his future with a somber demeanor. Every eye in the room fixated on him, eager to witness the unfolding of his destiny. With steadfast resolve, Jacob read the sacred words that had traveled across the vast expanse of the internet.

Each syllable hung in the air, as if honored by this pivotal moment. Anticipation, hope, and an underlying current of faith charged the room. We listened, captivated by the powerful words of the prophet, waiting for him to reveal his mission location.

Jacob's voice quivered, and the room seemed to hold its breath as he reached the sentence revealing the location of his sacred calling: the Cauayan Philippines Mission, speaking Tagalog.

A non-spiritual whoop rose from the group.

His pronunciation of *Cauayan* and *Tagalog* was off, drawing amusement and playful corrections from the crowd.

Aunt Vee, always quick with her guesses, enthusiastically declared that she had guessed the Philippines as Jacob's assigned destination in his guessing game and inquired if she won a prize. Mom responded, "No prizes," her voice almost drowned out by the boisterous excitement filling the room. It took Mom a full minute to restore a semblance of order, although, truth be told, she was the loudest among us, unable to contain her exuberance.

I grinned as I observed the shared joy and unity permeating our home. Despite Jacob's upcoming distant journey, the collective support showcased the unwavering strength of our ties with family and friends. Laughter gave way to a flurry of questions and advice. The room hummed with excitement, an air of adventure and cultural discovery electrifying the atmosphere. Those who had been to the Philippines shared tales about their experiences. Each person contributed their wisdom and vast love. I realized that Jacob's mission would shape his path and enrich our family's history.

The rest of the letter remained unread until our little family of four was alone. In the room, fifty-three people spoke, their voices buzzing over one another. My cousin sat at the laptop in the corner, scanning the live feed comments. He boasted that over two hundred people were on at one point. He read each comment aloud, matching the rambunctious energy of the gathering.

Our house was chaotic, and I wanted to hide. I looked at Jacob, who was giving Mom *Tinker Bell Kisses* on her perfect age spot and couldn't help myself. I wove through, around, and over people to reach my brother. Jacob was crying happy tears when I gave him the biggest bear hug I could muster. We're talking full-on, frontal hug, arms wrapped around bodies, unable to let go. That's it, my brother would be over six thousand miles away from me. I couldn't hold them back. Happy for him and sad for me, tears streamed down my face, matching his.

While Jacob accepted his congratulations, I snuck away and hid in my bedroom. That's where Mom found me. She had a little plate of treats and cocoa prepared just for me. She set them on my desk, sat on the edge of my bed, wrapped her arms around me, and let a few tears of her own fall.

Then she rubbed my cheek with her thumb and attempted to speak. It came out in an uncharacteristic, choked whisper, "We're going to be alright, you and me. Jacob will be the greatest missionary on Earth, and back here at home, you, me, and Dad will keep on keeping on. We'll fret for a few days, but then we will carry on. We'll live for each p-day when he calls home, and we get to see him."

I offered a tight, straight-lipped smile and nodded my head. She was right, but it didn't stop my tears of joy and heartache. I was going to miss my brother. I didn't think him calling once a week on preparation day was enough, but it was better than the old days when missionaries only called twice a year on Mother's Day and Christmas.

When I collected myself enough to leave my room, only a few family members remained at our house. My father's laughter filled the air as he recounted another tale from his mission days in Brazil. Though I'd heard these stories countless times, they never failed to captivate me, and Dad's laughter was always infectious.

I curled beside Grandma Evans on the couch and leaned my head on her shoulder. She reached up, patted my face, kissed the top of my head, and held my hand. Grandpa Evans threw in a few stories from his mission to the Louisiana Bayou in the 1970s. Over the years, I've heard only a few of Grandpa's stories. They were fantastic and different from Dad's, yet every bit as exciting and spiritual.

"Jacob," Mom said, her face glowing with pride, "your father and I are so proud of your decision to serve a mission. We know it won't be easy, but you can overcome all challenges."

"Thanks, Mom," Jacob replied, his voice steady and sure. "Serving a mission is what I am supposed to do. I have spent my entire life getting ready for this. I'm thrilled about serving in the Philippines. It's a country I never imagined."

Dad nodded, his graying hair catching the last rays of sunlight streaming through the window behind his favorite leather recliner. "Son, there will be challenges, language barriers, cultural differences, moments of doubt and fear, but remember, you're not alone. The Lord will be by your side, and we'll support and pray for your success."

"Speaking of which," Jacob said, a mischievous glint in his eye, "I searched for some videos of people speaking Tagalog. It's a crazy tough language to learn. Also, it's not the only language spoken in the Philippines. There are hundreds of dialects." Jacob pushed play on a video, then turned his phone around so we could see. We laughed at the fast-speaking Filipinos. We couldn't decipher where one word ended, and the next began. The words were big, and the Filipino pronunciations seemed impossible. I sighed in relief, thankful that learning the language was Jacob's responsibility, not mine.

"É bom ouvir isso," Dad replied, grinning. "That means *I'm glad to hear*, for those who don't speak Portuguese. It will be good to have something challenge this boy."

Dad winked at me, and I couldn't help but smile back. Long ago, Dad and I had discussed how Jacob was like Mom regarding education. They are too smart for their own good. All they had to do was look at a book, not even open it, and they knew everything in it. We didn't Google things; we Jacob'd them. Mom, too, was uber-smart, rattling off facts and details like she was born with them in her head.

I am more like Dad. We are intelligent, but we work our butts off for it. The difference is that once we learn something, we never forget it. Jacob and Mom come and go with what they learn and remember. They know a lot but tire of a topic and move on to learn another. They don't care about what they have learned before, so long as they can learn more. We call them learning junkies. Dad and I have minds like steel traps. Once it goes in, it stays forever. We never forget.

Like Dad, I thought it would be nice for Jacob to have something challenge him for once. Maybe he would comprehend what it's like for the rest of us mere mortals.

As the talks went on, I thought about the steadfast backing our family and friends gave Jacob on his journey. From assisting with his mission fund to purchasing necessary clothing and supplies, each family member played a role in his preparedness.

"Hey, Noah," Jacob said, pulling me from my reverie. "I know we'll be apart for a while, but I promise to write to you every week. When I return, we'll have countless stories to share."

"Deal," I replied, my throat tight. "Remember, Jacob, no matter what challenges you face, you've got an army of support back home."

"Thanks, little brother," he said, his look filled with gratitude and love.

As night advanced and the stars emerged in the heavens above, I held firm in the belief that our family would confront the upcoming changes with poise and grace. United, we'd stand by Jacob during his mission. We would rely on the Lord's guidance and our family's enduring love to get us through until he returned.

CHAPTER FOUR

THE DISTANT MOUNTAINSIDE GLOWED in the soft, warm evening light as Jacob prepared for his last day of work at his second job at the retirement home. His primary job as a hospitality aide had ended yesterday, the last day of January, but his secondary position, and by far his favorite, was his personal Grandpa Mike. Mike lived at the retirement home, but, according to him, he was too healthy to need a nurse. He declared he only lived there because he preferred the social life.

Jacob's responsibility was to stop by each morning and evening, five days a week, to ensure Mike remembered to take his medicine. If Mike needed help with laundry, dishes, or vacuuming while he was there, Jacob took care of it. Just after Jacob turned sixteen, Mike's relatives approached him at church. They asked for his help in taking care of Grandpa Mike. Jacob agreed quickly, seeing it as an opportunity for *easy cash*. It began as just a job, but two years later, Grandpa Mike was as much a grandparent as Grandma Bean. And what kid wouldn't want a couple of extra self-appointed grandparents?

"Hey, Noah, do you want to come? Mike's family approved an outing, so I can take him out for truffle fries and root beer floats. You'll have to sit in the back, but I'll buy."

"Heck yeah! Seriously, bro, truffle fries are my favorite, but are you sure Mike should eat them? Won't they clog his arteries or something? You're going to kill him."

"Nah, he's hard-core. It's his favorite spot. Before Betty died, Mike took her there every Thursday night since it opened. For him, it's more about the memories than the food. Plus, he likes to joke that he's so old he can eat whatever he wants, and no one can tell him otherwise. The man practically lives on Dr. Pepper."

Jacob glanced out the window, eager to leave. "I'll go start the truck and get it heated. Come out when you're ready. If you haven't noticed, it's snowing again, so be sure to grab your gear."

"Not again," I huffed. "I guess this means no Bermuda shorts?"

"Not today."

I snatched my shoes, coat, hat, gloves, scarf, and anything else warm I could scrounge together. The chill in the air reminded me that winter wasn't ready to let go just yet.

The air didn't have the biting chill that penetrated my bones during December and January, but the winds of the first day of February were still below freezing. Upon stepping outside, I drew in a deep breath and caught the scent of burning firewood. The smoke lingered in the valley's air. I shivered from the cold and cinched my coat tighter around me. It approached four in the afternoon, but dusk had already come and gone.

Jacob pulled up at the facility and parked the truck. "I'll leave her running for you. Please keep the heat on so it's warm when I bring Mike out."

"For sure," I said, holding my hands in front of the vents, now blowing warm air. I cranked the thermostat hot and high, no longer afraid of the cold air, and climbed over the console into the tiny backseat. I played games on my cell phone while I waited for them to return. It didn't take long before the facility door opened, and Mike hobbled forward. His back was bowed with age, and his movements were slow and deliberate. He wore a thick coat, a scarf wrapped tight around his neck, and a woolen hat pulled low over his ears. I didn't blame him. The cold outside was biting, especially for an old guy. Mike shuffled across the icy pavement, his right hand gripping a cane for support. Jacob stood to his left, steadying his back and ready to catch him should he fall.

Jacob opened the pickup door and placed Mike's cane inside. He then assisted Mike to climb in, since the truck was too high for him.

Observing Jacob and Mike was captivating. Their contrast was clear, one fragile and uncertain, the other confident and strong. Yet, their disparities faded now. They moved harmoniously, the younger man lending support and the elder sharing a wealth of wisdom and experience.

"Hey, Mike," I said as Jacob shut the door and ran around to the driver's side to get in.

My voice startled Mike, who hadn't noticed me, and he attempted to turn his stiff neck towards my voice.

I leaned forward in the seat, between the front driver and passenger seats, so he could see me better.

"Well, hello there," Mike greeted, his old voice a little shaky as Jacob jumped in and shut his door.

"Mike, you remember my little brother, Noah?"

"Little?" Mike questioned, looking me over. "He doesn't look so little to me. How old are you now, Noah?"

"Sixteen, sir," I replied, recalling my manners to avoid upsetting my mom and risking a wallop on my rear end. She was particular about us showing respect to our elders. She didn't really wallop. In fact, she never disciplined at all. Though her threats always seemed real. Particularly when Dad responded, *"Don't let Mom hurt her hand when she wallops you, or I'll give you one too."* That, I believed.

"Sixteen! Are you driving yet?"

"Yes, sir, I got my license the first Tuesday after I turned sixteen. It would have been on Monday, but the Driver's License Office is closed on Mondays." It still irritated me that my friend got his license on his birthday. I had to wait three days for mine since my birthday fell on the weekend and the driver's license office was closed on Mondays.

"He aced every test in the class with a perfect one hundred percent and nailed his driving test with a flawless score," Jacob boasted on my behalf.

"Why, your family's full of smarty-pants, isn't it?" Mike jested.

I smiled, proud that my brother had remembered my accomplishments. The reality was, Jacob's brilliance and talent sometimes left me feeling inadequate. His confident and dynamic persona stands out, and he receives abundant praise, while my more reserved nature sometimes fades into the background.

Jacob never made me feel inadequate, though. He understood my needs. When everyone sang his praises to the roof and back, Jacob would say *thanks,* find me, and lay them all at my feet. *I owe it all to you, bro. None of this would have been possible without your help,* he said.

I recognized his kindness, yet he was right. I had indeed accomplished what he said. Before his initial debate, the one for that real certificate he won, I quizzed him on his potential responses. After winning the state competition, I simulated a reporter's interview to help refine his camera presence. I also did his chores, giving him extra time to write his acclaimed paper and secure his fancy scholarship.

We were a team, a great one.

Jacob and Mike continued conversing until we arrived. Once he parked and turned off the pickup near the entrance of Milepost 111, our favorite restaurant in nearby Cashmere, Jacob got out and circled around to assist Mike.

I watched in awe of my big brother, so selfless and kind to a man sixty-eight years his senior.

Exiting the compact back seat, I slammed the old door and followed them. The dirty, icy ground crackled beneath my feet. As Mike transitioned from the parking lot to the sidewalk, he had to navigate a sizable mound of snow. His actions were slow and deliberate, and I noticed his legs trembling. He relied on Jacob for support to hoist himself up. I swear Jacob bore Mike's entire weight as he stood behind him, encircling him to assist.

I wondered *if I should assist from the other side or hang back and let Jacob handle it?* After they reached the sidewalk, I hurried ahead and opened the restaurant door.

"Thanks, Noah," Jacob said, leading Mike into the warmth of the building.

Jacob walked Mike straight to a table in the corner where he always sat, waving to the seating host who was helping other guests. The host nodded and then grabbed two menus after settling the other guests. We were just getting situated when he came over to greet us.

"Mike, my man, how are you?" he said, then, looking at Jacob and me without pausing, added, "I see you're still keeping company with *The Wilde Boys*. Careful now, these boys have a reputation."

"That's why I like 'em. They keep me young," Mike answered.

The host laughed and asked, "Your usual drink?"

"You betcha," Mike quipped.

The host looked at Jacob and me, and we both said, "Same."

Mike held up his menu as if he were inspecting it. "Jacob, what is this?" Mike asked, pointing at a picture of a pile of fries with tiny writing underneath. "My old eyes are failing me these days, and I can't quite make out what it says."

"Goodness gracious," Jacob declared. "I can't imagine why. The text is so small I can't even read it. Let's see here. Onion Rings are on the left, and Sweet Potato Fries on the right. Below them are the House Fries with the Blue Cheese Dip."

"Bah, where are my Truffle Fries?" Mike tossed the menu and declared, "You know what I want. I can't find them on that dumb thing."

I snatched the menu and turned it over. Right there, top center in bold lettering, was *You Have to Try Our Truffle Fries*. I pointed and said, "Here they are. Look, they're even gluten-free and vegetarian!" I laughed at the ridiculously obvious observation. Every farmer and orchardist in the world understood they were gluten-free, but the menu had to state it for the tree-hugging hippies who didn't know the difference between fries and pasta. Then again, they might confuse them with gnocchi.

"I don't give a flying leap about all that fancy stuff."

I almost laughed. Almost.

A server showed up with three mugs of Root Beer Floats in one hand and an enormous serving of Truffle Fries we hadn't even ordered yet. "Mike, good to see you. Look at what I have for you. On the house!" He set three mugs on the table, which Jacob passed around. Then he positioned the large platter of fries in front of Mike, settled five different condiments in little ramekins around the edge within reach, and, like magic, whipped out a smaller bowl with just a handful of fries and set it to the side, saying, "These are for Betty."

"She sure loved your Truffle Fries," Mike stated as he popped a small one in his mouth.

"I know she did." The server laid a hand on Mike's shoulder and squeezed. "We sure are glad you keep up the tradition."

"You keep making these delicious fries, and I'll keep eating them. Deal?"

"You got it, man. Anything else?"

Uncertain about the food status quo now that the fries and floats seemed to be free, I waited for Jacob's lead. "Wow, that's a ton of fries, but I have a mind for a burger. I'll take the Mile High Burger. What about you, Noah?"

"Awesome, yeah, I'll take the Milepost Burger."

"Mike, do you want anything else?"

"Nope, just my fries and float."

The server nodded and trotted off with our order. I heard him holler over the counter to the kitchen, "One Mile High, one Milepost."

The chef in the back confirmed the order with a muffled response.

Jacob leaned in and stole three of Mike's fries, dipping them in 111 Secret Sauce. "You're aware, they don't hand out a bowl of Secret Sauce to just anyone."

Mike pushed a few fries toward me and then nudged the sauces closer. He held up a white one I suspected was Ranch Dip. "You like this one?"

I nodded.

"Here, take it away. I don't like that one."

Jacob snickered. "Not even for your Betty fries? That was her favorite."

"The fries are enough. I'm not about to torture myself to eat them. I want to enjoy them. On second thought, here, you dip one in that sauce and eat it for her. That counts." He handed me a single fry from the Betty fries.

I silently laughed, or so I thought, until Jacob looked over at me and raised his eyebrows, mirroring my mirth. Naturally, we understood each other's thoughts. I reverently took the single Betty fry he offered and dipped it in the sauce. I held it up to salute her as if clinking fries like we would fancy drinks, saying, "To Betty."

Mike held a fry but refused to clink, responding, "I don't want that yucky stuff touching my fry."

I shoved the un-clinked fry into my mouth before my *yucky* sauce dripped onto the table. I nearly fell over. I was trying hard not to laugh. My sides and cheeks hurt from holding it in. Old men are hilarious. They'll say anything. I aspire to be just like Mike when I'm an old man.

It only took a few minutes to devour my burger when it arrived, but for another hour, Jacob and I listened to Mike's tales from the past. He shared stories of his childhood, his life with Betty, raising his kids, and watching his grandkids grow up. He described the joy of his great-grandchildren visiting, even if they concentrated on their phones and ignored him.

His comment made me glad I had resisted the urge to glance at my phone, not once, even to check the time. Dang, Mom would be so proud of me if I told her. I wouldn't tell her. I didn't need to. I no longer needed her to stroke my ego and tell me how awesome I was. I already knew it.

Mike concluded his story as he polished off his fries. By now, the winter sky was dark with hints of blue and purple. The bitter chill challenged us to leave the cozy confines of the restaurant and face the short but icy distance to the frozen pickup.

Mike fumbled in his back pocket, trying to pull out a wallet stuck between his baggy trousers and puffy coat.

Jacob waved his hand away, reached into the inside pocket of his coat, and whipped out his wallet. "It's on me, Mike."

With a single nod, Mike accepted.

While Jacob paid, I slid out of the booth and said, "Jacob, I'll warm up the pickup while you and Mike wait a few minutes."

"Need my keys?" Jacob asked, already reaching into his pocket.

"Got my own," I said, jingling my keys from my fingertips as I headed for the door. We shared the pickup, a vehicle ten years older than Jacob, that our Grandpa Wilde had given us after Grandma died. He kept her car and handed down his beloved pickup for us to look after. Without his generosity, I'm not sure we would have a *kid's rig*, as Mom called it, especially after the orchard finance debacle.

When Grandpa handed Dad the keys and title, I am sure he wondered how long it would last with two teenage boys driving. Dad didn't just give us the keys and let us go. As usual, there was a lesson to be learned. Mom decided it was the perfect time for a homeschooling lesson, as she did for everything learning-related. Dad led us to the garage, popped the hood, and spent four hours teaching us all he could. Mom lasted forty-five minutes, taking photos and joking about how spoiled we were. She warned us if she caught us doing any *funny business*, she'd take our keys and drive it herself.

I had no doubt she'd do just that.

Dad made us change a tire, check the oil, use jumper cables, and identify the warning lights on the dash. I was only 14. I believed that was the end, that I wouldn't have to endure Dad's truck lecture anymore. But when I finally got my permit a year and a half later, Dad guided me through the entire process again. I had to listen to it twice!

As Jacob and Mike shuffled their way back to the truck, it was warmed up just enough to take off the chill. Mike settled in and put his seatbelt on. Once Jacob had done the same, Mike said, "I bet you are happy to be going somewhere warm on your mission."

"Sounds good right now," Jacob chimed in, while I countered, "Until he's so hot even his eyeballs sweat."

"Aren't you a supportive brother?" Mike quipped.

"It's better than his guess on my mission game. He guessed I was going to get called to Siberia."

Mike laughed. "No need to go to Siberia. In the 1960s, I studied as an undergraduate at Rick's College in Rexburg, Idaho. One day I was at the Planetarium taking Betty on one of our first dates. We were stargazing and heard a professor mention the temperature was colder in Rexburg than Antarctica. You could have been called to Rexburg. That would make your mom happy. You would be only one state away."

"Idaho!" Jacob declared. "I'm glad I get to go further away than Idaho. I've been there before. We have family in Boise."

We laughed and talked some more until we returned to Mike's place. Jacob helped him inside, and I climbed into the front seat and waited for him to return. It took a while, but it was fine. I cranked the heat and blew the hot air straight on my face, trying to thaw my icy nose. In theory, Jacob was supposed to look after Mike today; however, Mike's family understood Jacob was leaving and had already hired his replacement. The new caregiver started Monday. Mike's family said today was to be a fun outing, a time for them to enjoy each other's company. They knew Jacob loved Mike as if he was his own grandpa, and they acknowledged the possibility of Grandpa Mike's passing before Jacob's return. Today might be their final meeting.

Jacob's kindness toward Mike was a testament to his enduring selflessness and generosity, traits sure to make him an outstanding missionary. Despite others making remarks about the elderly in our church congregation, Jacob never did. He sought ways to assist them. Every Sunday, I witnessed him talk to each widow and widower, always posing the same question: "How can I help you this week?"

It's up to me now. Can I be as brave and honorable as Jacob and do likewise for them? He was awesome; every little old lady in the ward loved him. They tugged on his tie, forcing him to lean over and hug them. He would wrap his arms around their frail shoulders and give them gentle pats on the back. My favorite was Sister Bean, or I should say pseudo–Grandma Bean. She wrapped her slender arms around his middle and squeezed with all her strength. Then she scolded him, telling him to hug her like he meant it, assuring him she wouldn't be so easily broken. Last week, she turned to me, grabbed my tie, and yanked me to her eye level. "This is it. Jacob's about to leave. Looks like it all falls on your shoulders. But I know you can handle it."

"Yep," I croaked out, trying to swallow as she'd missed both ends of my tie and was now choking me.

At last, Jacob returned to the pickup, and we headed home. I caught him wiping a little at his face, but tried not to notice. "Mike gave me a hundred dollars for my mission. I'm going to miss him." His voice choked up, and he fell silent.

"I know you are. I'll check in on him for you from time to time."

"Thanks." Jacob wiped his eyes again as we drove the rest of the way home in silence.

I couldn't help but marvel at Mike's powerful impact on my brother. These experiences had shaped him into the person he was now, a man ready to fulfill his divine purpose and be an effective missionary.

CHATER FIVE

Dawn hadn't even cracked the sky when I heard a movement in the house beyond my room. The sound seemed to come from the dining room. I rolled out of my warm bed, wrapped my favorite blanket around my shoulders, and padded through the house.

Jacob sat at the table, his fingers tracing the delicate pages of his scriptures with his left hand while his right followed along on his phone. I watched from my perch in the doorway, listening to the strange sounds escaping his mouth. When I realized what he was attempting, I marveled at his dedication. He was genuinely trying to learn the Tagalog language, emphasis on trying. Most newly called missionaries waited until their arrival at the missionary training center to begin their language training, but not Jacob; he wanted a head start.

"Dude, what are you saying?" I asked, flopping into the seat next to his at the table and laying my head on top of my folded arms like a pillow.

"I Nephi, having been born of goodly parents..." Jacob responded. "I found and downloaded a copy of the Tagalog Book of Mormon in the Gospel Library app. I'm trying to read along in my English scriptures, but I'm not doing very well."

I had never seen such a crestfallen look on my big brother's face.

"That hard, huh?"

"Impossible," he replied. "Here, look at this."

He turned his phone around. Huge, enormous, monstrous words loomed on the screen before me. My tired eyes couldn't adjust to make out any of them.

"Looks like gibberish to me."

Jacob sighed, "Yeah, me too. Unfortunately." He turned his phone back around and stared at it. I heard him sigh before he said, "Learning Tagalog presents its own set of challenges. The language has unique grammar rules, pronunciation, and sentence structures. They vastly differ from English. I keep hearing Mom's voice drilling us with the English language rules. I'm having trouble reconciling them with what I'm learning in Tagalog. The differences make it difficult to interpret the intended meaning. Look at this word," Jacob said, pointing to a word on his screen. "Say it one way, and it means *nothing*, but add a little inflection to your voice right here, and it means *everything*. I can't tell the difference."

He dropped his head and twined his fingers through his hair. No words came to mind, so I sat and waited. Then a thought struck me, and I responded, "Remember the prophet's words. They promise every missionary who reads the Book of Mormon in their mission language will become fluent. You keep reading and practicing, and you will learn. You have to. It's a blessing and a promise. God's truth is eternal. He sets forth the tasks and assigns the blessings. God must fulfill the promise if we accept and follow His counsel."

"Exactly! I'm relying on it." Jacob held up his phone and scriptures and waved them at me.

He continued to attempt his reading while I scrounged in the kitchen. Our mom was all about healthy, good, nutritious food. Where was the sugary cereal when you wanted some? I opened and closed every cupboard without success.

"Dude," Jacob said, waving at a top cabinet above the fridge. I opened the door and grinned like a Cheshire cat.

"Bro, do you always keep a stash up here? Why'd you do me dirty like that and not tell me? I'm hurt! Seriously, bro, wounded." I gangster-pounded my chest with my fist and gave him my best pouty face.

"Don't be such a drama queen. I will tell you my secrets with all the love I can muster. Mom's too short. She never uses or even looks up there. It's all yours. Fair warning, though, Dad monitors the stash and eats all the chips if he finds them. Many a Kettle Vinegar Chip has been sacrificed to the Pops!"

"You're my hero, man. I mean it H-E-R-O." With both hands in the air, one holding a cereal box, I gave him a hallelujah wave. Then, sauntering to the short cupboards that Mom could reach, I snatched out a bowl. Filling it with sugary goodness, I grabbed a spoon and hopped on the counter to sit.

Some moms may hate it when their kids sit on the counter, but our mom doesn't care. I've even caught her climbing on them to decorate all cutesy above the cupboards. Her only rule was to wipe it down and not leave it dirty. Add clean freak to her list of quirks.

I looked above the cupboard, unsure what cute items she kept there. I couldn't care less about the cutesy stuff, but she liked it. Oversized white platters, only used for holidays, rested against the rear wall. In front, there were a few old knick-knacks from Grandma. Above the stove, there was a big farmhouse sign declaring this the Kitchen. As if we didn't already know we were in the kitchen.

"Hey Noah," Jacob said, glancing at me from his reading, "what did you think of this week's *Come, Follow Me* lesson?"

"Umm," I hesitated, trying to recall the specifics of the lesson Dad led last Tuesday, as that was the best day for our family to fit in the lesson. "It was interesting how Nephi's faith helped him overcome his challenges. The Liahona was remarkable in its ability to function as both a physical and spiritual compass. It guided Lehi and his family through the wilderness and offered them spiritual direction. It's incredible to consider the immense power of that object."

"Absolutely!" Jacob added. "If they were righteous and obedient, both physically and spiritually, they led themselves in the right direction by using the Liahona, which is a symbol of God's guidance and mercy."

"That's a great point. I recall reading that the Liahona only functioned when they had faith in God. When they murmured and were disobedient, it ceased to work. It's a powerful reminder that our faith and actions are significant in receiving divine guidance."

"Definitely. The Liahona further teaches us the importance of aligning our will with God's. It serves as a reminder that when we are on the right path and seeking the Lord's guidance, He will direct our steps and show us the way. Like He did for Lehi and his family, I pray this happens on my mission. The Lord will guide those who seek truth and the gospel's light. I know the gospel will give their lives direction, as it has mine."

"I love how the Liahona provided more than directional guidance. It also contained written words of instruction from the Lord. God communicates with everyone in the way they need Him to. He adapts His words to our needs, sometimes through tangible means like the Liahona, and sometimes through the living scriptures. Without them, my life is incomplete. Since I started attending Seminary, I rely on these sacred writings in a way I never imagined possible. The thought of not having their guidance leaves me bereft of direction and counsel. They are every bit as special to me as my precious family."

"Yes, that's a crucial aspect to note. The Liahona provided physical direction and served as a source of spiritual nourishment. It also reminds us of the importance of seeking guidance from many sources. We can use both physical and spiritual sources to help us navigate life's challenges."

"Agreed. The significance of the Liahona is astonishing. I'm grateful for the opportunity to study and learn from it in our *Come, Follow Me* lessons. It inspires me to seek divine guidance in my life and strive to align my actions with God's will."

I watched as Jacob packed his scriptures and notebooks into his mission satchel. Clearly, he had dedicated himself to serving the Lord and was on the path to becoming an exemplary missionary. While I knew I would miss him terribly during the two years he would be gone, I also knew he was doing exactly what he was supposed to do.

"Hey, Jacob?" I asked, hopping down from the counter. "Are you nervous about leaving?"

"Of course, I'm a little nervous," he admitted, slinging his scripture satchel over his shoulder. "I've prayed a lot, and I know this is the path the Lord wants for me. Even though it's scary, I trust He will guide me every step of the way."

"Wow," I whispered, in awe of Jacob's faith and determination. "I hope I am half as brave as you when it's my turn to serve."

"You will be, Noah," Jacob said as he affectionately ruffled my bedhead. "I know you'll make an amazing missionary someday."

"Thanks, Jacob," I said. I smiled and a sense of warmth surrounded my chest in response to his words. If my brother believed in me, I could believe in myself even more.

"I'm going to shower and get ready for church now. I need the extra time to read over my talk. Catch you later." Jacob gathered his scriptures and phone and headed to the back of the house, where our bedrooms were. A few minutes later, as I was finishing my sugary cereal, I heard the water running.

WE MOVED IN UNISON, the clanking of our shovels against the concrete of the church sidewalks. My nose hairs were freezing, and the huff of my breath filled the chilly air. I cleared my throat between heaves and said, "Jacob, I've been thinking about something."

"Go ahead, Noah. What's on your mind?" Jacob stopped shoveling, straightened, and then propped a hand on his shovel, his breath coming in white puffs of steam.

"Remember how Dad always talks about the importance of paying tithing? About giving a tenth of our income to the Lord?"

"Of course. It's one of the gospel principles he holds dearest. He and Mom have received many blessings in their lives from tithing.

Pay tithing first, even if you're short; the Lord will provide the rest. He attests to the truth of this for his entire life."

"I did some quick math in my head. When you return from your mission, you will have dedicated a tenth of your life to the Lord. A life tithing."

"That's true. I hadn't considered it from that perspective before," Jacob responded.

"I thought it was an interesting analogy," I offered. I hoped my brother didn't think my idea was too weird.

He smiled and nodded, encouraging me to continue. I released a breath and said, "But what about the rest of our lives? How will we pay a full life's tithing for the upcoming decades? What are your thoughts on this?"

"It would be with true dedication to our callings. If we perform them to the best of our abilities, we will pay a full life tithe."

"And helping people like Grandma Bean and Grandpa Mike, and doing heavy lifting like this," I offered, as I bent my back low and shoveled another heap of snow.

"Christ preached we should care for the widows and orphans. *Inasmuch as ye have done it unto one of the least of these my brethren, ye have done it unto me.*"[1]

As we kept shoveling, I often glanced at Jacob. I couldn't help but notice the light in his eyes. Their sparkle mesmerized me as it proclaimed his unwavering commitment to his faith. He had always been a devoted member of The Church of Jesus Christ of Latter-day Saints, but he radiated with passion and purpose since submitting his mission application.

"Jacob, do you ever worry about the sacrifices you'll make during your mission?" I asked.

"Of course I do," he admitted. "But I also know any sacrifice I make will be worth it if I can help bring others closer to Christ. It's the purpose of being a missionary. I'm willing to face whatever challenges God deems necessary to fulfill this purpose."

"Like learning a new language or adapting to a different culture?" I ventured.

Jacob nodded in agreement. "I'm sure I'll be able to learn another language. If Dad can, I can too. I am eager to learn about another culture. But whatever challenges come with it pale compared to the blessings of serving God."

While shoveling the church sidewalks, my admiration for my brother grew. He chose the harder path, pausing his life to serve God, unlike his peers who pursued college or jobs. Many of his classmates were already enjoying a vibrant campus life, but not Jacob. Jacob focused on guiding God's lost sheep back to the fold. He devoted himself to providing hope and healing to those who had lost their way.

My heart swelled with pride as my voice rose with conviction. I declared, "Jacob, you have the courage and strength to do incredible things. I am in awe of you and know your mission will be exceptional."

"Thank you, Noah. I'll do my best to make you and our parents proud," Jacob replied. He placed a reassuring hand on my shoulder, gave it a squeeze, then we returned to shoveling.

Ten minutes later, the sing-song voice of fifteen-year-old Shelby Thurston broke through my thoughts. "Hi, Noah!"

I stopped shoveling, stood straight and tall, and looked over at her. She was adorable in her light pink Sunday dress. She always wore pink. It was her signature color, and she wore it better than anyone else. Her younger brother wrenched his hand from her and ran off, causing her to slip on the ice. She shrieked, and I reached out and steadied her. "Whoa there, don't fall. Here, I got you."

"Goodness, that would have been terrible!" she exclaimed, clinging to my arm. She righted herself on the shoveled walk and stomped her petite feet free of the snow that collected on the tips of her shoes. "Oh no, I'm sorry. I just messed up your shoveling."

I laughed she thought the handful of snow from her cute little feet constituted messing up my shoveling. I used the edge of the shovel to throw it off the sidewalk and declared, "There, all gone."

She giggled, and my heart squeezed.

"It might be slippery. Here, allow me to walk you to the door." I offered her my arm, and she tucked her hand into the crook of my elbow. She had a fuzzy white cape-wrap-thingy on and matching gloves. She looked angelic. As I walked her to the door, I kept expecting the clouds to part and rays of sunlight to pour over her. She would sparkle with goodness and glitter, and fairy dust. Specifically, Tinker Bell fairy dust, because walking next to Shelby made me feel like I could fly.

"Thank you, Noah."

Upon reaching the building entrance, I held the door open. Right as she was about to enter, a snowball struck her on the left side of her face.

She screamed in shock, and I whipped my head around to see another one of her brothers laughing like a madman. "Gotcha, Shelby!"

"John," I scolded with every ounce of sixteen-year-old authority I could muster. "That was unacceptable. Miss Shelby is dressed in her Sunday best and is not ready for a snowball fight. Say you're sorry."

Eight-year-old John Thurston stuck out his tongue at me, and hollered "Sorry, Shelby!" as he ran to the other door to go inside and avoid us.

"Here, let me help you." I released the door and removed clumps of snow from Shelby's hair and shoulder. Fuming with rage, she clenched her fists and gritted her teeth. She was angry, embarrassed, and flustered all at once. I'd never seen a girl look this perfect in all my life. "There, I think we got it all," I declared, opening the door again. "Why not go in and warm up?"

She nodded and walked past me without another word.

My eyes followed her walk up the corridor until she turned into the chapel. Then, I returned to shoveling.

Fifteen minutes later, Jacob and I rushed into the chapel. Jacob sat behind the bishop while I took a seat next to Dad. We had two minutes to spare. Nice! A glance at the front made me realize we needed priests to bless the sacrament. I took a moment to fix my tie, then stood up and walked to the front, taking a seat at the sacrament table. I relaxed on the pew, looking at the congregation, and found Shelby watching me. I nodded in what I hoped was a nonchalant manner, then looked at my hands in my lap, unable to meet anyone else's gaze.

When I could finally look up again, I saw the loving faces of so many family members looking back at me. Grandma and Grandpa Evans sat in the row with Mom and Dad, their smiles warm and reassuring. Grandma's eyes sparkled with pride, while Grandpa's weathered hands rested on his lap, a gentle reminder of the strength and wisdom he carried. Aunt Vee was there too, surrounded by her husband and children, who whispered and giggled as they shared their excitement for Jacob. Their presence felt like a comforting embrace, each face a testament to our family's unwavering support. I knew that even more family members were watching the Zoom call from Utah, their love stretching across the miles, adding to the collective warmth in the room. It was a bittersweet moment, filled with joy and nostalgia, as we prepared to send Jacob off on his mission.

This week was designated for Young Men's, not Sunday School, which meant I wouldn't see Shelby in our combined class. After church, Jacob was being set apart as a missionary, so I wouldn't get to talk to her before heading home, either. As I tucked my scriptures into Mom's SUV to lighten my load, I caught sight of Shelby struggling to wrangle her unruly brothers into their family's minivan. I waved, and she smiled and waved back.

After church, our home buzzed with the warmth of a big family dinner, laughter, and the clatter of dishes. But as soon as the last guest left and only the four of us remained, Mom shifted into business mode. With only two days left before Jacob's departure for his mission to the Philippines, there was no time to waste. While chasing down items for Mom, I spotted Jacob walking by. "Hey, Jacob, come look at this!" I called out, tracing my fingers along the map of the islands and imagining what it would be like to spend two years there.

Jacob walked over to the table, his thoughtful blue eyes scanning the map I had spread out before me.

"Look at all these islands. Did you know there are over seven thousand?" I asked, trying to distract myself from the impending goodbye weighing heavier on my heart each day we drew closer to Jacob's departure.

"7,641 to be exact, but only seven are main islands."

Of course, he knew the stats.

He leaned in to scrutinize the map more. "That's amazing. I can't wait to get there and explore my mission area and meet new people. It will be an unbelievable adventure."

The excitement in his voice was palpable, yet I could sense something else. Beneath his excitement was a little fear and trepidation. For a moment, he didn't seem like the larger-than-life older brother but a timid boy afraid to board a plane and leave his family. A boy who knew he would be gone for two long years, far away from his familiar life and the people he loved. When you thought about it, our little town was nothing compared to the Philippines.

Jacob extended his finger and pointed to one mountain range, then another flanking Cauayan City. "I will be right here in Cauayan, Isabela, Luzon. This is Cordillera Central, and this is Sierra Madre. I can't wait to get there, to see the countryside, and learn the Filipino culture. As I understand, travel can be difficult on the mission because of the mountains. It takes a long time to get anywhere. It's not like it is here." His finger ran up the map, tracing the mountains and then circling the imaginary boundary of his mission. The map was dry and rough to the touch. When he leaned his weight on his finger, it sunk into the thin parchment paper, leaving an impression. He leaned low over the map, studying the names of each city within his mission boundary. He attempted to say a few, but despite neither of us speaking the language, we knew he made a hilarious mess of their pronunciations.

Knowing Jacob my whole life as I did, I could see the veritable cogs of his brain working. He envisioned living in each of those cities, surrounded by Filipino people he hadn't met yet, and speaking a language he didn't understand. He couldn't wait to discover their traditions. He was eager to leave and begin this grand new adventure.

"Before my mission area, I need to go to the Missionary Training Center in Manila." He dragged his finger south, circled a little area, and tapped his finger over it. He grinned and slapped me on the back. "You know what? These are going to be the best two years FOR my life!"

"I know it will be. It sure was for Dad. It's been over twenty years since he served a mission in Brazil, and to this day, he talks about it like it was yesterday."

Jacob laughed at the truthfulness of my words.

"I heard my name. Are you talking about me?" Dad mumbled from his recliner, where he had been snoozing while *Music and the Spoken Word* played in the background.

"Just talking mission stuff again. Go back to sleep."

Dad adjusted his recliner to sit and pawed at his sleepy eyes. "I'm always up for talking mission stuff."

I chuckled and responded, "We know."

"Noah found a map of the Philippines. Come look at this."

Dad meandered to his feet, stretched his back like a tomcat, and lumbered to the table. He plopped into a chair and turned the map towards him. "Let me see this thing. Oh wow, isn't this cool?" He inspected the old map while Jacob repeated what he had already told me. Dad leaned close and continued to inspect the cities, mountains, and roads. He was wide awake and intent on the task at hand.

"I'm afraid to admit I Googled the Philippines, and a few scary articles emerged. Americans are frequent targets of terrorists or kidnappings, especially on these islands." I pointed at the islands further south on the map. The thought of my big brother, my protector, venturing into the unknown filled me with pride and fear.

"Yes, I read them too, but those islands are further south from where Jacob will be. His mission boundaries brim with tourist attractions and popular hot spots. As I see it, that makes it safer. The people there will love him as much as we do, and I am confident God will keep him safe."

"Of course," I said, glancing at the map key and gauging the distance from island to island. Dad was right; the more dangerous islands were a lot farther south. Dad had a way with words that eased my fears.

Just then, Mom ran by with her clipboard. The room became an instant whirlwind of bustling activity. Jacob left Dad and me with the map, trailing behind Mom as she bustled around preparing.

"Jacob, have you double-checked everything on this list?" Mom asked, waving the clipboard from where she settled on the couch surrounded by Jacob's belongings. She had red rims around her eyes, betraying the exhaustion and emotions of the past few weeks. She was our everything, and I knew for a fact we were hers. I could only imagine what her emotional state must be. Jacob was only my brother, but he was her son. Her firstborn. Her baby.

Mom worried all the time whether she needed to or not. When she and Dad traveled, be it domestic or international, she called us every night to check in. Once, I mentioned how dumb it was to Grandma Wilde, and she lectured me for ten minutes about a mother's love. Now I knew where Dad inherited his lecture abilities from.

"Let's go over it again," Jacob said, mostly for her. His voice was steady and calm, though his nervous actions gave him away. He fidgeted with his hands and tapped his right heel on the floor.

"Passport?" Mom checked off the item with a sigh of relief. It had arrived only two days ago, cutting it a little too close in her book. If it wasn't finished two weeks early, it might as well be late.

"Got it," Jacob said, patting the front pocket of his satchel where he'd placed it earlier that day.

"Travel documents?"

"Right here, triple checked." His eyes met hers with a comforting smile. I knew his smile well. It was the one he gave me when I was scared or unsure about something. It always reassured me and seemed to have the same effect on Mom.

"Alright... clothes?" Mom continued, her voice wavering.

"Six to eight pairs of pants. Ten white dress shirts, three long-sleeved, seven short," Jacob recited. He pointed at a folded stack of shirts and slacks in his suitcase, the creases aligned. He then proceeded through his garments, socks, ties, belts, shoes, and other items.

"Okay... toiletries?"

"Shampoo, soap, toothbrush, toothpaste, razor, shaving cream, deodorant. I believe that covers it." He rattled off the items as if he'd memorized them, which he had.

"What about the bug spray?"

"Got it."

"Thank goodness. The mosquitoes there are the size of small children."

I laughed from Dad's recliner, where I had settled to watch the spectacle and play games on my phone. Dad was now lying in the middle of the living room floor with his hands propped behind his head, staring at the ceiling and smiling over Mom's craziness. He just let her be her Wilde self.

"Other essentials? Scriptures, journal, pens..."

"Of course, Mom," Jacob reassured her, reaching into his satchel to show her the worn leather-bound scriptures and a brand-new journal. "You know I wouldn't go anywhere without my scriptures."

"Good, good." Mom glanced at the list, her finger tracing the remaining items. Tears filled her eyes as she gazed up at Jacob. "You know me. I need to ensure you have everything you need, sweetheart. I won't be there to help care for you for a long time. You're on your own after this," she whispered.

Jacob placed a hand on her shoulder, his expression tender. "Mom, I'll be okay. God will provide for me, as He always has."

CHAPTER SIX

THE FOLLOWING DAY, I woke to the sound of a howling wind and the sight of snowflakes swirling past my window. The weather forecast had warned us of an impending blizzard, but I hadn't expected it to arrive so soon. With Jacob's departure tomorrow, our world seemed to flip upside down.

"Snow!" Mom declared, exasperated, from the kitchen as I shuffled from my room. Bleary-eyed, I joined her at the window, my breath fogging the glass as I pressed my face close to see outside. "This will make it difficult to drive to Seattle tomorrow morning. We have two mountain passes to cross. I hope they get the roads plowed before we need to get Jacob to the airport."

There it was again. I could hear the worry in Mom's voice.

"We will make it. It will take more than a few snow flurries to deter Black."

Dad's big black Ford was a powerhouse. I thought it was unstoppable, but the February snow was record-breaking. I hoped I appeared more confident than I actually was as I reached around her and snatched a pancake from the top of her stack.

"A few snow flurries? That's what you call that, flurries?" Mom pointed out the window and gave me a wry, crooked smile before she returned to cooking breakfast. "Go wake up your brother. You two need to get started plowing. It's already over twenty-two inches out there and expected to persist snowing for three more days. Weather reports say this is one of the worst storms in history. It's expected to accumulate over three feet today, and it's already drifting. You know how dangerous that can be. It will be overwhelming if you don't plow as it snows."

As I headed to Jacob's room, I couldn't help but feel a sense of urgency in my chest. Here we were, about to say goodbye to my big brother, and now we had to battle a blizzard too. The universe tested our faith, daring us to continue trusting God's plan. Was this His plan? A vicious snowstorm that dared us to venture over two mountain passes to take him to the airport.

"Jacob," I called, pushing open his door. "Time to get up. We've got work to do."

"Already?" he groaned, pulling the covers over his head. "I swear, I just went to bed. Leave me alone. It's my last day to sleep in."

"Come on, Mom needs us to go plow everyone out," I insisted. I yanked his blankets off and threw them on the floor. "Besides, this will be your last chance to plow for a while. It doesn't snow much in the Philippines." I wryly laughed, knowing full well it doesn't snow at all in the Philippines.

"Alright, alright," he muttered, sitting up and rubbing his eyes. "Give me a minute to get dressed. How bad is it?" he asked, even as he stood and went to the window. "Gadzooks!" he blurted before I had time to respond.

"You're telling me. Mom says it's over twenty-two inches already."

Jacob groaned and pulled his flannel-lined work pants out of his bottom drawer. He hadn't packed them for his two-year stint in the Philippines. They'd remain in the bottom drawer until he came back and needed them once more. I returned to the kitchen with Mom until he emerged.

We bundled into our heaviest winter gear before braving the frigid air outside. Snow fell, obscuring my vision. It did not deter us. We trudged onward, determined to clear a path to get our trusty pickup out of the shop where we had parked. Despite Dad plowing before work, the ground had already piled up again with hip-high drifts.

"Can you believe this weather?" Jacob shouted over the wind as we pulled the shop doors open, our breath coming out in puffs of white vapor. "It's like God's sending me a going-away present!"

"More like a challenge," I grumbled, kicking at the drift blocking the door from opening wide enough to get the truck out. I knew Jacob was trying to stay positive, but I was freezing and didn't want to plow today. I was off work for a week, and since I'm homeschooled and my motherly teacher said she was too distraught over the impending loss of her eldest son, she couldn't properly supervise my education. As a result, I also got to skip school. "Want to pack me in your suitcase and let me tag along? A couple of years without snow sounds mighty nice right about now." I heaved against the door one last time, and the drift gave way. It rolled open.

Together, we pushed a mountain of snow off the driveway. The plow scraped along the icy gravel beneath. It was slow going, our progress hindered by the relentless storm, but we refused to give up.

It took us an hour to plow our drive, the parking area in front of the house and shop. Then, while Jacob ran to the house to grab us some snacks, I loaded the pickup with sandbags and salt. When he came back, I was throwing two shovels and a broom in the back.

"Looks like we're ready. Thanks for loading the sand and salt." Jacob threw a couple of granola bars and a small baggie of pistachios on the console between us, then tossed me a water bottle, which I caught.

"Thought I'd let you drive, since this is your last chance to play in the snow for a while."

Jacob laughed. "Play? Is that what you call this work?"

I shrugged and opened the water bottle, gulping down half of it without taking a breath.

"Alright, I guess we can play a little." Jacob raised the plow on the front as he pulled out of our driveway. He gave me a wry look, and in a voice that danced between audacity and exhilaration, he bellowed, "Don't tell Mom!"

His foot crashed onto the pedal, awakening the slumbering beast beneath the truck's hood. The engine roared, a primal symphony of power. In a heartbeat, the world outside blurred into a frenzy of white. The truck bounced as it climbed over the mounds of snow onto the road, which was piled high. The truck experienced a small spin-out, but when a couple of trees blocked the drifts and the bare road showed, the tires caught, and an explosion of snow followed. A glorious eruption that painted the winter canvas with a tempest of white. We charged forward, a force of nature unchained, and the snow danced and swirled in mesmerizing chaos, trailing in the wake of our furious escape.

Jacob wrestled with the wheel, summoning every ounce of his skill to command the truck through the snowy wonderland. Drifts beckoned us like adversaries, threatening to ensnare the truck's unwavering path. But Jacob was no mere spectator of fate's designs. He drift-busted like the pro he was. His focus was unbreakable, a laser guiding him down the middle of the road. The snow-laden abyss on either side yearned to swallow us whole, but Jacob defied the icy odds, deftly avoiding being sucked into their waiting arms and breaking their finger-like tendrils snaking into the road.

Adrenaline surged through my veins, igniting a fire within. Every heartbeat was a triumphant drumbeat, a reminder that we were alive. My brother was conquering the frozen world with sheer will and an old Ford F-150.

"This is awesome!" I shouted.

Finally, Jacob arrived at the highway. "We'll plow the road on the way home," he declared.

"I know!" I stated matter-of-fact. Then I grabbed the *Oh Crap* handle as he busted through the final drift and pulled onto the highway. The back of the truck fishtailed. Like a pro, Jacob steered and got the pickup back on course.

"Hold on tight. It's icy!" Jacob yelled, accelerating.

"Dude!" I shouted, bracing my feet against the floor and leaning back in my seat. The snow was pounding the windshield, impairing our vision by the time we sped up to a safe speed. "I feared we'd get stuck," I confessed as he accelerated.

"Nah, I got this," Jacob said, steering through the edge of a drift creeping onto the highway. The county couldn't keep up with the heavy snowfall, yet it was against the law for us to use our plow here. "Even if we did, that's where you come in. I stay toasty warm and drive while you get out and push."

"I know. That's why I was worried," I admitted with a laugh.

"Almost there," Jacob encouraged. "I'm sure we'll make it without getting stuck."

And we did. A minute later, we were in front of Grandma Bean's house. Jacob stopped and dropped the plow. I grabbed a shovel from the back. Without speaking, we both got to work. He plowed the drive, barnyard, and anywhere the plow could fit. He even plowed part of her front and side yards to keep the future melting away from the house. I tackled the walkways in the front and back of the house.

I was halfway through the back path that cut across the yard to the barn when I heard Jacob's crazy laugh split the surrounding air, and a mound of snow went flying over my head. The howling wind gobbled up and carried off his laughter. I admired how his legs, a little longer, and his arms, a little stronger, hefted the snow a little faster than mine. No matter how hard I tried, his shovelfuls were just a little larger than mine.

"What in the world are you two doing out there?" Grandma Bean shouted from her door.

"Shoveling your walks!" I hollered back, trying to be heard by her old ears over the howling wind.

"But it's still snowing."

"It's a lot of snow, and we'll be gone tomorrow. Remember, I'm leaving. If I don't help today, Noah has to shovel it all by himself tomorrow evening. Unless you'll come out here and help him?" Jacob found her expression amusing.

"You shovel. I make cookies and banana bread, remember!"

"Exactly! What is it today, cookies or bread?"

Her face fell a little when she responded, "It's too early. I didn't expect you. I haven't made anything."

"No problem," I responded. "This one's on the house."

She smiled in her wonderful way that I loved so much. Ever since Grandma Wilde had died, I appreciated Sister Bean being there in her place. We still had Mom's mom, Grandma Evans, but Sister Bean had a personality closer to Grandma Wilde.

"You better go back inside and stay warm," I warned her. "We'll come and say goodbye before we leave."

We finished ten minutes later, with plowed snow mounds higher than we were tall and walkway tunnels up to our hips.

After the last shovelful, Jacob grabbed my shovel from me and said, "I'll load these in the truck. You go inside."

I ran to the door and knocked. Grandma Bean answered as if she knew I was coming. She must have been watching us from the window.

"All done. I'll return late tomorrow or early Wednesday after we drop Jacob off at the airport. Call Bishop if you need anything before then. I'm sure he can scrounge up some other young men to come over and break their backs."

"I'll wait," Grandma Bean said. "I'm not going anywhere, and nobody takes care of me half so well as you Wilde boys." She beckoned out the door with a wave at Jacob. "Come here," she demanded in her loving but most strict old-lady-grandma voice. "Here, this is for you."

She handed Jacob an envelope covered with stickers and elegant, flowy handwriting. Then she pulled him into a big hug. "My goodness, I'm going to miss you. I remember when I first got to know you. You were four years old and in my primary class. Oh, how I loved you and your old-man prayers."

"Old-man prayers? What does that mean?" I inquired with curiosity.

"Your big brother memorized old men's prayers from sacrament meeting. So, when he prayed, it was never a little kid praying. He spoke like an old man. I bet he didn't know the meaning of half the words he prayed."

Jacob wrapped her in his arms and gave her a *Tinker Bell Kiss*. "I'm going to miss you too, but you'll still have Noah, and I'll be back before you know it. Don't forget to give Mom your email address, so you get my mission updates. If you visit our house on an occasional Sunday afternoon, I'll get to see you when I call. With the time difference, my p-day calls will be Sunday evenings here."

Jacob and I said goodbye and ran back up the walkway tunnel to our pickup. When I looked over my shoulder, Grandma Bean was still standing in the doorway, wiping a tear from her wrinkled cheek.

Our drive home was crazier than our drive there. County plows were nowhere to be seen, and drifts were halfway across the highway. At the turnoff, we dropped the plow again and cleared our road. Normally, it only takes two passes to plow the road, but our little plow took five today. We hoped it would still be clear when Dad came back from work in a few hours.

The house buzzed with activity all day and into the evening as we readied for Jacob's departure. We would leave at what Dad calls O-Dark-Thirty, meaning hours and hours before the sun graces us with its presence on the Eastern horizon.

It had continued to snow all day and still showed no signs of stopping. Following dinner, I had to face the elements once more, running road passes and plowing the drive.

Dad came in from the garage and peeled off his black coveralls. "I took her down, fueled her up, topped off the DEF, refilled the washer fluid, and checked the oil. She's ready for another adventure."

I loved how Dad referred to Black as *she*. I did the same with Old Gray, my pickup. It's completely normal for us to give names to our vehicles like Old Gray, Black, Papa Smurf, and Mom's SUV, Sunshine. I'll give you one guess what color they all are.

"Let's load the bags into the truck to save time in the morning. We can't put them in the back because Blewett and Snoqualmie Passes will both be a mess. We don't want them ruined before you get on your way. It's going to be cramped in the back with the two of you and all Jacob's luggage," Dad said. He grabbed the first oversized suitcase and headed out the door. He looked funny with his coveralls peeled halfway off and bunched at his waist. The suspenders hung to his knees.

I helped carry out the second suitcase as Jacob grabbed his carry-on. Dad tucked them in the middle and told us to hop in. "Make sure you fit on each side. You'll be half asleep when you get in. We don't want to rearrange in the morning."

We just fit.

"Please recheck the weather, Noah," Mom called from inside the house. "And make sure you charge your phone. It's your job to check the road conditions on the way."

"Got it, Mom," I replied, anticipating her subsequent request. "And don't worry, I also helped Jacob check his flights. Despite the weather, they're still running on time." My voice sounded confident, but inside, I wasn't so sure. The storm tested us at every turn, throwing everything it had at us before forcing us to say our goodbyes to Jacob. Dad was sure the snow would cease overnight, and we would have open roads in the morning, but I didn't agree, and neither did the weatherman.

"Perfect, I expected as much. Once we pass North Bend, there won't be any more snow. We'll only have the notorious Seattle rain."

No matter how hard I tried that night, I couldn't fall asleep. I tossed and turned, knowing my brother would be gone at the end of tomorrow's trip. A little before midnight, I snuck into Jacob's room with a pile of blankets and my pillow and lay down on his floor.

"Noah, dude, is that you?" Jacob asked in a sleepy voice.

"Yeah, I couldn't sleep. I want to have one last slumber party. Go back to sleep."

"Sounds like a plan," Jacob responded. He reached over the side of the bed and patted my shoulder before rolling over and falling back to sleep. His light snoring lulled me to sleep like it had when we shared a room when we were little.

At 3:30 a.m., the house stirred, each of us willing ourselves to face the dark, chilly morning. Snowfall persisted throughout the night with a greater accumulation than the previous day. It looked terrible, and I wasn't sure what Dad would decide.

"Okay, everyone," Dad said, rubbing his eyes as he gulped his orange juice. "Let's hit the road. We need to get Jacob to Seattle before his flight takes off."

"Will we get out of the driveway without plowing?" Mom asked, cupping her eyes against the window to look outside.

"Of course we will," Dad said. "Once we make it to the highway, and then it's smooth sailing to Seattle. I bet we have clean roads the entire trip."

Mom studied him doubtfully. "I think we should say a quick prayer."

Dad said the prayer, albeit not swiftly. By the end, I found myself with sore knees, my butt up in the air, and my face pressed against my pillow resting on the floor. It had started on my lap; I swear.

As soon as the prayer was over, we all opened our eyes, but before I moved, Mom slapped my rear end, waving in the air. She laughed and whooped, "I couldn't resist!"

I deserved that.

I heard the wind howling outside the garage door as we left the house and climbed into the truck. It whipped the snow into a frenzy. The storm swallowed the world outside our tiny bubble, giving the impression that we were the only people left on Earth.

The garage door opened, and Dad gunned the truck in reverse, crashing through the drifts. He reversed almost a hundred feet, angling down the driveway and backing into the shop yard before shifting into drive and gunning Black towards the road. With a swift motion, Mom reached over and hit the button to close the garage. She watched to make sure the door closed all the way. Dad crashed out of the driveway like Jacob had done yesterday; he drift-busted like a pro. The whole time, Mom clasped the door handle and threw out cautions to Dad. He responded, "Yes, dear," as he always did. He had to ignore her protests. Slowing, even slightly, we risked getting stuck, which would prevent us from getting Jacob to the airport on time.

We weren't alone on our daring journey, though only a few other vehicles had ventured before us. On the highway, snowplows and salt trucks carved through the darkness with blazing headlights. Fellow drivers inched forward, their cars hugging the road's edges as if wary of the uncharted. In contrast, Dad piloted Black with a blend of caution and conviction. Amid it all, safety enveloped me, a reassuring cloak woven from years of trusting Dad's driving and the brawn of our powerful truck.

"Look at that guy," Dad muttered, pointing at a car crawling along at a snail's pace. "Some people don't know how to drive in the snow."

"Give 'em a break, Dad. Not everyone grew up driving in mountain snowstorms like you," Jacob cautioned.

"Or have a sturdy truck like Black," I added.

I watched the snowflakes dance in the headlights, mesmerized by how they swirled and twirled before disappearing into the abyss. Thinking about Jacob being thousands of miles away in a snowless location seemed strange.

"Hey, Noah, you okay?" Jacob said, nudging me.

"Yeah," I replied, forcing a smile. "I'm just thinking about you being so far away, that's all."

He nodded and returned his attention to the front, letting me become once again lost in my thoughts.

"Keep your eyes on the road, Dad," Jacob said. "We don't know what's around the next bend." My breath fogged the window as I leaned close and wiped the glass with my sleeve. I don't know why I bothered. Snow swirling in the depths of a dark night created a vast expanse of nothingness. The blackness beyond the back window rendered sight futile. No glimmer or flicker illuminated the path for the wary traveler. Nothing except the truck's headlights. Like a beacon, they illuminated the night in front of us. The absence of light beyond engulfed my senses. It was a palpable cloak of impenetrable blackness.

As I strained to see beyond, the air seemed thicker, heavy with the weight of unseen mysteries. The stillness whispered secrets I wanted to unravel. Even though I had driven these roads countless times, I was currently lost.

"Yup, can't afford any surprises in this weather," Mom chimed in from the front seat. She fidgeted with her cell phone, glancing at the pass reports and checking traffic when she had adequate reception. Furtive glances betrayed her worry. I knew she was praying for our safety on this treacherous journey.

"God is watching over us," Jacob murmured, as if reading her thoughts.

"Of course He is," Mom replied, her voice softening. "He won't let anything happen to us, especially not today. We have a set-apart missionary on board. That's our ticket to safety."

"I'm glad we seem on time," I mused. "Luckily, you made us leave early. It's taken at least an extra hour over our usual travel time to make it this far."

"Definitely," Jacob agreed. "I should be alright either way. I'm slated to be there three hours early, but I'm sure I'll be ready and waiting at the gate for over half of that."

"True, that's always the case, especially on these international flights," Dad said.

Mom leaned back in her seat, reaching over her left shoulder to grip Jacob's hand. They didn't need any words. She just wanted a reassuring love squeeze.

"You know, Mom, I would have been lost if you hadn't created all those checklists for me."

We all knew he just placated her, but we didn't care.

"Did you remember to pack your scriptures?" Mom asked, her voice suddenly sharp. "You'll need them in the Philippines."

"Yes, Mom," Jacob reassured. "They're safely tucked away in my suitcase."

"Good," she sighed, relaxing back into her seat. "One less thing to worry about."

"Is there anything else on your mind, Mom?" I ventured, glancing at the reflection of her eyes in the rearview mirror. "If there is, tell us before it's too late."

"Everything will be fine, Noah," she said. "All we need to do is get Jacob to the airport on time and trust God will take care of him for *the next two years*." Her voice caught in her throat, and the words came out choked.

Dad released the steering wheel with his right hand and took Mom's left. He held her hand for a minute before returning it to the steering wheel.

"Sounds like a plan," Jacob grinned. Reaching across the pile of luggage, he gave me a reassuring pat on the shoulder. "Imagine the stories we'll have to share when I return."

"Two years is a long time, Jacob," I said, my voice wavering like Mom's. "I'm going to miss you."

"Hey, remember what Bishop said?" Jacob responded with excitement in his voice. "This is a once-in-a-lifetime opportunity. I'll be doing God's work and helping others in need. You wouldn't want me to miss that, would you?"

"Of course not," I sighed. "I just wish it didn't have to be so far away and without me."

"Distance is nothing when you have love and faith," Mom said. "We'll be together in spirit, even if we're thousands of miles apart."

Mom almost lost it at the word *thousands*, and I must admit, I swallowed hard and had to fight the thud in my chest. Dad seemed to be the only one holding it together, at least on the surface. When I studied his eyes in the rearview mirror, I saw he looked tired and seemed aged since yesterday.

"Besides, we'll always have our memories of shoveling snow at Sister Bean's place, won't we? Nothing can take that away from us."

"True! This is one epic snowstorm," I agreed, a touch more optimistic.

"Speaking of which," Dad interjected, gripping the steering wheel tighter as he navigated an icy curve. "Let's focus on getting through it, shall we?"

As we continued our journey, the hours seemed to stretch into eternity. The monotonous hum of Black's engine was interrupted only by my thoughts. Each one pondering the same question: *How will life be without Jacob?*

CHAPTER SEVEN

THE SNOWFALL CONTINUED, BUT it was dwindling, and Dad was picking up speed. No longer were we moving at a turtle's pace. I mused a little to myself. *At least it wasn't a snail's pace. Then again, which was slower, the snail or the turtle?* I concluded a snail moved slower because of its smaller size. It made sense in my tired mind until I remembered the tortoise and the hare tale.

The snow blanketing everything wasn't as thick as when we were on the pass, but we were still in a winter wonderland. My heart fluttered with excitement, pride, and anxiety as I realized how close we were to Seattle. I sensed the gravity of the moment as a hint of dark blue pierced the black sky. The day struggled to wake up. We had been on the road for two hours already. With the snow easing up and Dad maintaining his new speed, I estimated we had an hour left.

"Hey, Noah," Jacob whispered, leaning in around the suitcases and bags as near as possible so only I could hear him. "When I'm in the Philippines, you better keep Mom and Dad entertained, alright? They'll need your humor and energy."

"Of course, I'll do my best," I replied, acknowledging the burden of responsibility settling upon me.

"Good," Jacob said, flashing me a quick smile before restoring his attention to the road ahead.

As we navigated the slick roads of I-90, the Seattle Temple emerged through the swirling flakes of the winter snowstorm, its gleaming spire just visible against the white backdrop. I glanced up at Mom and Dad. Mom was looking at the beautiful edifice. Dad gripped the wheel with steady focus, eyes fixed on the road ahead. I wasn't sure if he even noticed we were passing the temple. "Can you believe you got married there?" I asked, the question slipping out as easily as the snowflakes drifting past the window.

Dad chuckled, a warm smile spreading across his face as he joined Mom's gaze at the temple, then exchanged a knowing look. "Yeah, it seems like it was only yesterday," he said, his eyes drifting back to the road.

As we passed, I craned my neck around until I lost sight of the temple. Its marble facade reminded me of my parents' vows, a promise sealed in that sacred place. A swell of pride rose, knowing our eternal family had started there.

The last leg of our journey was a breeze compared to the beginning.

"Almost there," Dad announced. "Another twenty minutes."

"Thank goodness," Mom sighed, her face pale and drawn from worry. "This storm is something else. And we still need to return home."

"God is watching over us," Jacob reassured her. "We'll make it there safe and sound, and you will be fine going home. The drive home will be easier now that the sun is up."

"Indeed," Mom agreed, offering him a wan smile.

Finally, the familiar exits approached, and Dad expertly maneuvered Black through traffic to the one we needed.

"Do we drop him curbside or go in with him?" Dad asked.

I knew he was kidding, but Mom must have thought he was serious. Had she been standing; she would have cocked her head with her hand on her hip and huffed. But here in the truck, she whipped her head towards Dad and stated her obvious answer. "Are you kidding me? Why would you even ask? Park the truck. I'm going in with him."

Relief washed over us as Dad pulled into the airport parking lot. He maneuvered the truck into an empty spot near the entrance.

"Made it," he said, cutting the engine and allowing the silence to envelop us again.

"Thank you, Lord," Mom sighed.

"Alright," Jacob said, clapping once as he looked around the truck. "Let's get these bags out and get going."

I could feel his excitement. He was buzzing with energy. He was ready for this adventure.

We all climbed out of the truck. I stood on the balls of my feet and stretched to the parking garage ceiling. I yawned, my sleepless night on Jacob's floor catching up with me.

Dad jostled between my stretching form and the door to pull out Jacob's suitcases. Mom reached over the center console and pulled his carry-on out through the front.

As we unloaded Jacob's luggage, I sensed the weight of the moment. It was unfolding too quickly, if you asked me. My brother was leaving home to pursue his calling halfway across the world. My heart raced like the storm beyond.

"Ready?" Dad asked, giving Jacob a solemn nod.

"Ready as I'll ever be," Jacob proclaimed.

"Before we go, let's have another prayer," Dad suggested as we huddled beside the truck. We wrapped our arms around one another in a tight family circle and bowed our heads. Mom sniffled, trying to hold back her tears.

"Our Dear Gracious Eternal Father in Heaven, we thank Thee for our safe arrival at the airport. Please watch over Jacob as he embarks on the next leg of his journey. Keep him healthy as he serves the magnificent people of the Philippines. Keep him safe, strong, and focused on his purpose. Help us all find peace and comfort during this time apart. In the name of Jesus Christ, our Lord, and Savior, Amen."

"Amen," we echoed, the words hanging in the air.

We each grabbed a piece of Jacob's luggage and began walking toward the airport terminal. The glass skywalk into the airport offered a view of the storm here. Seattle rain drizzled against the windows, a stark contrast to the vicious snowstorm in the mountains.

The fluorescent lights on the skywalk flickered and cast an eerie glow against the windows. The day was upon us, but the heavy storm over the mountains kept the clouds low. A thick fog engulfed Seattle. Gazing out through the floor-to-ceiling windows lining the bridge, it was challenging to see the cars on the road right below us. They would have vanished without their lights shining through the rain and fog.

We exited the sky bridge into the airport, taking the escalator to the terminal level. Airline counters, ticket kiosks, and baggage checks as far as the eye could see. It was still very early in the day and not the most common travel day. Thankfully, there were few people at the airport so early. Those who were here with us were polite and friendly. It seemed unreal, considering our last adventure at this very airport. Last Thanksgiving, we visited our Wilde relatives in Utah. That experience had been an absolute nightmare. Nightmare with a capital N. Today, everyone was keeping their distance from one another while still wearing friendly smiles.

Despite being surrounded by my family, a sense of loneliness pervaded me. Time stood still as Jacob and Mom debated where to go. I would miss this, the way their brilliant minds worked together, using logic to unravel the puzzle of where to find the international Delta desk.

They chose a direction, and we walked. The thud of Dad's boots echoed against the polished floor. The even tempo of his footsteps was the only sound as we moved forward. It oddly comforted me, a calm and steady heartbeat amongst my inner turmoil.

"There it is. Someone should move that thing," Mom said as we passed a large posterboard blocking her view. She waved her arm at the poster in a flourish, which only seemed to bother short people like her. She continued walking but shook her head, treating the poster as the most abominable object in the world's history. It was a testament to the actual state of her mind.

I knew she needed a hug, but the timing wasn't right. As soon as we had a minute, I would hug her so tight she could scarcely breathe. The type of hug she always wanted at the worst moments in life, like when Dad's mom, my grandma, died.

Mom, Dad, and Jacob moved ahead when we arrived at the baggage check while I hung back. I took a moment to absorb everything around me. I sensed Jacob's clashing emotions of excitement and concern emanating as he neared the front of the ticket line.

Traveling was a constant in our family. Mom and Dad cherished adventure, taking us across the country nine times, from coast to coast. I had already explored thirty-eight states, surpassing my seventy-year-old grandpa's record of twenty-three. Traveling was Mom's favored way of learning. A fitting pursuit for our homeschooling family during winter breaks from orcharding.

I stood a few feet away, yet could still hear everything happening at the counter.

"Is this your first time flying alone?" the attendant asked Jacob as she scanned his passport and printed his boarding pass.

"First time flying solo, yes." It was, but none of us had realized it until now. He and I had visited grandpa together, flying to Utah without our parents, but I had been with him. It was something.

"And first time traveling so far from home," Jacob offered.

I heard the mix of excitement and nervousness in his words.

"Manila, huh? That's quite a trip. You'll have a two-hour layover and change planes in South Korea," she said as she attached bag tags to Jacob's luggage. "You're all set. Have a great flight."

"Thank you," Jacob said, taking his boarding pass and pocketing his passport.

"Hey, big brother, you better come back with stories that'll make us laugh until our sides hurt," I choked out around the growing lump in my throat.

"Absolutely," Jacob said as we walked towards security.

Jacob's departure hung over me like a heavy storm cloud. I waited with bated breath for it to release its torrential downpour. I clenched my fists, grappling with the surge of emotions as we headed toward security. We'd shared countless adventures during our lives. From minor injuries to gut-wrenching laughter. Our lives to this point were one. We had always walked the same path.

"Quite the send-off, huh?" Jacob teased, trying to lighten the mood. But beneath his smile, I read the uncertainty in his eyes.

The number of people in the corridors had doubled in the thirty minutes since our arrival. The airport was now bustling with activity. People rushing to catch their flights. Families hugging goodbye, and announcements echoing. My heart ached, knowing soon my brother would be among those boarding the plane, leaving us behind.

"Let's make sure you have everything," Mom said, her voice steady despite her emotional state.

Dad laughed, "It's too late now. He checked his bags. If it's missing, he can't get it now. Offer your hugs, and let's be on our way."

He tried to lighten the mood, but his words sounded harsh with the rawness of our emotions. Mom stiffened and crumbled a little. I walked over and wrapped my arms around her. It was time to give her that hug she so desperately needed.

"I'm sorry, sweetheart, I didn't mean it." Dad realized how his words had sounded.

"I know, I know. Emotions are running high."

Mom wiped at the tear slipping from her eye and called out, "Group hug!" Her voice wavered as she fought back the waterfall of tears that threatened to follow the trickle already running down her cheeks. Mom wrapped her arms around Jacob, and Dad enveloped them both in a hug. Determined not to be left out, I joined the Jacob sandwich. We squished him between us, pouring as much love as possible onto him before he left. We huddled together, arms entwined, holding each other as tight as possible. Wishing we could somehow transfer our strength to Jacob. Offer him two years' worth of hugs so he didn't miss any. We needed to give him all our love, so he never forgets what he means to us.

A tear slipped down my cheek, yet I clung to my brother. We would face a long separation. His handsome face was tear-stained as he patted my cheek. Then he cleared his emotion-choked throat. I expected him to speak, but he remained silent.

I bent my head low and wiped my tear-filled eyes on the shoulder of his suit jacket. With a rueful smile, he turned and glanced at me. "Yo bro, don't stain my fancy new suit with your boogers!"

I gasped with a laugh-cry combo, shooting the previously absent boogers straight out my nose and all over my face.

Dad laughed, Jacob wiggled away from me, and my precious Mom offered the sleeve of her sweater. I dropped all dignity and wiped my runny cry boogers on Mom's sleeve. Sheepishly, I looked at her and whispered, "Thanks, Mom."

She steeled a straight-lipped smile, and I noticed she was fighting actual sobs. Quietly, I moved behind her and encircled her with my arms. I looked over her head and watched as Jacob waved goodbye. I didn't let go. Mom needed my hugs right now. She needed them as much as she needed air. Jacob, her firstborn son, was leaving her protective arms for two full years. Her heart was breaking. A chunk of it would be missing until he returned.

"Stay safe, son. We're proud of you," Dad murmured into Jacob's ear as they shared a brief, heartfelt embrace. Dad wasn't fooling anyone. His eyes had red rims, and I heard him sniffle at least twice. "Remember, Jacob," Dad said, leaning back from the embrace to see his face, "prayer will be your lifeline while you're away. Lean on the Lord for strength and guidance. I couldn't have made it through my mission without wearing callouses into my knees."

"Yes, Dad, I know how important prayer is to my mission." Jacob's voice was steady and filled with conviction despite his matching tear-filled eyes.

I glanced down at Mom and over at Dad. Raw emotions played across their faces. Pride, sorrow, and admiration all rolled into one.

I tried to memorize this moment. How my brother looked with his steadfast purpose and unwavering faith. Jacob knew his mission to the Philippines would test him in ways he'd never experienced. Yet, through all the preparations leading up to today, he remained dedicated to serving the Lord. He never, not once, considered quitting.

"Jacob," I choked around the large lump in my throat. "I don't know what I will do without you."

"Hey now," he said, squeezing my shoulder. "You're going to be fine. You've got Mom and Dad here, and I'll be praying for you daily."

My vision blurred as waterfalls of tears fell. We're talking about the Niagara Falls of tears running down my cheeks. I let go of Mom, and Jacob hugged me tight. His chest heaved with emotion. That set me off all over again.

"It's not goodbye forever," he whispered. "Think about all the amazing stories we'll have to share when I get back. Remember absolutely everything. When I return, we will have some long nights talking. I expect you to tell me all the details, day by day."

"Okay," I whispered back, my voice thick with emotion.

Surrounded by our prayers, Jacob shouldered his bags and left. His faith would be his strength, guiding him through challenges and triumphs ahead. Our unyielding love and dedication to the Lord would endure despite the distance.

As he moved towards the security line, we watched, aware his resolute steps carried the weight of his commitment. With a last wave amidst tears, Jacob's firm voice declared, "Love you all!" Then, he blended into the crowd, leaving us united to face our emotional turmoil without him.

Unrestrained tears flowed down Mom's face, her large tears obscuring the place Jacob had previously occupied. Dad embraced her, his shirt dampened by her tears and his own cheeks glistening.

"Lord, guide, protect, and use him for your glory," Mom's whispered plea resonated. Amidst growing distance, our familial bond and shared faith remained unshakable.

CHAPTER EIGHT

After exiting the airport, we headed east out of Seattle. The truck was oddly silent as melancholy washed over us due to Jacob's absence. By daylight, the snow's ferocity appeared less intense, but it was deceptive. The storm still raged, as evidenced by the accumulation on the road once we left the metropolitan area.

As Dad drove, I realized we were each lost in the recesses of our individual thoughts. Occasionally, Mom's mindless chatter broke the silence. Her offering an unyielding stream of stories, laughter, and heartfelt advice provided an escape from her own thoughts. Sometimes bordering on the mundane, her chatter had an undeniable magnetism. She captivated Dad's and my attention, pulling us into the orbit of her lively narration. Her words could unravel our emotions and return us to the life we would all carry-on living. She was determined we would not end the day with gloominess. It was a day of rejoicing. Celebrating this large step in Jacob's life. It helped Mom to talk about Jacob, to cry over him. Mom's tears spilled a little less with every spoken memory, and she captured a sliver of more control over her emotions.

I soon realized her words weren't just helping her; they were helping me too. I felt good, so much better. In the cocoon of the truck cab, the gentle hum of the engine surrounded us. The rhythm of the road beneath our wheels was a balm. It was there we took the first step toward healing. We would learn how to live for the next two years without Jacob's daily presence.

The summit of Snoqualmie Pass was a picturesque winter wonderland. With the lifting fog and full daylight, we could see the surrounding beauty despite the heavy snowfall. The ski lifts were running, and while many considered the snow a burden, others were enjoying it to the fullest.

The whistling wind and the crunching snow beneath the tires drew my attention back to the road. Since getting my license, I'd found myself drawn to watching the trip ahead out the windshield, envisioning how I would react if I were the one driving.

The snow-covered trees wore thick white fluff, while the rock faces along the road formed a tunnel of snow crystals. Frozen branches, bare and leafless, reached out like claws. They made the forest look menacing. The wind whipped, causing the trees to sway and rock back and forth. Snow swirled around us, forming a frosty cyclone, yet Dad skillfully navigated the truck through it all. With every mile, we were closer to the safety and warmth of home.

The peak of Blewett Pass lacked the vibrant winter playground that Snoqualmie had. The highway was less traveled, and despite previous plowing efforts, fresh snowfall had obscured the road once more. Outside the truck, the ongoing blizzard was even more intense. Tree branches bowed under the weight of heavy snow. Occasionally, a plume cascaded from the top to the ground below, landing in a heavy mound.

"This is beautiful," Mom said as she admired the scenery. Her endless chatter had finally settled an hour ago around Cle Elum, and I could see how exhausted the mix of emotions had left her. She would sleep well tonight.

"Yeah, it's like something you'd see on a postcard," Dad agreed.

Dad was doing alright, but he carried his emotions across his neck and shoulders. I caught him reaching up and rubbing his neck a few times.

I took it all in, watching as the snowflakes hit the window and melted away, leaving behind wet trails. It seemed odd, but there was a sense of comfort being surrounded by the winter wonderland. I closed my eyes, took a deep breath, and calmed my last remaining frazzled emotions. The closer we got to home, the more settled our emotions became.

I opened my eyes when I heard the speed of the windshield wipers increase. Dad set them to full speed, but they still struggled to keep up with the increasing snowfall. Visibility was next to nothing, yet the icy road seemed to stretch on forever.

"Where are we?" Mom asked. The never-ending snow made it difficult to know our whereabouts, despite our familiarity with the highway.

"We passed Liberty awhile back, so we're on the downhill stretch. Not much further, and we'll pass the old Blewett townsite and then the 97 Rock House Café," Dad answered.

"Oh good, about ten miles then." Mom sat back, relaxing now that she knew how close to home we were.

As I sat behind Dad, I peeked between him and the door. I saw him rub his hand over the top of his leg and pound his fist twice on his knee. I glanced at Mom to see if she noticed. She hadn't. Good.

The action was one of Dad's tells. Something was happening, but he endeavored to conceal it.

"Dad, why is the snow swirling like that?" It seemed like we were continuously driving into an enormous wall of snow. I'd seen nothing like it.

"That's a big rig in front of us. It's throwing up snow. We're at least three hundred feet behind it, but you are exactly right; it is like driving into a wall."

Dad gripped the steering wheel, his knuckles turning white.

Then, a stream of four cars came toward us, breaking up the wall of white and allowing me to better decipher shapes and objects. The cluster of drivers stayed close together, as if driving in a caravan would keep them safer. The last car in the lineup, a little white one, fishtailed and swerved as it passed the big rig. It slammed against the back tires of the trailer, sending the trailer into a jackknife in front of us. The brake lights illuminated the snowy scene in bright red, but they were not where they should be.

I gripped the left armrest and right seat's edge. My eyes widened as fear took hold of me. I braced my feet against the floor and leaned back in my seat.

"Hold on," Dad yelled, pumping the brakes hard. He hugged the road's right side, as far as he dared. The back tires on the passenger side slipped off the edge twice, but Dad recovered before we veered off the side of the road.

The little car that hit the trailer catapulted into the snowbank on their side of the road. I craned my neck to see if they were alright, but the puff of snow made it impossible to tell.

The big rig careened down the road ahead with its trailer perpendicular. Dad pumped the brakes to stop our truck while being overrun by a whirlwind of snow.

The trailer hit the rocky mountainside on the right. Jackknifing in the other direction, the force threw it back as a spray of rock hit us, cracking the windshield in two places. The semi-trailer barely missed us as it pendulum'd. Dad kept control of Black but struggled to stop us amidst the mayhem of the steep downhill grade. I prayed the truck would slow down faster and that God would send angels to stop us.

Fear etched itself onto Mom's face when I glanced at her, but she remained silent. With her feet braced against the floor and her back straight, she clung on for dear life.

My heart raced faster and faster with every skid of Black on the snowy road. My anxiety reached an unprecedented peak, jolting through my veins like lightning.

Dad teetered on the verge of stopping. The semi-truck ahead jackknifed into oncoming traffic, careening down the mountain out of control. I prayed there wouldn't be anyone coming in the other lane. I didn't want anyone to get hurt.

Just when I thought we were out of danger, another tractor-trailer appeared out of nowhere and collided with us from behind. The impact thrust us forward, launching us toward the jackknifed trailer that Dad had miraculously avoided moments earlier.

The force threw me sideways in my seat. My head hit my window hard. I launched myself to the right, attempting to distance myself from the window as much as possible. My seatbelt buckle cut into my right hip. I burrowed into the blanket and pillow I had brought. The truck continued to slide as Dad crammed the brake pedal to the floor, trying to stop us before we slammed into the jackknifed tractor-trailer. Black shook, the tires locked and squealed, and the engine emitted unfamiliar sounds.

The semi-truck behind us slammed on its brakes, riding our back bumper down the mountain. I heard gears grinding and smelled brakes burning. Sliding down the mountain, time seemed to slow.

I had just enough time to wonder about Dad's driving ability. He was attempting to use our big ole' truck to stop the tractor-trailer barreling down the mountain behind us. It couldn't stop, and now neither could we. Then a surge of elation filled my heart when we broke free until I realized that may not be a good thing. I grasped the severity of how bad our situation was when the semi-truck behind us collided with us a second time, propelling us forward once again.

I prayed, oh, how fervently I prayed, that Dad would find a safe way off the road. I prayed the semi-truck behind us would stop. I prayed the semi-truck ahead of us could get under control. I prayed it would end. I prayed we would all survive. I prayed Dad would receive the inspiration he needed to save us. Then, with the jackknifed tractor-trailer right in front of us, when I thought the big rig behind us would crush us under it, Dad shouted, "I love you!" He jerked the steering wheel to the right when an opening appeared in the guardrail. It was our last chance to avoid being crushed between the two semi-trucks. I hoped we would crash into the soft, powdery mountainside like the little car. At the last moment, another impact resonated with the sound of crunching metal as Black was struck a third time from behind.

It's funny what your brain considers during horrific situations. Science lessons about centrifugal force and inertia spun through my mind. I braced myself to spin right, hoping the seats back would support me as we went off the road. Then, all at once, we spun left, opposite of what I expected. I was thrown forward, followed by a jerk back caused by my seatbelt locking. At that moment, I realized we were back in the middle of the road. I snapped my head to the left and caught the semi-truck driver making eye contact with Dad. Then the driver closed his eyes, jerked his truck left and slammed into Black's side at the font of the truck and Dad's door, sending Mom's side straight into the jackknifed truck ahead.

Sparks and shards of glass exploded from shattering windows, spiraling around us in a flurry. My world swirled into a void of endless nothingness.

I GASPED FOR BREATH as the darkness lifted, and light appeared at the end of a long tunnel. My heart pounded with fear as I fought back the flood of terror threatening to overwhelm me. I awoke to the surrounding wreckage.

The sound of screeching brakes and the look of horror on the big rig driver's face replayed in my mind, hammering away at my consciousness. When I tried to move, I could only open my eyes. Chaos filled the scene. Smoke filled the air, shattered glass and debris covered the inside of the truck. I perceived the sound of voices shouting in the distance. Men filled every broken window when my eyes focused. I looked at the man closest to me and tried to speak. He sighed with visible relief.

"Hold on, son. Help is on the way. We're getting you help."

I thought I moved, but all I did was blink.

I heard Mom gasping in pain.

"Mom," I attempted, but my words came out as a painful cry.

"Noah," she shouted. Her words seemed clearer than mine, but her immense cry of pain and fear turned out to be much more severe.

"Don't move or speak," another man instructed. He stood at Mom's broken window.

"Help her," I squeaked out, trying to push myself up. I winced in pain, acknowledging the mangled state of my left hip and the intense pain in my neck and head. I looked toward Mom, but my eyes wouldn't stay focused. I sensed her suffering, and though the men professed to be aiding us, no one attempted to open our doors or get us out.

I squeezed my eyes shut and willed them to open in focus.

I didn't want to, but I knew I needed to look at the driver's seat where Dad sat. Dad's lifeless body lay trapped in a mangled mess. I didn't recognize the gray blanket covering him. One arm hung over the center console, and I reached for his hand. I wanted to hold his hand. I needed to touch him one last time.

"Dad?" I called into the void. I knew he wouldn't answer, but I still held onto hope. I believed in miracles, after all. Jesus is a God of miracles. The primary children sang that song in sacrament meeting, and the comforting chorus came to mind.

"It's alright, son. Stay there. Try not to move," the man at my window advised.

"Dad, wake up," I called, my voice shaking. "I need you. Wake up. There's too much left to do."

Dad's silence made my heart sink. I didn't want to believe he was gone, but reality was setting in. My father was gone, taken far too soon. I was left behind.

I tried to sit up again. Some of my movements were coming back. I raised my head and looked at Dad. My neck ached and my head throbbed, but I needed to see him.

Fear clenched my heart as the enormity of what had happened settled in.

"Help them," I cried again, looking at the man by my window.

"We can't. We already tried," he replied sadly. "But help is coming. Lots of help is coming."

My eyes finally focused, both a blessing and a curse. Mom's voice and breathing indicated she had severe injuries. When I focused on her, her body contorted in a way no human should ever experience. Blood poured from the wounds on her face. When I looked closer, I noticed large shards of metal lodged in her throat and chest. Although Mom's life had been spared so far, I feared I might still become an orphan if she didn't receive help soon.

Panic welled up in me. The iron taste of blood filled my mouth, and bile rose in my throat. The sweat and spinning sensation that accompanied my nausea forced me to turn my gaze, or else I'd vomit.

Sitting in the frozen wasteland, we were trapped with my dead father and my dying mother just beyond my reach. Unable to touch Dad and will his breath back with a miracle from God, a wave of despair engulfed me. Mom was also out of my reach. I longed to hold her hand and comfort her. Yearned to embrace her, to hug her tight and let her know I was here, and I loved her. *Tinker Bell Kisses* came to mind. What if I could never give her those sweet kisses again? I wanted to whisper for her to stay with me, to make her promise she wouldn't leave me behind like Dad had.

I could hear people yelling again. This time, the sounds clearer.

Layers of snow covered the road, some even came through the window, leaving a small layer on my leg and injured hip. I wanted to wipe it off, but I couldn't move my arm.

In my desperation and fear, I prayed, and then I sang in my broken and pained voice.

> *I am a child of God,*
> *And he has sent me here,*
> *Has given me an earthly home*
> *With parents kind and dear.*
> *Lead me, guide me, walk beside me,*
> *Help me find the way.*
> *Teach me all that I must do*
> *To live with him someday.*[2]

When the enormity of the words struck me, I cried out in anguish, mixed with pain. Dad was gone. He was now in heaven with God. He was gone, and I was left behind—almost alone.

"Help me, Lord," I prayed out loud. "Please spare my Mom's life."

As my senses sharpened and my mind cleared, the stench of diesel, engine oil, and blood filled my nose, making me gag. Bile welled in my throat again, and I tried to sing more church songs, desperate to push down my fears.

> *I have a fam'ly here on earth.*
> *They are so good to me.*
> *I want to share my life with*
> *them through all eternity.*

Fam'lies can be together forever
Through Heav'nly Father's plan.
I always want to be with my own family,
And the Lord has shown me how I can.
The Lord has shown me how I can.[3]

I couldn't finish the verses. I wanted to scream. All the church songs I remembered spoke of eternal families and heaven; now, that was all I had. Without eternal families, my family was broken. Dad was gone. *Oh God, why did you take him and leave me behind? He was the piece that made us whole. Without him, everything has shattered, and now we're nothing but the broken fragments of what remains.*

Suddenly, I became dizzy and disoriented once more. I clutched my head as sharp, stabbing pain brought back patches of blackness.

"Son, son, are you okay?" the man asked, his voice swimming toward me through the haze.

"I don't know. My dad..." I replied, my words slurring as the blackness took over again. The last thing I heard was Mom shout in agonizing pain, "Hold on, Noah, don't you leave me too."

Mom's screaming brought me around. Her pain was severe, and no matter how thick the blackness was, I had to get out of it to help her. I ran hard and fast, but heavy, unseen mud clung to my feet, weighing me down. My legs refused to respond to my commands, but I was nearly at the light. Just a few more steps, and

I would be at Mom's side. Finally, I broke free from the darkness of my jumbled mind.

"Mom," I said, turning my still-blurry eyes toward the sound of her voice. I could hear grinding, and as my vision focused, I saw sparks flying around like beautiful fireworks. I couldn't distinguish between reality and imagination, but Mom's screams were unquestionably real to me.

At last, my eyes focused. I saw police, firefighters, paramedics, and tow trucks. The sparks came from tools and machinery cutting metal.

They almost had Mom's door off, and someone had replaced the gray blanket over my father with an official-looking blue tarp. His arm had even been tucked under it. I wanted to scream, to get that vile thing off him, but I couldn't. I tried to reach forward and pull it off myself, but I couldn't quite reach. I could brush my fingers against it but couldn't quite grab hold.

All at once, my door opened. I hadn't even realized anyone was working on mine. Then someone touched me, and I shrieked in pain. I tried not to, but I couldn't help it.

"Noah!" Mom wailed in response, her voice thick with both pain and agony.

"It's okay, Mom, I promise," I cried. The last thing I needed was for her to focus on me. She needed to focus on living.

A stretcher was laid on the ground as four men carefully lifted me from the truck and onto it. The pain was more excruciating than anything I had ever endured. I fought to suppress my screams, not wanting to worry Mom, but tortured sounds escaped my lips, more desperate than any cry. A woman placed an oxygen mask over my face, while another wrapped a heated blanket around me.

The warmth enveloped me, an incredible relief, and I had a sudden realization of just how cold I had become.

They lifted me into the back of an ambulance, and I begged them to stop until I knew Mom was free. No one paid attention to what I wanted.

I noticed a pinch in my arm and heard a paramedic say, "Dispatch, this is Paramedic Unit 7. We are leaving the scene and en route to Central Washington Hospital. Minor on board in need of immediate medical attention. Over."

"What is the nature of the patient's condition? Over."

I strained to hear the answer, but my world went black again. This time, a cocoon of warmth spread over me from head to toe. The pain that had wreaked havoc on my body just moments ago subsided, and sleep enveloped me.

A blissful, warm, pain-free sleep.

CHAPTER NINE

Beep. Beep. Beep.

Good grief, turn off the stupid alarm. I wanted to yell at whoever had set it. I could imagine how much Mom would detest it if I was already annoyed. She despised weird sounds, while they rarely bothered me. But this one did. It bothered me a lot.

I attempted to emerge from the deep sleep that had overtaken me for far too long. Waking up and turning off the alarm seemed like an endless struggle for days.

There. I opened my eyes a sliver, just enough to search for my alarm, and shut it off before Mom came in, irritated. I didn't see it. *Where is it?* Honestly, even if I found it, I wouldn't be able to move to turn it off.

A stabbing pain erupted behind my eyes, and the back of my head pounded like a drum.

It was too much to handle. I closed my eyes and slipped back to sleep. Or at least, I thought I did.

WHERE DID THESE PEOPLE come from? I wondered when, what I thought was only a moment later, I heard voices.

"The chart shows elevated brain activity right here. It seems he woke up for a minute or two a few hours ago." A petite woman, not much taller than Mom, pointed at a chart over the top of a tablet that a tall doctor held low for her. It reminded me of how Dad held things for Mom.

Oh, there's that pain again.

More beeping. This time, the rate increased.

The nurse and doctor looked my way in unison.

"Hello there," the cheerful little nurse said, her large smile revealing perfect white teeth.

"Welcome back, Wildcat," the doctor chimed in. I lacked the energy to clarify that I was homeschooled and, even if I wasn't, the mascot was from the high school in the city where I didn't live.

Then I realized it didn't matter. I couldn't speak with tubes stuck down my throat, but I blinked.

The doctor handed the tablet to the nurse and walked over. He pulled doctor instruments from his pockets and around his neck. Then he tested every vital and reflex I had. He asked a million questions but, thankfully, answered them all himself. The nurse stood nearby, tapping away on the tablet, taking notes on my e-chart.

"Looks like you've been through quite an ordeal, haven't you?" I nodded or thought I did. It didn't matter. He kept talking. "Well, now that you're awake, we can see how you're really doing. You were lucky, no broken bones or anything too severe. The worst injury is your hip, but it looked worse than it was once we got you into surgery. It will heal, but you'll have an impressive scar. Lots of cuts, scrapes, and bruises to go with it. The nastiest injury is that concussion of yours. Head injuries can be scary. Do you play sports?" Once again, he didn't require an answer. "Luckily, nothing's going to hold you back long-term. I'll have you back on the court, field, track, or whatever you play in no time. Soon you'll be as good as new, but you'll have to take it easy at first."

Shut up, I wanted to yell. *Stop talking about sports. Who cares about sports? What is going on with Mom?*

Then I heard a voice I recognized.

"Doctor, what's happening?"

Grandpa Wilde entered.

I blinked furiously, tried to speak, and attempted to move my arms. I could move my arm a little this time, but no one noticed. Horrific noises came from my throat.

Grandpa rushed to the side of my bed and took my hand.

"Noah, hey there, you're awake. I've been so worried about you."

"Mom," I screamed. The tubes made it impossible to speak or make any decipherable noise.

"Calm down. I'm here. Uncle Jared's here too. We hopped on the first flight out of Salt Lake as soon as we heard."

I lifted my arm and tried to tug at the tubes in my throat. This time, it moved.

"Oh no, don't do that," the little nurse said. She came over and pressed my hand back to the bed.

"Mom," I tried again, but no one understood me.

Grandpa started talking to the doctor about their plan for me. I listened to their conversation, hoping to hear something about Mom, but not once did they bring her up.

I tried one more time, slower and calmer. "Mom."

Although I caught their attention, they remained oblivious to what I was asking.

I hoped it was only the word "Mom." I tried again. "Dad. Jacob."

"It's alright, Wildcat. Stay calm. Tomorrow, if you're still improving, we'll take the tube out, and then you can talk to us. Until then, rest up. I'll have the nurse give you something to help with the pain. I know you've got some."

He took the tablet, made a note, and handed it back to the nurse, who glanced down. As the doctor left, she nodded.

"I'll be right back," Grandpa Wilde said, and then followed the doctor out.

"This will help," said the nurse. She filled a syringe with a liquid and injected it into the tube already in my arm. I presumed it was pain medication. She took a moment to straighten my blankets and brushed aside a long lock of hair that had fallen onto my face. It reminded me of how Mom would do the same whenever my hair fell across my face. The memory made me want to cry.

"There now, you're going to be alright. You have family here to help you. You'll get to see them tomorrow. Today, let's have you rest a little more."

My eyes grew heavy as I listened to her gentle voice. Then warmth and peace once again surrounded me.

THE WARM SUN ON my face made waking up the next morning easy. I opened my eyes, facing the window. Frost crystals covered the tree branches outside.

"Hey, Buddy," Grandpa Wilde said.

I jerked my head toward him. He sounded like Dad. Only Dad called me Buddy. Grandpa had never called me that before. It was Dad's nickname for me, and I wanted to tell grandpa he had no right to use it. I wasn't his *Buddy*. I was only *Dad's Buddy*.

Uncle Jared walked into my room, his arms laden with a tray from the cafeteria and a bag from a nearby fast-food place. "I brought you some food, Dad."

Tears sprang to my eyes and cascaded down my face. I thought Grandpa sounded like Dad, but I was mistaken. His voice was older, deeper, and had more baritone. Uncle Jared sounded just like him. I hadn't realized it before, but he also looked like him, *exactly* like him.

I had to look away.

"Everyone says your dad and I sound and look a lot alike. We're the closest of all the brothers. It's been a while since I last saw you. You've grown. A lot." Uncle Jared understood what no one else did.

He came closer, and I dared to look at him. I could see Dad's same twinkling eyes and crooked smile through my tears. But the smile was different. He didn't have Dad's little scar above his top lip, the one he got when I was nine. A tire jack had slipped and hit him in the face while he was changing the tire on his pickup. Seeing Uncle Jared hurt my heart. I had to avert my gaze once more.

Now Grandpa understood. He pulled his seat closer and looked at me. I cried and cried. He held my hand and tried to comfort me, but when his tears fell, I knew we were both lost in our grief.

"It'll be okay. You'll be okay. I'll be okay. We'll be okay." Grandpa babbled until his voice trailed off. I wasn't sure I agreed. With my broken heart over Dad and no one mentioning Mom, I doubted whether I would be alright.

I tried another tactic.

Raising a heavy hand to my head, I touched my hair and struggled to wave it like a woman's long, wavy hair.

Once again, Uncle Jared was my rock star. "You want to know about your mom?"

Grandpa looked at me, surprised he hadn't understood what I was asking until now. Uncle Jared pulled at his neck, thinking about what to say. Grandpa clamped his mouth shut, shook his head, and closed his eyes.

"No!" I screamed around the tube in my throat. The word was indecipherable, but my meaning was clear. I balled up my fist and pounded it on the bed.

"Whoa, whoa, whoa," Uncle Jared said, raising and lowering his hands to calm me. Grandpa's eyes shot open. "She's alive. You misunderstood. Dad, be careful how you respond," Jared scolded. Uncle Jared came closer as Grandpa stood and moved to the foot of my bed. "Your mom got terribly hurt in the accident. We haven't seen her," Uncle Jared informed me. "When she first arrived at the hospital, she had to undergo multiple surgeries. She needs another one. Despite her uncertain condition, doctors are optimistic about her outcome. They've put her in an induced coma for now. Your Grandpa and Grandma Evans are with her. Noah, you're at North Central Washington Hospital in Wenatchee, but your mom is at Harborview in Seattle."

Finally, I knew she was alive. But then his words registered. She was so far away, unreachable in my current state.

Uncle Jared came over and put his hand on my shoulder. He bent close and said, "Noah, your dad's burial is tomorrow. I've taken care of everything, but there won't be a memorial until you and your mom are ready."

Tomorrow? Tomorrow was too soon. I didn't get to say goodbye. I hadn't hugged Dad enough. Jacob's not here. Tears flooded down my cheeks. I couldn't stop them.

"That's not all. Your bishop sent word to Jacob through the MTC president about the accident, but he only provided general information, not specifics. The bishop said they would contact him when they knew more. When Jacob arrived at the Missionary Training Center in Manila, he sent one message through Messenger. We responded as if we were your mom."

His words horrified me. Jacob was being kept in the dark. Dad was dead. Mom was fighting for her life. I lay helpless in a hospital bed. Our family didn't know Jacob very well if they hadn't told him the truth—all of it. He would be furious when he found out they had lied to him. Lying by omission was fundamentally the same, especially to someone like Jacob. Then again, what could he do? He was over six thousand miles away.

Grandpa noticed my expression and spoke up, "We all agreed it's best to wait and tell him everything at once. We need to answer all his questions. You know how he is. We would've told him about your dad if we had known more about you or your mom's conditions. We didn't have any details to tell him, and he couldn't do anything about your dad. All we would've done was frustrated him when he already has enough to worry about in a foreign country. Right now, he's still focusing on missionary work. He'll have to make a tough decision soon. We want him to have all the information he needs to make the right one."

I contemplated Grandpa's words, but I knew the answer. Dad had ingrained in us our entire lives to stay on our missions no matter what happened back home. *"Nothing brings you home. You remain and do the Lord's work and somehow, sometime, you'll reap greater blessings for it."* I knew what Jacob would choose. He would stay and serve. He would continue the Lord's work.

My entire life, I had agreed with Dad. I promised him I would do as he said and stay on my mission, no matter what. Jacob had pledged to do the same. But now, the situation stared us straight in the face, and I wanted Jacob to come home. Who cared what we had promised Dad? This was different. Dad was the one who died. I'm sure he only meant those words if someone else died. Not him, though. He only made us promise because he would be here with me. Dad would wrap his big, strong arms around me and comfort me. That way, I didn't need Jacob, and he could stay on his mission. Not now, though. Dad was gone, and I wanted my brother here with me more than anything else in the entire world. I didn't want him to come home; I needed him to.

When Grandma Wilde died, Dad comforted us by saying she was now one of our guardian angels. I repeated his words and applied them to him, but they didn't help. They made me mad. Jacob and I didn't need another angel by our side. We needed Dad alive and at home with us. *Famous last words, Dad,* I thought wryly.

I wanted to ask more questions about Mom, but it proved impossible to inquire further. Longing for peace, I closed my eyes and wished for Grandpa and Uncle Jared to sit down. Or better yet, go away. I had to calm down and free my mind from the horrors. Right now, the best remedy was sleep. I faked sleeping, until finally, it overtook me.

I woke up to a different nurse, not the little one I had encountered earlier. She wasn't as friendly and went about her business in a precise, clinical manner. Her demeanor matched our present mood. When she finished, she declared, "Everything looks good here. Let's get some people in here to remove your tubes and give you your voice back."

Hallelujah, I wanted to shout.

Grandpa settled back in his chair and pulled out his phone to text. He kept everyone in the family, except Jacob, updated on my status. After hitting send, he tucked his phone into his shirt pocket. Then, he pulled out a science fiction novel from what seemed like thin air. I hadn't noticed he had a book folded in half lengthwise and tucked into his pocket until now. His treatment of the book would horrify Mom.

I lay there, my body trapped beneath countless medical implements. The agonizing wait for the medical team's arrival seemed like an eternity. My labored breaths punctuated the minutes and hours of silent waiting. Breathing ought to have been effortless with the breathing tube, yet I struggled against it. I couldn't wait for its removal once and for all.

The distant sound of footsteps echoed through the hospital corridor. They grew louder until they reached my room, and an army of nurses entered. With a precision born from countless hours of training, they disentangled me. I watched, their hands a blur of movement. One by one, the sterile tools detached from my body, their absence bringing a newfound sense of relief. At last, I was no longer bound to my bed. A wave of liberation washed over me. I took a deep breath, savoring the sweet taste of independence as oxygen filled my lungs. Swallowing, drinking, and talking again became a possibility. My throat throbbed like nobody's business, a persistent reminder of what I had endured.

With the nurse gone again, Grandpa and Uncle Jared seemed more comfortable. We fell into a lull, each of us lost in our individual thoughts.

Uncle Jared cleared his throat, breaking the silence. "You want to try talking?"

I hesitated. My throat was raw, but I gave a small nod. Uncle Jared handed me a cup of water, and I took a tentative sip. The cool liquid soothed my dry throat, and I swallowed again, testing my voice.

"H-how's Mom?" My voice was raspy, barely more than a whisper, but it was enough.

Grandpa looked up from his book. "She's stable, like Jared said. The doctors are optimistic, but it's going to be a long recovery."

I nodded, but my chest tightened at the thought of her lying in a hospital bed far away from me. It was all too much to take in. Mom was hurt, Dad was gone, and Jacob was half a world away. Despite wanting to believe the doctors, the fear persisted that she wouldn't make it.

Uncle Jared patted my shoulder. "You'll see her soon. As soon as you're cleared to travel, we'll get you to Seattle."

But when? I wanted to see her now. Every second she was unconscious was a loss, a second together that I couldn't get back. But I couldn't voice any of that. My throat still burned, and I was too tired to argue. Instead, I took another sip of water and nodded. Then, summoning all my strength, I mustered a wan smile and attempted to describe the indescribable tragedy I'd experienced. I knew what they wanted to know but would not ask about.

"I remember dropping Jacob off at the airport. Then we were driving home," I said, my voice trailing off.

Sharp pain interrupted my thoughts, and I groaned in discomfort.

"You don't have to continue if it's too hard," Uncle Jared comforted me.

"It's not that," I said. "My head is pounding. Like the worst migraine of my life."

Grandpa stood up and pressed the nurse's button. This time, the little nurse who reminded me of Mom came trotting in.

"Wahoo! Look who's getting back to normal. It must feel good to have all those tubes out and equipment off."

I nodded and attempted to smile at her jovial mood.

"What's not nice is his splitting headache. Is there anything he can take?" Grandpa said.

"Of course. I'll be right back." She grabbed the tablet hanging from a strap around her back and made some notes as she walked out of the room. Moments later, she came back with pills and a little cup of water. "Can you swallow yet?"

I nodded, though I wasn't sure if I could. So far, no one had offered me anything beyond liquid to swallow. I figured I could man up and get the pills down. I did.

Grandpa stood up and stretched. "Let's give you a few minutes to let the medicine take effect. I'm going to stretch my legs." He stepped out, leaving me alone with Uncle Jared.

Uncle Jared leaned back in the chair, his eyes scanning me. "You're a strong kid, Noah. You've been through a lot, and you're still here."

I didn't feel strong. I felt weak and broken, but Uncle Jared's words gave me hope I could overcome this.

"You'll need to lean on a lot of people. Your mom, she'll need you too when she wakes up. We're all going to be there for each other."

I blinked, fighting back tears again. I didn't want to think about all the weight that would fall on me once Mom woke up. I just wanted to survive today, and tomorrow... Dad's burial. I wasn't sure I could survive that.

Uncle Jared must have seen the worry on my face because he sat forward and put his hand on my arm. "It's okay to take things one day at a time. No one expects you to have all the answers."

I closed my eyes, his words sinking in. I didn't have the answers. But maybe I didn't need to. For now, surviving each day was sufficient.

We sat in silence for a while longer. The only sound was the steady beep of the monitors next to me. I listened to the rhythm of my heartbeat—steady, slow.

Tomorrow would bring more grief and more questions. But for now, I was still here. And that had to be enough.

The silence was comforting, almost like a blanket wrapping around me. Despite the lingering ache in my chest, Uncle Jared's presence brought some relief, if only for a moment.

I took a deep breath, trying to steady myself. "Uncle Jared, what happens now?"

He sighed, leaning back in his chair. "Well, tomorrow's the burial. After that, we'll focus on getting you home and then to Seattle to see your mom. She'll need all the help she can get, and you'll need to take care of yourself, too. The next few weeks... months... they won't be easy."

I nodded, my heart heavy. I already knew it would not be easy, but hearing it said out loud made it more tangible. "And after that?"

Uncle Jared was quiet for a moment, considering his words. "We proceed gradually, one step at a time. You'll have school, but no one's going to rush you into anything. We'll figure out a plan for everything else once things settle down a bit. Right now, it's just about surviving tomorrow."

I looked down at my hands, clasped tight in my lap. Tomorrow. The burial. The final goodbye and I wouldn't even be there to give it. Uncle Jared was taking care of everything. Only he would attend. My throat tightened again, and the familiar sting of tears surfaced.

"I don't know if I can do it," I whispered, barely loud enough for him to hear.

Uncle Jared leaned forward, his expression soft but firm. "Noah, no one expects you to be okay right away. You are not in this alone. We're all here for you: me, grandpa, your Evans grandparents, your mom when she's ready. And Jacob, even though he's far away. You also have your aunt and cousins and everyone else who loves you. Grandpas already received half a dozen calls from your friends and youth group. You have so many people to stand with you and help hold you up. We'll all get through this together."

Together. The word hung in the air, both a promise and a lifeline. I wasn't ready for tomorrow, for any of it, but I had to hold on to that, together.

Uncle Jared squeezed my hand and stood up. "I'm going to let you get some rest. You've been through a lot. I'll be right outside if you need anything, okay?"

I nodded, watching him as he walked toward the door. As he reached the threshold, I called out, my raspy voice growing stronger. "Uncle Jared?"

He turned, waiting.

"Thank you."

A small smile touched his lips. "Anytime, kid."

As the door closed behind him, I lay back against the pillows, my body aching with exhaustion. Tomorrow loomed like an insurmountable mountain, but for now, I had made it through today. And that had to be enough.

I closed my eyes, letting the sounds of the hospital fade into the background. There would be more heartache, more moments where I wasn't sure I could go on. But as I drifted into an uneasy sleep, Uncle Jared's words echoed in my mind.

Together.

CHAPTER TEN

A WHIRLWIND OF MEDICAL personnel swept through like a tornado. Dedicated doctors and nurses conducted a blur of examinations over the following days. My room teemed with a mix of emotions, like a colorful kaleidoscope. Many people united, all determined to cheer me on and help me feel better.

My young men's quorum visited Wednesday night. They stood around, shuffling their feet, looking uncomfortable and acting awkward. I knew they cared, but they clearly wanted to be anywhere except here. My face, marked by cuts and bruises, was so awful that no one wanted to look at me. They kept their eyes on their feet, the window, or the door. Their longing to escape was obvious.

Then, on Friday, a horde of young women flooded my room carrying balloons, handmade cards, and a giant get-well banner. The decorated banner sported messages of encouragement, hearts, and flowers. It was adorable, and I loved it.

The girls were so much more caring. A few sat on the edge of my bed and fussed over the blankets. Two girls fluffed my pillow, one on each side of the bed near my head, while two others offered me goodies. Rummaging through a bag, one produced a bottle of apple juice and a Tupperware bowl. She popped the seal, and I recognized the famous green Jello from every ward party. The girls spoke a mile a minute, asking tons of questions. I couldn't keep up with their endless chatter, so I just listened. I soon realized they didn't need answers, they just wanted to talk, to show they cared. I appreciated it. One question made me laugh a little: "When will you get out?" The way the young girl phrased it made it seem like I was escaping from prison. It felt wonderful to laugh.

Shelby Thurston stayed at the back of the crowd, but as the other girls got bored and drifted away, she edged closer, her eyes reflecting a mix of compassion and shyness. "Noah, I'm sorry about your dad," she whispered, her sincerity carrying weight. "I've been praying non-stop for your mom. I carry a prayer in my heart, and I know she will get better real soon." She smiled, a glimmer of hope in her expression, and continued, "And guess what? I'll whip up some delicious cookies with my mom and bring them over as soon as you're back home." She pointed to her mother in the group of girls. Her words held a genuine warmth that touched my heart, a testament to how much she cared.

She even stepped close and gave me a *Tinker Bell Kiss* on my cheek, just like Jacob and I always kissed our mom. Bruises, scrapes, and who knew what else marked my purple cheek. I was sure I looked dreadful, but she wasn't afraid to kiss me.

Unbidden, I blushed from the roots of my hair to my toes.

I remembered almost nothing else anyone said during the last five minutes of the girls' visit. When they sashayed out of my room, giggling and promising to see me soon, my gaze followed Shelby.

She paused at the door, the last girl to leave, and waved. I waved back.

"Well, well, isn't she a cute one?" Uncle Jared said, from the furthest corner. He had remained hidden while the girls pranced about like a flutter of glorious butterflies. "Are you going to ask her on a date?"

"She's not sixteen," I responded. I hoped he would drop it.

"I reckon she will be soon. What is she, about fifteen and a half? Three quarters?"

"I don't know," I shrugged. I tried not to encourage him.

"She reminds me of your Aunt Megan. Shy, timid, cute at first, but I bet if you let her into your heart, she'll tip your world upside down."

"She's feisty," I admitted. "She has three younger brothers she helps her mom with. The littlest one is a handful."

"I see. Shy at first, then they go all feisty on you. Those feisty ones can surprise you." Uncle Jared leaned back in his chair and stretched his arms toward the ceiling. "They've got a fire inside them that keeps things interesting."

I nodded, remembering how Shelby's eyes sparkled when she teased her brothers. "She knows how to handle them. It's like she's got a secret superpower or something."

Uncle Jared laughed. "Sometimes it takes someone with a bit of a superpower to handle us too, you know? I swear Megan has a superpower and wields it over me daily."

I shifted, noticing my cheeks become warm again. Uncle Jared raised an eyebrow, a mischievous smile playing on his lips. He was about to say something else when his phone rang. "Speaking of Aunt Megan." He gave me a knowing look before he answered his phone and exited the room. "Hello, Beautiful." I heard him say before his voice faded down the hallway.

A mix of emotions flooded me as I sat there, contemplating Uncle Jared's words. Shelby's kindness, her sweet *Tinker Bell Kiss*, and how she made me feel at ease were undeniable. *Could there be something more between us?* It might be worth exploring when she turned sixteen.

With a sigh, I leaned back against my pillows. I'd been in the hospital for ten days, six of which I was awake. My health was improving, but I was anxious about Mom.

"Aunt Megan and the kids send their love," Uncle Jared said when he flopped back in his seat after his call.

"Next time you talk to them, tell them I love them too."

"I told Aunt Megan about your visitors. She's happy the kids in your ward care so much."

Fortunately, Uncle Jared dropped the Shelby discussion, though I noticed a few sly smiles exchanged between him and Grandpa. Grandpa returned to his novel, absorbed in the adventures playing out on the pages. Uncle Jared scrolled through the endless nothingness of social media, occasionally holding up his phone to show me something he thought I'd like.

"Do you know where my phone is? It was in the truck," I asked.

"It's at your house. I got everything I could from the truck and put it in a box. Do you want me to go get it for you?" He leaned forward, ready to go now if I asked.

"Nah, not now. But maybe tonight you could charge it and bring it tomorrow. Also, could you bring the cable plugged in at my desk in my bedroom so I can keep it charged?"

"Sure thing," he said as he settled back into his chair.

"Grandpa," I asked. He looked up from his book. "When can I go see Mom?"

"Hey, Buddy, it might be a while. You haven't even busted out of this joint yet."

He said it again. He called me *Buddy*. I wanted to scream at him *to stop. To never call me that again.* It hurt my heart more than anything else. A knife stabbing right in the middle, twisting left, right, and left again. I wanted to tell him. I really did. But I didn't.

"What about a video chat?"

Grandpa tugged at his neck. I'd never realized that was his tell before. He looked me straight in the eyes, tugged again, then finally caved. "Let's call your Grandpa Evans and see what we can figure out."

When he hesitated to make the call, I prompted, "Can we call him now?"

Grandpa sighed, leaned back in his seat, pulled his phone from his pocket, and dialed.

"Hello."

I could hear Grandpa Evans's voice boom over the phone when he answered. His baritone was deep and reassuring.

"Hi, Rick, it's me, Allen. Noah wants to know if we can arrange for him to see Leah."

It seemed like an eternity since I had last heard Mom's name. Jacob and I never called our parents by their names. Even Mom and Dad addressed each other as "Mom" and "Dad" when they were around us. At church, people called them "Brother" and "Sister" Wilde. It was odd to hear Mom's name spoken so casually. I rolled it over and over on my tongue: "Leah." Her name was beautiful. For the first time, I realized how much I loved Mom's name. Then a pain shot through my heart as I thought about what Dad's name was: *Adam.*

Distracted as I was thinking about Mom and Dad's names, I forgot to eavesdrop on my two grandpas' conversation.

Grandpa Wilde hung up.

"Well, what did he say?" I inquired as unease crept in.

"Not today, Buddy. Perhaps later this week."

My ire rose, and I snapped, "Don't call me that. Only Dad can call me that. It's his name for me. I'm not your…" I couldn't repeat my nickname. The word wouldn't come out, but tears did, lots of hot, angry tears.

Grandpa's expression became crestfallen. He studied his hands in his lap, uncertain how to calm me down. Grandpa Wilde was bad at conflict. He always shuts down. This was no exception.

I regretted snapping at him, but I wasn't ready to apologize. Not yet.

Grandpa took a few deep breaths, then, ignoring my outburst, continued. "Grandpa Evans said your mom's surgeries are complete. She came out of the last one today and returned to her room. He said they will keep her in a coma for some time yet. Let's see what the doctors say, and then we will arrange a call."

It was not the answer I desired. I didn't want to be that irritating toddler throwing a tantrum, but I needed to see her.

"Call him back. Let me talk to him." Then, as an afterthought, I added, "Please."

Grandpa Wilde eventually took his phone out of his pocket, pressed send, and handed it to me.

"Hello."

"Hi, Grandpa, it's me, Noah."

"Hey there, Buddy, how are you doing?"

I bristled. Grandpa Wilde noticed. Why were they all calling me by my dad's nickname for me? Did they think it would help me?

"I'm fine." It wasn't an outright lie. Physically, I was recovering, even if mentally I wanted to hurl my brain like a football. I prayed I could forget everything I had seen. A black abyss of an empty head would be preferable right now. I longed to erase the memory of my father's lifeless hand. Also, the horrifying tableau of my mom amidst her scene of distress. Her screams echoed, especially in my dreams.

"I'm glad to hear it. Grandma and I are so glad you are ali—safe." His voice choked up, but he recovered. Grandpa Evans had always been the rock in the family, tough as nails, when we all needed someone to hold us up.

"Grandpa, can I please see Mom?" I wasn't beating around the bush. Grandpa liked things direct, to the point, and not wasting his time. I needed him to let me see Mom.

"Noah, I don't know. I don't want you to see her like this. Remember her as she was and give her a few more days to recover. Let's have you see her when you can talk to her."

Determined to stay calm, I explained my perspective. Grandpa would respect that more. "Grandpa, if she's not screaming in the most excruciating pain of her life, with metal protruding from her neck and blood spurting from her head, I promise you she's better off now than I remember. Every time I close my eyes, I see Mom as she was in the truck. I can't sleep without the sight haunting me. Grandpa, I need to see her safe, healing, and on the path to recovery."

I heard a sharp intake of breath from all three of my grandparents. Grandma Evans cried out, and I heard Grandpa attempt to calm her. He must have held his hand over the phone to stifle her reaction. I could only hear every third word, and even those sounded muffled.

My words were straightforward, matter-of-fact, but they were hard, and I had a tough time holding my emotions in check. I determined that no matter the cost, I would not lower myself to a fit of teenage rage. It wouldn't work, anyway. Temper tantrums, for that's all teenage rage was, never worked in our family. But if I was honest, I wanted to throw a toddler whopper. I wanted nothing more than to lie down on the floor, kicking and screaming, until Grandpa surrendered. Grandpa Wilde might, but not Grandpa Evans. He might hang up on me.

I didn't throw a tantrum or rage into a fit of teenage pique. Instead, I waited. And I waited. And I waited.

"Very well, Noah. Call back in fifteen minutes. I'll be ready to let you see her."

I hung up, relief spreading through me. Grandpa Evans had agreed. In fifteen minutes, I would see Mom.

"Noah, my heart, it's good to see you," Grandma Evans said as she joined Grandpa on the little phone screen. I could tell she was on her last frazzled nerve. Grandma, our family's matriarch, always felt deeply. I recalled how often Mom complained about Grandma worrying and fretting constantly. Mom did the same, but differently. Mom's worry and fret came with energy and vitality, action to take charge and not allow troubles to overcome her. Grandma Evans' worry came with sorrow and bouts of depression. She let it control her, which slowed her down.

Observing her now, it was apparent that she had aged since the last time I saw her less than two weeks ago.

Grandma blew me air kisses, and I blew them back, offering air hugs as well. She laughed, but it didn't reach her eyes like it usually did. I'd do anything for Grandma's hugs and kisses to be real. This was my first time seeing her since Jacob's farewell, and I was desperate for a hug. In fact, I wanted ten of them. I loved Grandma so much, and though I was talking to her, I missed her, desperately. More so because of the present situation than I normally would have felt under regular life circumstances.

Grandpa turned the phone so I could see Mom. I knew she had suffered severe injuries, but I wasn't prepared for the extent of what I saw. She looked so fragile, lying unmoving in her bed. Tubes ran from her mouth to a machine that kept her breathing. No joke, they wrapped, bandaged, and monitored every part of her body. My two or three machines were nothing. Mom had a wall of monitors.

Grandma sat at Mom's bedside, and I saw her touch the strands of hair that poked out from Mom's bandages. She brushed them back, just like Mom always did for me. I shook as the tears began again. Dang it, would I ever stop crying?

"Grandpa, please put the phone by Mom's ear," I choked out.

Grandpa didn't question me. He placed the phone near Mom's ear. I could see half of her ear, the rest obscured by bandages. It didn't matter. I leaned close to my phone and whispered, "Please get better, Mom. I love you so much." As I rested my head on the pillow, I envisioned us sharing secrets on the trampoline. Mom was the one person I could tell anything to, and she never told a soul. Those secrets stayed just between us, and I needed her here to talk to. She loved to laugh and tease me about girls, and I wondered what she'd say about Shelby giving me a *Tinker Bell Kiss*. That would be the first secret I'd share with her as soon as she got better.

I wanted to lie there forever. I wanted to climb through the phone, up onto Mom's bed, wrap her in my arms, and hug her until she got better. If I could, I would take away all her pain and heal her. Was this how the Savior felt toward us? I would do anything for her.

"Have you given her a blessing?" I blurted as the thought came to me.

"Yes. She was in surgery when we arrived, but I gave her one the moment she was out, and we could see her. One of the ER doctors who operated on her is a member. He anointed, and I blessed her," Grandpa explained.

"Please give her another. Find someone and give her another with us on the phone. We aren't there with you, but Grandpa Wilde and Uncle Jared are here listening. They can repeat the blessing in their minds and combine their faith with yours. We will combine all our faith. Please, Grandpa, I want to hear it. I know you can make a miracle happen. Please, Grandpa, command a miracle."

"Noah, we already gave her one," Grandpa Evans began, but I interrupted.

"Please." I rarely begged, but this was more of a plea.

"Hold on, let me see what I can figure out. Here, talk with Grandma for a minute."

I heard Grandpa leave the room, but Grandma wasn't much of a conversationalist today. She didn't say a word, just held the phone so I could see Mom.

About ten minutes later, Grandpa returned with a hefty male nurse in dark blue scrubs. Grandma turned the phone around so we could see them. Grandpa introduced the nurse, then delivered the most humbling blessing I had ever heard. It was beautiful, but he didn't promise or command a miracle. A little agitated, I uttered, "Do it again. The prophets command miracles and teach that we can, too. Please, Grandpa, command a miracle. I need my mom." I laid my head back on my pillow and squeezed my eyes closed as hard as I could. I begged, "Please, God, heal her. Please give us a miracle. You took my dad. My brother is far away. Mom has to live."

I acknowledged the ugly truth of my selfishness. Uncle Jared came over and tried to take the phone from me.

"No, let me keep it. My mom is still on."

Grandpa Evans's tear-streaked face came into view, taking up the entire phone screen. It was an unusual sight, Grandpa Evans crying.

"Noah, dear boy, listen up."

I didn't want to listen. Grandpa would surely offer a churchy platitude meant to placate me and bring rest to my troubled soul. I had no desire to hear him.

"Why isn't she waking up? I believe in miracles. I know they happen today and not just in ancient times. Grandpa, I have faith." I wiped hard at my eyes and sniffled. Then the thought came to me: *Tell Jacob. He has great faith. God answers his prayers. You've seen it happen. Jacob needs to pray for Mom. God always answers Jacob's prayers.* I was sobbing so hard I couldn't say another word.

The people on the phone and in the room with me cherished me in a way no one else did, but at that precise moment, it didn't suffice. They weren't who I wanted. I longed for everyone I couldn't have. Dad. Mom. Jacob.

Then I realized that Jacob, my big brother, had always been my strength. He was the person I turned to when no one else could ease my troubled mind. Jacob's faith was always the faith I relied on. Did I even know what my own faith looked like?

My mind swirled with wonder. I believed, but did I truly know? Faith is just the beginning. Where the rubber meets the road is when we step beyond faith into knowledge. That's when the mustard seed explodes, and the mountains rise and walk to where we command. Knowledge is the bedrock of miracles—the foundation upon which they are built.

Jacob knew, but did I?

An overwhelming sense of helplessness threatened to consume me, a sensation that loomed if I allowed it to linger too long. Yet, even as sadness pressed in, a tiny flicker of hope sparked within me. Giving up on my mother was not an option. The darkness would not overpower or abandon us. Staying strong for her was my only choice. Believing she would wake up, that she would recover from this accident, became my anchor. I clung to the belief that my faith could carry me through. That faith would sustain me until the moment the knowledge arrived. The instant Mom's eyes opened, and I would know God had given me a miracle. Yes, my faith would be enough to get me there. It had to be!

Grandma Evans sobbed, and I watched her run across the screen behind Grandpa as she fled the room. I could see the nurse standing near Mom's head in the background. Did he wipe his cheek, or did I imagine it? Uncle Jared moved to the chair in the corner. Grandpa Wilde stood at my side and gripped the bed rail.

"Noah," Grandpa Evans addressed me gently. He stood beside Mom in a hospital room halfway across the state, the air thick with uncertainty. I could perceive it even through the phone. His voice softened as he continued, "Faith teaches us that trials can be difficult, but they're ultimately for our good. They shape us into who we're meant to become."

I looked up, clutching the phone as Grandpa spoke. I knew all this. Really, I did. But it wasn't the answer I wanted. "Grandpa, we've already had our *big bad thing*. Dad died. Right now, I don't need more lessons. I need a miracle. I get these principles are supposed to teach us, but I'm angry. I don't want bad things to keep happening to good people. I don't need more shaping. I've had enough. All I want now is a miracle."

Grandpa took a deep breath and responded, "I know you do. We all do. The answers aren't always easy, are they? Sometimes trials help us grow, teaching us important lessons and strengthening our character. Remember Joseph from the scriptures? He faced incredible trials. Ultimately, he became a great leader and helped many people because of those trials. Our faith reminds us to trust God's plan, even when it's hard to understand."

As I nodded, my gaze moved toward Mom's motionless figure next to him. "I know, and I understand. I just don't like it. It is never so well understood how horrible of a statement that is until it happens to you. I will never use it to comfort anyone ever again." I bowed my head, defeated. "Grandpa, don't let her die. I can't lose my mom. I can't."

My words hung in the air, and all I could hear was the beeping of the monitors in the background. I closed my eyes again and focused on a single word. "Mom." That's what I wanted; that's all I wanted.

"Noah, don't let this break your faith," Grandpa Wilde added.

I didn't answer him as he took the phone from me and hung up.

CHAPTER ELEVEN

I ONLY HAD TO stay in the hospital for twelve days. Upon my release, Mom remained in an induced coma at Harborview. Uncle Jared returned home to his family in Utah, while Grandpa Wilde stayed behind with me.

Tomorrow, Jacob would call, and it would be time to tell him everything. The stake president contacted the MTC president, informing him my grandpas and I would update Jacob with tragic news. He intended to be with Jacob during the call.

Both grandpas promised I could be the one to tell him what happened. It was what I wanted. Soon I would see Jacob. Soon I would have someone who understood what I was going through. Only Jacob could understand the extent of my suffering, for he was my brother. They were his parents, as well.

"Grandpa, should we go to Seattle?" I asked, as Grandpa Wilde helped me into the house after being released from the hospital.

"The forty-five-minute drive from the hospital to the house nearly did you in. Your head and hip still can't handle the journey, and the doctors haven't cleared you to travel over the pass since your concussion."

I was stir-crazy. The time ticked by at a turtle's pace. After lunch, Grandpa suggested, "Why don't you sit in the recliner? I'll put on a movie for you. It's more comfortable than the couch and easier to see."

"That's Dad's chair."

Grandpa stared at the chair for a moment, then vanished behind me. I refrained from turning around to see what he was doing. A moment later, I heard water running in the kitchen.

Grandpa had been sitting in the chair since we arrived home, and I was determined not to behave childishly over it. After declaring it as I had, I might as well have thrown a tantrum. My meaning had been clear, and Grandpa never sat in Dad's chair again.

I fell asleep on the couch that night, not bothering to hobble to my room.

The next day, I kept the Messenger app open and my phone volume on high, unsure when Jacob might call. With a fifteen-hour time difference and no idea of his missionary schedule, I didn't want to miss him.

Then, late afternoon, before evening settled in, the phone rang. I limp-ran as fast as possible without my crutches to the dining room table, where I had left the phone before a bathroom visit. I snatched up the phone and accepted the call. Of all the times to get up and use the bathroom! I had held my bladder all day, and he called right when I gave in to nature.

"Jacob!" I would have climbed into the phone and transported myself six thousand miles if I could have.

"Noah," Jacob gasped. "Oh, my goodness, Noah, are you alright? They told me there was an accident, but no one knows anything else. I am worried out of my mind, but I am just supposed to keep working. What happened?"

His concern and love poured through the video chat. It embodied everything I admired and valued in my big brother. His voice was music to my ears. I hadn't even answered his question when five more about Dad, Mom, and the accident flooded out.

"Noah?" Jacob's voice veritably begged.

I couldn't speak. I hung my head in my hands and cried.

Then another box popped up on the screen, splitting it into three, and Grandpa Evans joined the call. Grandpa Wilde moved his chair closer so Jacob could now see him on the shared screen.

Grandpa attempted a minute of mundane pleasantries, but Jacob would have none of it. Distress showed all over my countenance, and my big brother went into protection mode. He wanted to know why Grandpa Wilde was at our house and why Grandpa Evans was on the line. He demanded to know where Mom and Dad were, and he was getting upset. Jacob rarely got upset, and his fear and reaction broke my heart all over again.

A sob escaped. A loud, choking sob.

Both grandpas stayed silent. I had insisted I would tell Jacob, and they had relented. I needed to speak soon.

A few moments later, when I still couldn't speak, Grandpa Wilde took the phone from me. He propped it in the center of the table. The line fell silent. We all knew the tough discussion that needed to take place. Even Jacob knew something terrible was coming. He wiped tears from his cheeks, his back ramrod straight in his seat.

"Jacob, I hope all is well with you?" Grandpa Wilde spoke formally.

"Yes, Grandpa, it's great. What's going on? Where are Mom and Dad? Noah, is he alright? What's going on?"

Tears streamed down my face as I gasped for air, the sobs catching in my throat. It had been nearly two weeks since the accident and Dad's passing, and Mom's ongoing battle for survival was something I endured daily. Yet the sound of Jacob's voice made it all feel intensely present. His pleas reopened the raw wounds within me.

I wondered if I could handle this conversation after all. This was my choice. I had insisted on being the one to tell Jacob the news. *Man up. Do the hard thing.* Now, I wasn't so sure.

Grandpa leaned forward, ready to take my place, but I raised my hand to stop him. With a deep, unsteady breath, I gathered all the determination I could muster. "Jacob, we were in a horrible accident coming home from the airport after dropping you off. Dad died in the accident, and Mom is in a medically induced coma." By the time I finished speaking, my voice was little more than a whisper.

"No!" Jacob's tears mixed with a wail through the phone as he pitched forward onto his arms.

"We are not sure when she will be well enough to wake up, but everyone is very hopeful." My voice spoke the opposite.

Jacob cried some more, and then we heard a knock on his door. His companion rushed across the screen behind him to open the door. The MTC president and his wife walked in.

The kind-looking man stepped up to Jacob and pulled him into an embrace. I was glad. Jacob needed a hug, I could tell. I wished I was there to be the one to give it. The president's wife rubbed Jacob's back and soothed him as only a woman could. When they sat back down, the MTC president and his wife sat on either side of Jacob, offering support. He was still crying, but far less desperate.

"And you? Noah, were you injured?" Jacob leaned close to the phone, pawing the tears out of his eyes.

"I was, but not as serious, and I'm healing quickly. Most of my bruises are already fading, except for a couple." I leaned in, pointing to a few spots on my face. As I turned my head to the left, he saw the large gash and the bruising that would take longer to heal. He gasped, but I continued before he could respond. "My hip is the worst injury. When the wreckage shattered my window and mangled my door, my hip took the brunt of it. Thankfully, there are no long-term injuries. I also hit my head hard and was unconscious for four days, then heavily sedated for another two. They'll monitor my concussion until I am given a clean bill of health. They expect that I'll be recovered in six weeks."

Talking about myself was easy, and I felt my emotions ease.

"Six weeks!" Jacob exclaimed, his voice wavering in disbelief. He took a deep, steadying breath before continuing, but his composure quickly shattered. "It's been nearly two weeks since the accident. Why didn't anyone tell me sooner? This isn't something you just keep from me!" His voice cracked, rising in anger and pain. "I had a right to know! You don't keep news like this from someone. Why was I left in the dark?" He breathed hard now, his frustration palpable through the phone.

Grandpa Evans sighed, leaning closer to the phone. "Jacob, there was nothing you could have done from the Philippines. We didn't have reliable information at first, and we didn't want to worry you more than necessary. Everything was chaotic. No one knew if your mother would make it through those first days. We thought it was better to wait until we knew more before telling you. I know it wasn't fair to keep this from you, but we were trying to protect you. Believe me, it was the hardest decision I've ever made." His voice was heavy with regret.

I swallowed hard, struggling to keep my emotions in check as his next words echoed in my ears. "What about Dad's funeral?"

Every emotion surged back in a flood. I shook as I spoke, my words punctuated by tears and wracking sobs. "We didn't have one. We were in the hospital. Uncle Jared came and took care of everything. Dad's already buried. Jacob, I didn't get to hug him goodbye. It was impossible to reach him in the wreckage. I tried. I could see his hand, but I was trapped and couldn't get to him. When they cut the doors off and got me out, they wouldn't let me see him. I didn't get to say goodbye. Then they took me to a different hospital than Mom. Jacob, I can't go see her either. My hip is too injured to travel, and even if it weren't, I'm not allowed to cross mountain passes with my concussion. Not yet, at least. No matter which route we take, we have to drive over the mountains. They don't want the increased pressure on my brain."

I folded my arms over the table's edge and leaned on them, sobbing uncontrollably. In my despair, I shot snot from my nose onto Mom's clean floor below me. It didn't matter to me.

Jacob wiped his face with the back of his hand, sniffled, and struggled to steady his voice. "Is she... is Mom nearby? Can I... can I see her?"

Grandpa Evans exchanged a glance with Grandpa Wilde on the video call, the weight of their unspoken concerns plain. "Jacob, I don't think that's the best idea right now," Grandpa Evans said gently. "She's in a very fragile state, and..."

"She's not awake, Jacob, and she wouldn't know you were there even if she was, with all the medicine they have her on," Grandpa Wilde added, his tone equally firm but soft.

Jacob's face crumpled, his eyes filling with a fresh wave of tears. "Please. I just want to see her. I need to see her."

"No," Grandpa Evans said, shaking his head slowly. "It might be too much for you right now, son."

I couldn't hold back any longer. My fists clenched at my sides as I pushed myself up straighter, meeting their eyes across the screen. "You can't keep hiding everything from him!" I said. My voice trembled, but I was resolute. "He has a right to see her, to know what's going on. He needs to see her, just like I did."

Both grandpas turned their attention to me, taken aback by my outburst. Grandpa Wilde opened his mouth to protest, but I pressed on before he could get a word out. "You can't protect him from this, not forever. Let him see her, Grandpa. Please."

A heavy silence settled over the call. After what felt like an eternity, Grandpa Evans nodded, sorrow etched across his face. "Alright, Noah. Jacob, if you're sure this is what's best."

We nodded with combined determination. My heart pounded in my chest. They turned the camera toward the hospital bed, and Jacob leaned forward, his breath catching in his throat.

When Mom's image filled the screen, Jacob went silent, his face paling. Tubes and wires surrounded her, and the rhythmic beep of the machines echoed through the phone as Grandpa approached her. She looked small and fragile beneath the stark white hospital sheets, her eyes closed, her face bruised and swollen.

Jacob's lip quivered, and his hand flew to his mouth as if to hold back a scream. The agony on his face was raw and gut-wrenching, a pain so deep that I felt it like a knife to my heart.

"Jacob, let's talk about what you want to do," Grandpa Evans said, breaking the stillness.

"What do you mean?" Jacob wiped his eyes and attempted to steady his breathing. His words came out filled with anguish, catching and hitching in his throat. If I had looked, I would have seen red eyes and tears on the faces of both grandpas, the MTC President, and his wife.

"I assume you'll want to come home, at least for a while. No one would blame you if you stayed home and didn't return to the mission field."

"No, Grandpa! How can you even ask? I'm staying. It's what Dad would have wanted." Jacob's words were solid and final.

"Even with your mother as hurt as she is?"

"Will her condition improve by me being there?"

"No, but I assumed you'd want to be here with her. She is not out of the woods yet."

"Of course, I want to be there, but we can call down more heavenly blessings through my service than by me coming home."

The MTC President looked like he wanted to speak. He cleared his throat, and we all listened. "Elder Wilde," he turned to Jacob, "the choice is yours. If you go home, you may return to the Cauayan mission if it is within your original two-year timeframe. Or, should you choose, you can request reassignment to a United States mission. Your family requests your presence. You should take the time to pray and reflect before deciding. This is a crucial juncture in your life. Consult with your Heavenly Father so you have no regrets over your decision, whichever it may be."

"Stay! It's what Dad would have wanted. Mom would agree with me if she could. She knows what Dad ingrained in us our entire lives." My words held confidence, even if my voice trembled.

"Alright, I will take some time to pray over it and talk to you next week." Jacob's voice quivered with vulnerability. I had never recognized this side of my strong brother.

"Tomorrow," the MTC President declared. He had a kind face that held years of wisdom and understanding. "You will not wait an entire week for your decision. The Lord will tell you immediately, and we will act as soon as you decide. Brethren," he addressed my two grandfathers, "expect another call soon. If Elder Wilde wants to return home, we can have him on a flight within 24 hours. If he stays, I hope you will send him more frequent updates about his mother's progress. I will allow him to check messages on Messenger daily instead of waiting for p-day. Elder Wilde, if you stay but later decide you want to go home, just say the word."

The MTC President cleared his throat, sitting with an air of tense authority. "The decision of what to disclose to Elder Wilde rests with your family, but if I were in your position, I wouldn't delay communicating important information. Providing all necessary details is important for timely and informed decision making. Elder Wilde is a grown man. The Lord trusts him to feed His sheep on another continent. You should trust him with all family information."

If it had been within my power, I would have reached through the phone and hugged Jacob's MTC President. I wanted to raise my hands and shout, *Amen, Brother!* He got it. He understood Jacob deserved the whole truth from the start. Jacob was a grown man, not a child. I couldn't have said it better.

Jacob nodded and wiped his eyes one more time.

"Jacob, pray for a miracle. God always answers your prayers. Please, I need you to pray hard. God is not answering my prayers, but He will answer yours." My words carried an emotional weight, revealing my inner turmoil and exposing the shattered fragments of my faith.

"I will, but Noah, He answers your prayers too."

I twisted my face in disagreement and shook my head. I had doubts about whether God was hearing and answering my prayers.

"Noah, He is too!" Jacob insisted. "Don't you dare lose faith. Mom needs your prayers, too."

I stiffened my back and sat up straight, but didn't answer him. I couldn't, or else I would cry again.

Grandpa Evans asked Jacob questions about his transition to life in the Philippines, inquiring about the culture, language, food, and his studies. I had to commend him for his efforts, but Jacob revealed little. The conversation felt stilted after such a heavy discussion filled with high emotions, and it ended all too soon.

"Do you think he will come home?" Grandpa Wilde asked after we hung up.

"Nope."

Struggling to stand from the rigid dining room chair, I steadied myself on my sturdy leg. I snatched my phone off the table and tucked it into my pocket before limping into my bedroom. Despite my exhaustion, I didn't sleep or cry as I collapsed onto my bed. I had spent all my tears, every last one.

I stared at the ceiling, not wanting to do anything or feel anything. Yet, after a lifetime of praying, the habit was hard to break. So hard, in fact, that even when I wasn't sure if my prayers were being heard, I still caught myself praying. Even when I didn't want to give Grandpa, Jacob, or God the satisfaction of being right, those thoughts came unbidden.

I repeated my pleas to God for a miracle. That Mom would wake up and be her fabulous self again. This relentless, unbidden pleading was making me angry.

The longer I pleaded, the more upset I became. I was furious that the doctors were keeping Mom in a coma. Maybe the miracle was being prevented. I wondered if she would already be awake and healed if it weren't for the medication keeping her sedated. No, that wasn't it. God could wake her up even from an induced coma.

It was incredibly late and the sky outside my window was pitch black when I bitterly rolled over and attempted to sleep. I didn't say my personal prayers that night. I had prayed enough.

CHAPTER TWELVE

Maybe Mom would wake up, and everything would go back to normal. Perhaps the doctors could heal her, restoring her as good as new. There was even a possibility that Jacob would come home, and we could face this together. Deep down, I didn't expect him to return. Part of me didn't even want him to. Well, I did, but I didn't. You understand, right?

I squeezed my eyes shut and took a deep breath, trying to push the negative thoughts away.

As I predicted, Jacob called at the same time as yesterday. He announced he was staying. The MTC President sat beside him, committed to supporting his decision while offering reassurance that he was free to change his mind at any time.

It didn't surprise me; in fact, it made me proud. I agreed with him, and I told him so.

After we hung up, I struggled into my usual seat on the couch, grabbed the remote, and started movie menu surfing.

"Someone's here," Grandpa Wilde exclaimed as he leaned back and peered through the curtains. "Here they come," he said with a smile. "One of them looks like that girl who visited you at the hospital. What was her name, Shelly?" Grandpa stood and started for the door.

Blood rushed to my cheeks as I corrected him. "Shelby."

"That's right, Shelby. I need to remember that."

My cheeks ablaze, I raked my fingers through my untidy hair. When was the last time I combed it?

A moment later, I heard little kids' feet running on the porch. "Can I ring the doorbell, Mom?" the high-pitched, squeaky voice of a child called out. I couldn't catch his mother's less lively reaction, but Grandpa opened the door before he could ring the bell.

"Welcome, welcome!" Grandpa Wilde greeted with a flourish.

In a voice as sweet as honey, Shelby answered, "Hello, Brother Wilde. I heard Noah is home. I promised I would bring him some cookies."

"Hear that, Noah? Your friend brought you some cookies!"

"They're for you too," she added with a smile.

Grandpa chuckled as most of the Thurston family rushed in past him. Over their heads, he winked at me, understanding that the young girl holding the cookies hadn't made them for an old man like him.

"Hi, Shelby! Come on in. Hey, Steven, how are you?" I greeted her brother as he walked in behind her.

"Noah, we came too!" Daniel piped up, racing over to my couch and bouncing up and down in front of me. His brother, John, joined him, less lively but still enthusiastic about being here.

"Hi, Daniel, John! I'm glad you came." I reached forward and ruffled Daniel's hair before throwing off the blanket from my legs and standing up.

I stood up faster than I should have, and pain shot through my hip. Right, I needed to remember to rise in a more gentle motion.

"No need to get up," Shelby said, her voice laced with concern and compassion. I settled back on the couch but didn't reach for the blanket. "We brought some freezer meals. My mom thought they would help you and your grandfather."

My heart skipped a beat at the sound of Shelby's voice. I briefly shifted my gaze to her mother, who carried a bag full of homemade dinners in each hand. Steven held up two more full totes.

"You didn't have to do that," Grandpa replied, leading her to the freezer in the kitchen.

"I know we didn't, but we wanted to. It's not much, but it should lighten your load right now."

"There's enough here to feed an army!" Grandpa laughed, stacking the meals in neat piles in the freezer.

"I know how it is feeding growing boys, and mine are half the size of Noah. I wanted to make sure you don't go hungry."

Their voices faded into the background, and I returned my attention to Shelby. "That's really nice of your mom to make those for us."

"I helped!" she replied proudly.

"Oh yeah? I can't wait to try one. Which one is your favorite?"

I watched her, mesmerized by the sparkle in her eyes, as she talked about something as mundane as dinner.

"Do you want me to heat one for you now?" she offered.

I vaguely recalled what she said and sat there trying to figure out how to respond.

"Um, no, my grandpa can do that later. Didn't you say you brought some cookies?"

"Yes!" Her eyes lit up even more, if that was even possible. She set a plate covered in aluminum foil on my lap. "They are chocolate chip, my specialty."

"Thanks!" I lifted the plate and peeked under the foil. "Can I have one now?"

"Of course!" she laughed.

Her voice was musical and warmed my heart.

Seizing the plate from my hands, she removed the aluminum foil. After studying the collection of cookies for a moment, she reached for a giant one in the middle and handed it to me.

"That's the biggest one!"

"I want one! I want one!" The two youngest boys jumped up and down, begging for a cookie.

"Those are for Noah," Sister Thurston called from the kitchen. I hadn't realized she was observing us. It was one of those supermom powers. I guess all moms had them.

My chest clenched a little, but I shook it off.

"It's all right. They can have one," I answered. Then, a little quieter to Shelby, I added, "But if they eat them all, you'll just have to bring me some more."

A smile the size of Texas erupted across her face. Her smile could light up the darkest room, and I liked it. I smiled back at her as I took a bite from her giant cookie.

"Mm, this is delicious."

I didn't believe it was possible, but her smile grew even bigger.

Meanwhile, Shelby's two mischievous little brothers, John and Daniel, bounced around like energized puppies, munching on their cookies and scattering crumbs all over the living room floor.

"Hey, Noah," John called out with a playful grin. "You know, Shelby talks about you all the time. She thinks you're a-mazing!"

My cheeks flushed, a mix of embarrassment and elation washing over me, along with a hint of self-satisfaction at the revelation. Shelby blushed too and cast her gaze downward.

Daniel, the youngest, poked his head out from around the bookshelf. He attempted to whisper, but it came out more like a shout. "Hey, Noah. Do you have any cool stories to tell us? I heard you were in a car accident! Our dad said your truck is all mangled and wrecked."

I winced at the mention of the accident, a pang of grief surfacing and choking me.

"No, Daniel. It's been a tough time for me. I can't talk about the accident yet. Maybe another time."

"Okay, later then."

Luckily, we dropped the topic, and before the atmosphere could grow heavy, John picked up his previous thread and interjected gleefully. "Shelby thinks you're cute, Noah! She says you're her knight in shining armor!"

"Daniel, we don't ask questions like that! And John, how dare you tell lies?" Shelby scolded, her cheeks flushing.

"Why not? And it's not a lie! I overheard you telling Mom when you were making cookies."

"Go to Mom, NOW!" Shelby pointed her finger toward the kitchen, giving her younger brother the Big Sister look she had mastered. It screamed, *Don't say another word and get your butt out of here before I kill you,* all at once.

He raced to his mom, tattling on Shelby before he even reached her.

"That's it. We need to go," Sister Thurston declared a split second later. Like every other mom on Earth, the visit was over as soon as the fighting started.

I had never known embarrassment until that moment. But if my face turned red, Shelby's was redder, red as a ripe tomato. She fidgeted with her hands and refused to look at me.

I reached out and touched her cool hand, prompting her to look up. "When do you turn sixteen?" I asked. I was nervous and didn't know what else to say. The words rushed out like an unstoppable avalanche.

"July twenty-first." She looked up at me through her long eyelashes.

"So, this summer. Good to know," I said, relieved to shift the focus.

"Your birthday is in September, isn't it?"

"That's right," I replied, happy she already knew.

Grandpa Wilde stepped forward, a twinkle in his eyes. "Why don't you leave Shelby and Steven here? They can watch a movie with Noah, and I can bring them home later. They can all hang out a little while longer. Noah could use the distraction."

"Yes! Can we, Mom?" Shelby asked sweetly.

Steven nodded beside her, eyes wide with excitement.

"If you don't think it's too much of a burden?" Sister Thurston questioned Grandpa.

"Not at all! It will be good for Noah to have some friends around."

"All right, you can stay."

"Me too?" John and Daniel declared in unison.

"I think not! You two rapscallions are coming home with me," Sister Thurston replied, hands on her hips.

She picked up her empty totes and headed for the door. The mischievous duo grumbled but scampered off after their mom, leaving Shelby and Steven behind.

"Want some popcorn?" Grandpa asked, his voice cheerful.

"Sure! Thanks, Grandpa," I answered.

"Do you need some help making it?" sweet Shelby asked, always ready to lend a hand.

"No, I got it. You pick a movie with the boys."

I flipped on the TV and asked, "Disney, Netflix, Prime?"

"Disney. Is that all right?" Shelby asked, her joy evident.

"Sure. Disney it is. Jacob and I love *Star Wars*."

"Shelby loves *Beauty and the Beast*," Steven chimed in.

"Cartoon or live action?" I asked.

"Live action."

"Live action it is." I clicked on Disney and waited as the channel loaded, my heart skipping a beat, grateful they had chosen a movie I secretly adored. "Why do you like it so much?" I asked, curious.

Shelby's face lit up as she leaned back against the cushions. "Well, I've always loved the story of *Beauty and the Beast*. It's a tale of seeing beyond appearances and finding the beauty within. And the live-action version captures that so beautifully."

She turned toward me, a gentle smile playing on her lips. "Plus, Emma Watson did an amazing job as Belle. She portrayed her as smart, strong, and independent, an admirable character."

I listened intently, my admiration for Shelby growing with every word she spoke. Her passion and insight captivated me, drawing me in even more.

"Yeah, Emma Watson was great, and the visual effects in the movie are stunning. It's such a magical experience. My mom once mentioned that the Disney animated *Beauty and the Beast* was the first movie she ever saw in a theater. During her freshman year of high school, the students went as a seminary group. She loves this version as well, but deep down, I know the cartoon is her favorite."

It felt good to talk about Mom, though my heart ached a little, sharing something personal about her.

"Really? That's so fun," Shelby replied, her eyes bright with interest.

"I like Gaston. He's hilarious!" Steven chimed in, pulling our attention away from each other.

I scrolled until I found *Beauty and the Beast* and pressed play.

As the movie loaded, I glanced at Shelby. I felt nervous with her sitting beside me on the couch, though an entire cushion separated us. Every so often, I caught the scent of her sweet floral perfume. I liked it. Steven plopped down on the other couch.

"Here you go," Grandpa said, setting a big bowl of popcorn on the couch between Shelby and me.

"Steven, there are more bowls in the lower cupboard to the left of the sink. Grab one so you can take some of this popcorn over there," I suggested.

"Sorry, I didn't think of that." Grandpa followed Steven to the kitchen.

As the movie started playing, Shelby's and my eyes locked for the briefest of moments before we both looked away. I calculated the days until her sixteenth birthday, five months, give or take. That wasn't too bad. By then, I assumed Mom would be home, and I would have healed. I wondered if she would go on a date with me. My chances were looking pretty good.

Shelby couldn't help but share her enthusiasm during her favorite parts of the movie. I loved it when she patted my hand and exclaimed, "I love this part!"

She sang along to every song and encouraged Steven and me to join her. Never had I enjoyed watching a movie so much as I did today.

Shelby's pleasure exuded innocence and joy that I found charming. Her passion for the movie mirrored my growing admiration for her. I couldn't help but feel a connection forming.

We reached into the shared popcorn bowl twice, our hands bumping knuckles.

"Sorry, you go first," I said.

She smiled back and grabbed a handful.

"Steven, I can't believe you like Gaston. He's horrible!" she pointed at the screen as Gaston locked Belle and her father in the *crazy wagon*, what Dad used to call it. I smiled at the memory, chasing away the twinge of pain around my heart.

"What can I say? He's the most entertaining because he's such a dork," Steven replied, shrugging.

"That's one word for him. I can think of a few others," Shelby grumbled.

Her enthusiasm was infectious, and my appreciation for the film grew with each passing minute.

As the last notes of the movie's iconic theme played, I turned to Shelby, a soft smile tugging at the corners of my lips. "Thank you for choosing this movie. I can see why you like it so much. I've always liked it too, but I like it even more now."

She blushed, her gaze meeting mine with surprise and delight. "I'm glad."

As the credits rolled, Grandpa appeared from the back of the house. "Movie over already?"

"Thank you for letting us stay with Noah," Shelby said, her voice warm.

"Of course! Come by anytime."

They gathered their coats, and then Grandpa asked, "You going to be all right here while I drive them home?"

I nodded, then plucked up my courage and hollered after Shelby, "Thanks for the cookies. Feel free to visit next time you make more!"

"Okay," she smiled and waved goodbye.

CHAPTER THIRTEEN

Every day, I called Grandpa Evans, who would hold up the phone so I could see my mom. After each call, I'd send Jacob a quick video message over Messenger, keeping him in the loop. He usually sent a short reply or just a thumbs-up, but it felt good knowing he was with me in spirit. This routine went on and on.

As the weeks slipped by, each day's sunset seemed to fade my grip on hope. One month after the accident, the doctors had begun a countdown. Soon, they'd have to bring Mom out of her coma. Regardless of her readiness, keeping her sedated posed a danger. Time was slipping through our fingers.

For weeks, I'd been on my knees every morning and night, but my prayers had thinned out, turning bitter. It had been three days since I'd prayed, and I thought my silence with God was my secret. But that illusion shattered when Grandpa Wilde turned to me one evening and asked, "Have you prayed today?"

I didn't respond, and before I knew it, Grandpa force-fed me the words. No one had intervened in my prayers since my Sunbeam days. Managing them on my own had been a point of pride until now.

When we finished, Grandpa Wilde's gaze softened, and he leaned back, taking a steady breath. "Noah, I spoke with your doctor today. He cleared you to drive to Seattle."

My heart leaped. "Really? I can be packed in five minutes. How soon can we leave?"

"In the morning," he said with a gentle smile. "They're planning to wake your mom in two days. Grandpa Evans and I both think you should be there."

I jumped from my seat, grinning, and rushed to pack. My hip felt a little better every day, and it had been four days since my last headache. It felt like my prayers, even the ones I skipped, were being answered.

The next morning, the hum of Mom's SUV felt steady beneath me, a reminder of why this trip mattered. I sank into the worn leather seat, ignoring the aches that surged as we started down the road. I wasn't about to let on that it hurt; the last thing I wanted was for Grandpa Wilde to change his mind.

Grandpa's hands gripped the wheel, his weathered fingers firm and unyielding, his gaze focused. Determination and love were etched deep in his features, guiding us both toward Seattle, where my mother waited, ready to awaken from her deep slumber.

As we rolled down the driveway, I turned to the window, and a beautiful sight unfolded. The once-white blanket of snow had vanished, uncovering the earth beneath. Trees that had been bare and lifeless now bore the first signs of spring. Delicate buds dotted their branches, painting the landscape with fresh greens and soft hues. It was a quiet symphony of renewal, a testament to the shifting seasons. I felt a small swell of hope as winter's frost gave way to the promise of warmer days.

"I know it's a longer route and the roads are fine, but let's head to Vantage instead of taking Blewett Pass. The elevation's lower, so there'll be less pressure on your head. Best for this trip, don't you think?"

Bless my thoughtful Grandpa. He understood, maybe better than I did, that I might not be ready to face the accident site. The idea of passing it still gripped me with fear. He read my mind.

The tires hummed against the pavement, a delicate sound weaving through the quiet that wrapped around us. Now and then, Grandpa would ask a gentle question, his words lingering between us when he noticed me shift or wince from a jolt on the uneven road.

I wasn't alright. The pain was relentless, but I wouldn't let him know. I couldn't risk him turning the car around and taking me home.

Outside, the scenery blurred by in a wash of colors and shapes, until massive tractor-trailers loomed on the freeway, casting shadows over my fragile heart. Every time we passed one, my chest tightened, my breaths turned shallow and erratic. Memories of the accident, of the impact, the twisted metal, rushed back. In every looming truck, I saw a potential collision that could shatter everything once more. Fear clenched around me, squeezing the air from my lungs.

Grandpa must have noticed. Without a word, he reached over and laid his rough hand on mine, warm and steady. Through that touch, I felt the weight of his love, an unspoken promise to help bear my burden.

As the miles stretched on, fatigue seeped into my bones. The ache from my injuries intensified with every bump and shift. My seatbelt pressed into my torso and felt like a vise, a reminder of the one that had kept me trapped, unable to reach my father. The urge to get out was overwhelming, but my need to see Mom kept me grounded. *Just a little longer,* I told myself.

Grandpa glanced over and his gaze softened, concern etched into the lines around his eyes. His voice, gravelly but gentle, cut through the heavy silence. "Hang in there, Noah. We're almost there. Your mama's waiting for you."

His words held the weight of a thousand promises, casting a glimmer of hope through the darkness that threatened to consume me. I clung to those words, to the image of my mother's face, and to the warmth of her embrace waiting at this journey's end. I knew she would wake up and hold me. I'd hold her. We would hold each other, and I wanted that moment more than anything else I'd ever wanted. The thought of her hug filled me with strength.

With each passing mile, my fear eased, replaced by a steady determination. The sight of a tractor-trailer no longer paralyzed me; instead, I took a deep breath, holding my gaze steady as it passed. I was stronger than my fear.

As the city skyline came into view, anticipation surged within me. Grandpa Wilde's hands tightened on the steering wheel, mirroring my resolve. We had made it, on the verge of a new beginning, where love and healing waited for us.

When Grandpa guided the car into the hospital parking lot, my emotions danced in the space between us. The outside world felt distant. This journey was about more than a destination. It was about finding the strength to face my fears. The time had come to wake Mom. I needed to know if my faith and my prayers for miracles would be enough.

With a soft thud, the car came to a stop, and Grandpa's presence anchored me, steadying my racing heart. A wave of gratitude surged within me, unspoken words catching in my throat. I hadn't told him how much his being here with me meant.

I turned to him, my voice thick with emotion. "Grandpa, I never told you how grateful I am that you came after the accident. I couldn't have done this without you. I love you."

His hand, weathered but still strong, cupped my cheek with a gentleness that said everything. "I know, Noah, my boy. I love you too."

Overcome, I leaned across the console and wrapped my arms around him in a fierce embrace, holding on a moment longer than usual. Finally, with a deep breath, I climbed out of the car, my determination propelling me forward. Each step toward the hospital doors felt heavy with anticipation, yet our shared strength carried me. Inside those walls, amidst all the unknowns, I trusted miracles awaited.

I hadn't moved this fast in weeks, not since the accident. Now, clutching Mom's room number, I pushed through the ache in my hip, each step sending a jolt up my leg, through my hip, and into my lower back. Counting each step, each stab of pain, kept my mind steady. I could do this just a little farther.

Grandpa Evans met us in the hall, stopping me with a warm hug and a few hurried questions I was too impatient to register. My mind focused on the door ahead. My heart hammered as I stood just outside her hospital room, a tempest of longing and fear swirling within me. Weeks had passed since the accident, weeks filled with yearning and hope. Video calls with Grandpa Evans had helped, but nothing compared to being here, on the threshold of her room.

I froze, paralyzed by the thought of going in. I stood on the edge, desperate to see Mom, yet fearful of what I'd find. I wished Jacob was here to go first. If he led the way, I could stay behind, hidden, only looking when I was ready. I could peek over his shoulder to reassure myself she was alright.

I inhaled deeply, then pushed open the door and stepped inside, my gaze landing on the figure lying in bed. Mom looked pale and thinner than I remembered, her delicate features softened by the toll of the accident. But to me, she was more beautiful than ever. Just seeing her, I felt a rush of longing so fierce it made my heart ache. A fragility emanated around Mom that tugged at something deep within me, a pull to protect her that was stronger than any fear. She was here, alive, and now that I was by her side, I would do everything to help her heal. I needed her. She needed me. We needed each other.

As I walked closer, a lump formed in my throat, and my legs wobbled beneath me. Her eyes, peacefully closed, hinted at the promise of waking. A reunion I had dreamed of every night. She looked like *Sleeping Beauty*, waiting for love's true kiss to bring her back. But then, reality struck: *Dad was gone. He couldn't be here to kiss her awake.* My throat tightened at the thought, and I pushed it away.

The monitors on the wall behind Mom's bed beeped, a steady reminder of her current state. But I refused to let fear overshadow hope. This was my mom, my only remaining parent.

Tears blurred my vision, but I held them back, reaching for her pale hand. I expected it to be cold, but her skin was warm beneath my touch, grounding me. She was real, alive, tethered to me in this silent moment. My voice trembled as I spoke, hardly more than a whisper. "Mom, it's me, Noah. I'm here. I've missed you so much."

Time seemed to slow as I waited for something, anything. A flutter of her eyelids, a twitch of her fingers. I held my breath, willing her to respond. I had convinced myself that all she needed was for me to be here, that the miracle I'd prayed for would happen the moment she felt my presence. I'd thought maybe it was the phone or the distance that had prevented it, but now, standing beside her, surely God would answer my prayers. I was positive He was waiting for me to be the one to usher in the miracle.

But there was no response. No miracle.

A wave of defeat washed over me, mingling with a surge of guilt. For weeks, I'd thought Grandpa Evans' faith must not have been strong enough and that only my touch, my voice, would bring her back. Now, as I stood here without a sign, a hollow ache filled me, as if hope itself was slipping away.

I leaned down and kissed Mom's forehead. Since the first video call, some of her bandages had been removed, a sign that her body was healing. Even if her healing was slower than I wanted, it was something. A small comfort and a glimmer of hope I clung to. But as I pulled away and stood up, something felt off. A forehead kiss seemed distant, wrong somehow. What Mom needed was a *Tinker Bell Kiss*.

I pressed my lips to that familiar spot, my favorite place on her cheek, then waited, heart pounding, watching for any sign, any stirring.

Nothing.

Overwhelmed with emotion, I collapsed into the chair, laying my head on the bed beside her. Strangely, I didn't cry, not even as a hollow ache settled deep within. My faith felt like it had slipped through my fingers, leaving me empty. God had abandoned me. Numb and broken, I just lay there, staring ahead, unseeing.

In the thick silence, a steady stream of medical staff filtered into the room behind Mom's doctor. He wore the weary look of someone who'd spent hours on rounds, his white coat rumpled, but his expression was kind as he approached.

"Hello, you must be Noah. I've heard a lot about you from your grandpa," he said, extending his hand. His voice was light, almost out of place in the room's weighted atmosphere, thick with unspoken worry. Behind him, Grandma spoke with a nurse; they seemed to know each other well.

"I'm glad you made it here," he continued, his tone steady but gentle. "I've reviewed your mom's condition, and it's time to discuss the next steps." He directed his statement at me as though I held authority over the situation, and somehow, that brought a flicker of reassurance. "Your mom has recovered enough for us to wean her off the sedative. We'll assess her healing once she's awake. I know it's hard, but Leah won't wake immediately. It could take hours, maybe days, even longer. Every patient responds differently. But she's showing promising signs, like breathing on her own, so we'll monitor her carefully."

He paused, giving me space to absorb his words. I glanced at my grandparents, who gave me encouraging nods, but I could feel the weight of their exhaustion behind their expressions. Swallowing back the doubt clawing its way in, I forced a steady tone. "We've all been praying for her. I believe God will bring her back to us."

Dr. Mitchell gave a faint smile. "Your support has been tremendous for Leah. We just need to stay strong and patient. It's a waiting game now, and Leah's body will let us know when she's ready."

The hours blended into days, each stretching longer than the last, as we took shifts beside Mom's bed. When exhaustion finally overtook me, I would rest on the nearby couch, never leaving her side. The constant rhythm of the machines and the soft hum of hospital noises became a backdrop to our watchful waiting. Her breaths, slow and steady, became the fragile thread holding our hopes together.

At first, we clung to faith, the initial optimism carrying us. But as the days passed with no change, hope felt like a brittle thing, bending under the weight of reality. We all coped differently, each of us frayed around the edges in our own way.

Grandpa Wilde drifted between the waiting room and the condo where Grandpa and Grandma Evans were staying, his presence a quiet but comforting shadow. Grandpa Evans, silent and withdrawn, kept the TV on mute all day, reading the scrolling subtitles of the news. And Grandma Evans, restless and worn, wandered the halls, striking up conversations with nurses and patients alike. She couldn't sit still any longer; the waiting gnawed at her, and distraction became her solace.

I clung to my place beside Mom, my fingers curling around hers, searching for warmth, for reassurance, anything to remind me she was still here. The hospital room became our sanctuary and our prison, each breath and each heartbeat a fragile bridge between hope and despair.

Day in and day out, I sat at Mom's side, holding her hand. I talked to her, making promises of the things we'd do when she woke up. I read to her from her favorite book, *Pride and Prejudice*. As I held my phone, reading the tiny words on the screen, I felt a blend of curiosity and skepticism. This was a classic by an author from a different era, a timeless novel that meant everything to her.

At sixteen, and the son of a bookworm, I'd devoured my fair share of novels, but classics were uncharted territory. This was Mom's domain, not mine.

The language was challenging, but I pushed through. I remembered how Mom once compared Dad to Jane Austen's heroes, insisting he was most like Mr. Knightley from *Emma*. I wondered why *Emma* wasn't her favorite novel instead. After reading *Pride and Prejudice* to her, I found *Emma* in her Kindle library and started reading it.

I was determined to persevere through this literary journey. The first words transported me to a world of elegance and societal complexities, so far removed from my own. The language was rich, the prose intricate, and the pace slower than anything I was used to. But as I read, I uncovered layers beneath the surface, a craft that breathed life into each character. The further I got, the more I found a strange connection to this world, where matchmaking, social expectations, and subtle nuances governed everything.

I struggled at first to connect with *Pride and Prejudice*, but *Emma* felt different. The gossip, the plotting over who should date whom, it was just like high school. Some things, it turns out, never change.

Every time Mr. Knightley appeared, I read a little closer, searching for the reasons Mom saw Dad in him. Mr. Knightley was unlike the others. He held a quiet integrity and a moral grounding that didn't waver. He never bent to superficial pressures or followed the crowd. Dad had always been the same. I could see why Mom loved him for that. She was right, Dad was like Mr. Knightley.

Sometimes, I forgot to read aloud, losing myself in the story. Mr. Knightley's intelligence, his way of perceiving motives and emotions that others missed, reminded me of Dad's perceptiveness. Yet for all his wisdom, Mr. Knightley was humble and kind. He treated people with compassion and patience, never placing himself above them. His loyalty and unwavering support for those he loved left a lasting impression on me, a reminder of the importance of being there for the people who matter most.

Like Dad had always been there. And like I was now, by Mom's side.

I could not agree more. Mr. Knightley was exactly like my father, or my father was exactly like Mr. Knightley. Never had I loved a story as much as I loved *Emma* at that moment.

As I reached the last page, closing the book felt like a challenge. Mr. Knightley had left an unforgettable mark on me, and finishing the story brought a pang of sadness. I wanted to know more about him, believing that in understanding his character, I might uncover more about Dad. I yearned to reread *Emma*, hoping to discover additional layers in the character who so closely resembled my father.

"Mom, I agree. Mr. Knightley and Dad are a lot alike," I said softly. As I looked into Mom's face, I noticed something subtle, a flicker, perhaps? Were her eyes moving beneath their closed lids? I scanned her body from head to toe and back again, and I saw a twitch of her little finger on the hand nearest me.

I looked around, expecting to see Grandpa Evans watching the news in the corner, but he wasn't there. No one was there, just me, alone with my mom, who I hoped beyond hope was finally waking up. Instead of running for help, I remained at her side.

"Mom, I read your book. Did you hear me? You were right, Mr. Knightley is most like Dad. My favorite part was how patient and caring he was. Dad was the same way, wasn't he?"

Mom's eyes fluttered again.

I searched for Grandpa Evans once more, but he still wasn't there. I didn't want to leave Mom's side. The thought of her waking up alone was unbearable.

"Mom, do you think I'm like Dad? I think so. I've learned to be patient, and I care a lot, especially about you." Unsure if she could hear me, I whispered, "Yes, I think I'm like Dad. Just like him."

Oh, how I longed to be like my father, perfect in every way. I would always remember him that way.

"Yes, you are."

I froze, then snapped my head up, eyes wide in disbelief. Had she spoken? Her voice was so soft, I could hardly hear her. I held my breath, watching for any signs that I wasn't imagining this.

Her eyes remained closed, her body still and unmoving. Even her breath was barely perceptible. I must have imagined it. Doubt and disappointment washed over me. With my head resting on the bed beside her, I closed my eyes, holding back tears, determined not to cry again.

Then, her index finger twitched against my head, but I didn't move. I didn't want to be disappointed again. The doctor warned us about muscle spasms, and I was sure that was all it was. But then her entire hand moved, flopping onto my head. Her fingers closed around my hair, and she spoke my name.

"Noah."

I jumped up and shouted for anyone who could hear me. I pressed the nurse's call button at least ten times, praying that multiple presses would bring help faster.

"Mom, you're awake! I knew you would come back to me."

I stared into her pretty blue eyes, just like mine and Jacob's. She focused on me, recognition shining in her gaze, and I felt an overwhelming wave of gratitude. But then her eyes fluttered closed again, and she didn't respond. I begged her to come back. I was still pleading and praying when the nurses came running.

"She woke up. She spoke to me. She moved her hand, but she's gone again! Help her! Bring her back!" I cried.

"That's wonderful!" exclaimed the nurse I liked. But she didn't shake or command Mom to wake up again, as I had expected.

"But she's not responding anymore. Please, do something!"

"Like the doctor said, we have to wait. It's a great sign she woke up and spoke to you. Was she understandable?"

"Yes, she said my name."

"Excellent!" She jotted down notes on her tablet. "I'll call the doctor. You stay here in case she wakes up again. If I were waking up like this, I'd want to see my baby."

I liked her for that. She was right. Mom would want Dad, Jacob, or me. No one else. It had to be me she saw first. I was all she had right now.

"If you see my grandparents, can you send them in?"

"Yes, of course."

The nurse left, and moments later, Grandpa Evans came running. I knew he could hustle, but I'd never seen him run. Mom stirred again when he raced through the door.

"Look, see? Mom is waking up. She already said my name once and touched my head. Grandpa, she's going to be alright."

"Let's hope so, Noah."

Grandma arrived a few minutes later, and Grandpa Evans called Grandpa Wilde's phone for him to join us.

Everyone was present when Mom opened her eyes again. A collective gasp filled the room. At first, her gaze seemed disoriented, then she focused on our faces. We surrounded her bedside, her eyes darting left and right, seeing the others but never resting on them. Then she stared straight at me and cried.

Relief flooded the room, and tears of joy mingled with exhaustion and grief, mirroring Mom's. I understood her pain.

There were bursts of laughter and tears when she spoke, recognizing everyone. Nurses stood in the doorway, their hearts and faces swelling with a sense of triumph and gratitude. Each nurse rejoiced as they witnessed the culmination of their unwavering care and service to my mom.

Mom observed everyone with greater scrutiny this time. When her gaze settled on Grandpa Wilde, she blinked rapidly, and a steady stream of tears fell once more.

"Adam looked so much like you." Her words were slow and labored, but clear and understandable.

He nodded, pursing his lips back and forth before licking them and pressing them together tight. He was so choked up he couldn't respond.

"How is Jacob?"

Mom knew us well. She didn't question his whereabouts or whether he had come back; she just wanted to know if he was alright.

I whipped out my phone and loaded the Messenger app. It rang twice before a groggy Jacob sat up in bed. The room was dark except for the phone's glow that illuminated his face.

"Noah, is everything alright?"

"Jacob, Mom's awake. She woke up a few minutes ago. She's asking about you."

"She is? Can I see her?" Jacob's voice was urgent as he pleaded.

"What is it, Elder?" his companion asked in the background.

"It's my mom. She is awake from her coma."

A second young man's face popped into the screen from a bunk bed overhead, upside down in the corner as I turned the phone around to show Mom.

"Jacob, darling," Mom rasped. "It's good to see you."

Jacob burst into tears, mixed with a few sobbing laughs, just as we had experienced earlier. "I knew you would wake up. I knew it. I felt that if I worked hard and stayed faithful, you would be alright. Mom, I love you."

She nodded. The few words and many emotions overwhelmed Mom again. She had little energy but asked, "How is your mission?"

He took a deep breath and sighed. "I love it here, but it is tough. I admit, my worry over you has made me a little distracted. Which has made it harder to learn the language, but now that I know you are safe and recovering, I can focus more."

I knew that had to be hard for Jacob to admit.

"Dad will help you. He is your guardian angel," Mom whispered. It was the limit of what she could handle, and she closed her eyes, exhausted.

We all rejoiced together, and Jacob promised to call the next day after he updated the MTC president. We hung up.

Five minutes later, the doctor came running down the hall. The nurses had called him, and he rushed here as fast as possible.

When he entered the room, a smile a mile wide erupted on his face. I will never forget that smile. I felt a surge of hope.

At that moment, Mom's room transformed into a sacred space, the sterile scent of antiseptic mingling with the faint, floral aroma of a wilted bouquet in the corner. Boundaries of life and death blurred as hope surged among us, intertwining our fears and prayers. Mom's journey was far from over, but this chapter, filled with uncertainty and waiting, had ended. As she blinked away the remnants of her slumber, a renewed spirit flickered within her, igniting the love and dedication of our family who had never wavered in their faith.

I knew my mother was a fighter. She had always been strong and resilient, and I refused to give up on her. I leaned closer, taking her hand in mine, desperate for her to feel the unwavering love and support radiating from me. Her head rested on the pillow, eyes closed, but she squeezed my hand, a loving squeeze, a silent promise that we were still connected.

The most significant unknown had been amnesia. Now that she was awake and remembered us, my fear dissipated like morning mist. Mom recalled the crash. She remembered Dad was gone. She knew Jacob was halfway across the world, and most of all, she remembered I was her baby. The relief was palpable, washing over me like a warm embrace.

I stayed at the hospital with Mom day in and day out. I slept on the little couch near her bed and only went to the condo for a shower and a change of clothes before returning to my spot. Grandpa Evans wanted me to return to the condo and stay there now that Mom was awake, but I couldn't bear the thought of leaving. I pleaded to stay, my voice quavering with emotion. The friendly nurse, now my favorite, hugged me sideways and whispered assurances she'd keep a close eye on Mom for me. Grandma Evans couldn't stand my distress and sweet-talked Grandpa into letting me stay, saying, "What can it hurt?" I whooped a little, caught up in a whirlwind of joy, and in a moment of spontaneous affection, I leaned down and gave both Grandma and the little nurse a *Tinker Bell Kiss*.

Grandma smiled as she was used to the kisses, but the little nurse startled a little, then laid her hand over her cheek and exclaimed, "Why, aren't you a doll?" After fussing over Mom and adjusting the bedclothes, she left, and I pushed the small couch as close to Mom's bed as possible, using the accumulated pillows and blankets from the past month to create a makeshift nest.

I took Mom's hand, cherishing the delicate strength of her grip, and fell asleep. For the first time since the accident, I slept. Really slept. No nightmares tore me from the depths of slumber, no tears stained my cheeks when I woke. I didn't even dream, just collapsed into a fitful rest meant to restore my weary body and soul.

CHAPTER FOURTEEN

I'D BEEN AWAKE FOR over an hour when Mom's eyes fluttered open the next morning. Yesterday, when she woke from the coma, she was calm. Today, panic flared in her eyes and her breathing increased as she took in her unfamiliar surroundings.

I dropped my phone on the couch and hurried to her side. "I'm here, Mom. You're not alone."

Her fear stirred something deep within me. In that moment, I became the man my father and brother needed me to be for her. The others loved her, but they would come and go. Grandpa Wilde would eventually return home. So will Grandpa and Grandma Evans. But I would stay. I would be here until she could wake up without fearing the light.

Slowly she turned her head, her red, puffy eyes hinting at tears shed in sleep. Guilt washed over me that I hadn't noticed her sadness sooner.

She tried to sit up, struggling with the weight of it, and I helped, adjusting the bed until she was comfortable. For the next hour, we sat together, saying little. The silence was companionable, laced with understanding.

The nurses came in twice, their steps quick and lively, assuring us the doctor would arrive by nine to check on her. Their enthusiasm was contagious; hope seeped into me with each update. Today was the day. The doctor would share the next stage of Mom's recovery plan. Bucketfuls of hope filled the hearts of everyone, especially me.

At eight-thirty, Grandpa Wilde arrived, explaining that Grandma and Grandpa Evans would be along soon. They had woken up late, the weight of relief finally allowing them to rest.

Just before nine, Mom doubled over, a sudden fit of coughing wracking her thin frame. Her hand shot to her mouth. When she pulled it away, it was streaked with blood.

I rushed to her side, and Grandpa Wilde leaped to his feet and ran to the door, shouting, "Nurse!"

Panic gripped my chest as Mom's breaths grew labored. Her skin paled, then darkened: red, purple, then blue. She looked like she couldn't breathe, like she was suffocating.

The room burst into a flurry of movement. Nurses swarmed around us, their faces tight with concern. They eased her back, slipping an oxygen mask over her face, but it didn't seem to help. The doctor rushed in, his eyes meeting mine for a brief, loaded moment before turning to her.

Without a word to me, he ordered a series of tests, his focus unyielding. The nurses moved with practiced precision, adding equipment, inserting tubes, responding to his commands with silent urgency. The doctor made a call, and within seconds, they whisked her away, vanishing into a maze of sterile corridors.

I moved to follow, but Grandpa's firm hand held me back.

"Grandpa, what just happened?" I whispered in a trembling voice.

He took a breath, his gaze heavy. "I think it's her lungs." His words settled over me like a shadow.

When Grandma and Grandpa Evans arrived, Grandpa Wilde filled them in. I couldn't speak. Fear gnawed at my insides, doubling back stronger than ever, gripping me as if it would never let go.

Time crawled forward, each minute an eternity. At last, the nurse I trusted passed by, and I asked for news.

"The doctor will be here soon. He'll explain everything." She clasped my shoulder, her hand lingered, and my stomach tightened; that kind of touch from a medical professional usually meant bad news. Something was wrong. I knew it in my gut.

When the doctor returned, I leaped to my feet while everyone else remained seated, rooted in dread. He shook my hand, his expression shifting from concern to grim seriousness.

"Leah has internal bleeding, and a collapsed lung. The bleeding didn't show up in earlier scans. It must have been too deep. When she moved, it started. The accident caused more damage than we initially detected. Her lungs were weak from the trauma, and the coughing triggered the collapse. I'm confident we can repair it, but we need to act immediately to stop the bleeding and stabilize her condition. She's being prepped for surgery now."

The floor seemed to fall out beneath me as his words sank in. The fragile thread of hope that had been holding me up trembled, fraying under the weight of it all, threatening to snap.

After the doctor left, I bolted from the room, ignoring Grandpa Wilde's concerned calls. I couldn't take it. I had to get away, to find somewhere beyond the suffocating walls of that sterile room. My legs carried me down unfamiliar halls until I stumbled into a small indoor Japanese garden tucked away from the hospital's noise. The scent of blooming flowers drifted around me, but their beauty was a cruel mockery, offering no comfort to my aching soul.

My legs gave out, and I collapsed onto a worn wooden bench, shaking. Each sob tore through me, raw and unrestrained, echoing off the walls like a cry for help no one could answer. I was drowning in the pain, my cries a haunting reminder of the helplessness that threatened to consume me whole.

"Why, God?" My voice broke, caught between anger and anguish. "How could You let this happen? She just woke up, and now she's in danger all over again. Are You even listening? Do You even care?"

My words hung in the still air, unanswered, the silence pressing down on me, deepening my frustration. Anger simmered, fueling a doubt that had been waiting, a bitter ache I could no longer ignore. *How could a loving God allow so much suffering?* The thought poisoned what little faith I had left.

Despair twisted inside me, and I balled my fists, pounding them into my thighs over and over. Each hit a release, an accusation. Then I froze, struck by a memory of my father doing the same. He'd been hitting his leg just minutes before the accident. My fists tightened, and I dug my fingernails into my palms. The weight of everything was suffocating.

I knew, deep down, that I should turn to God, that I needed to pray. But bitterness took root and held me captive, sealing my lips, making prayer feel impossible.

As despair pulled me further into its darkness, a gentle voice interrupted, cutting through the turmoil like a light breaking through fog.

"Noah," Grandpa's voice was soft but steady, "it's okay to be angry. It's okay to ask questions. But remember, God isn't the source of our pain. He's our comforter, our rock in times of trouble."

I met his gaze, his steady eyes filled with understanding and faith that had stood the test of years. This was the man I'd always looked up to and tried to emulate. He was a man who had shown me what faith could be.

"But why, Grandpa? Why would God let this happen?" The question came out raw, vulnerable.

Grandpa Wilde sighed, sorrow and hope mixed in his gaze. "I don't have all the answers, Noah. I wish I could take away this pain. But I know God and our Savior are with us, even in the darkest valleys. Our Savior doesn't just stand apart from our suffering, He weeps with us, and He carries us when we're too weak to stand. All we need to do is talk to Him, to ask Him to be with us."

My throat tightened. With a trembling voice, I whispered, "I don't know if I can pray right now, Grandpa. I want to believe He's still there, even when it feels like He's so far away."

Grandpa nodded, a gentle smile gracing his weathered face. "That's okay, Noah. Sometimes our prayers are only the whispers from our broken hearts. Maybe we can't utter a single word, but our hearts call out to God, and our minds search for His comfort. God hears them all. Let's trust together, my boy, and lean on each other as we weather this storm."

In that garden, amidst the fragile blooms, I found solace in my grandfather's love. I needed the unshakable foundation of his faith now more than ever. Though I hadn't let my anger consume me completely, it hadn't loosened its grip either. All I could do was cling to Grandpa and his faith because I couldn't find my own. It felt like I'd lost it somewhere behind me, too far back to retrieve. I would have to build it anew. My foundation of faith had been cracked, shattered even. I wasn't sure the ground beneath was strong enough to hold me.

After Grandpa returned to the others, I stayed behind in the garden. I didn't pray, but I didn't cry either. Instead, I sat among the colorful flowers, allowing my thoughts to settle. I sifted through every memory on the surface, filing them away. I examined each emotion, choosing a few good ones to hold on to and letting the others pass through me.

It felt good to let my mind quiet, allowing peace to settle on the surface. Although I had read my scriptures a few times, I hadn't been to church or seminary in over two months. Dad wasn't here to lead our *Come, Follow Me* lessons, and I hadn't read them on my own. The constant fear of the next round of bad news had kept negativity at the surface, but now I was taking charge, tearing down those walls. I couldn't let them harden around my heart, keeping out the good forever.

Deep inside, a faint flicker of faith persisted, refusing to be snuffed out. I sensed it, a small flame gasping for oxygen to come alive. I beckoned it forward, blowing softly to fan it into life, and prayed. "Dear, gracious Eternal Father in Heaven..." As soon as the words left my lips, a warmth flooded me, bringing a peace and serenity I had never felt so strongly. "My Lord, my God, don't leave me. I feel Your embrace, and I need it now more than ever."

I felt my Savior's arms wrap around me, His love and tenderness unmistakable. I knew He was carrying me through this, another dark moment. Then, I felt something soft on my cheek, the light flutter of a *Tinker Bell Kiss*.

A smile formed as I received words spoken to my heart that would forever heal my soul. The assurance that God loved me, and my Savior loved me, was as certain as my own heartbeat.

I held perfectly still, listening to the words whispered by the still, small voice. *"Noah, My child, I am here with you in your pain and struggles. I know every tear you shed and understand the weight of your burdens. Only I understand the depth of your sorrow, for I have known your loss and suffering. I remember, My son. I weep with you, and I carry the ache of your heart within My own.*

"Even in your darkest moments, when your faith wavers, I remain steadfast. Though you may question why certain trials come, trust that I weave all things together for your good. Amidst your pain, I am creating a tapestry of beauty and redemption, even if you cannot see it now.

"Hold on to hope, for I am the giver of hope. Trust that I have a purpose for your life, and I will guide you through this season of darkness.

"When you struggle to pray, know that I hear the whispers of your heart. Your cries do not go unheard. Rest in My love and find comfort in My presence.

"You are never alone, dear Noah. I am always here, and I will carry you through this storm. Trust in Me, and together we will navigate the trials ahead."

The words faded from my mind, but the warmth surrounding me was pure joy, more profound than I could ever imagine. I sat on the bench, basking in it.

A butterfly landed on my knee. I studied its delicate wings, and then it hovered inches from my face before fluttering away.

I watched until it disappeared. With a deep breath, I then took my first hopeful step back to Mom's hospital room to wait.

As two nurses entered to prepare the room for Mom's return. I glanced at the clock; it was after two in the afternoon. Soon, it would be morning in the Philippines, and Jacob would wake up to see the message I'd sent after visiting the Japanese Garden. I wanted to have news for him, and for me. Rising from the uncomfortable chair, I stretched my legs, stiff from hours of waiting.

The nurse I liked passed by and mentioned that Mom was awake but groggy, drifting in and out of consciousness. Anesthesia was always tough on Mom. Her petite frame overreacted to even the smallest dose. She reassured me that Mom would be back soon and that the doctor would give a full update.

Before the doctor arrived, they wheeled Mom back into her room.

Tears welled up as I took in her pale face, framed by strands of hair clinging to her damp forehead. Tubes and wires snaked around her, connecting her to machines that beeped, monitoring her every vital sign.

"Hey, Mom! I've been waiting for you." I attempted to keep the tremble out of my voice.

Her eyes fluttered open, a faint smile touching her lips. "Noah, I knew you'd be here," she murmured. Her voice was weak, but full of love.

I pulled a chair close to her bed, holding her hand as her eyes drifted shut again. Every line of her face showed signs of exhaustion. The steady beeping of the machines provided a rhythm both soothing and unnerving. I prayed a quiet prayer of thanks to God for bringing her through the surgery and asking for strength in her recovery. This time, I felt certain God heard me, and that my Savior was holding my hand as I held hers. I can do all things with Christ.

When I messaged Jacob with our good news, he replied with a heart emoji. I double-tapped it, watching the heart explode into a spray of tiny hearts in return.

The days blurred together as I kept vigil by Mom's side. All three of my grandparents stayed close by, their presence a constant, supportive background. I focused all my attention on Mom. Her health consumed every waking thought.

One afternoon, while Mom slept, I went to the hallway to grab a snack from the vending machine. As I waited, I overheard Grandpa Evans talking to the nurse at the station.

"Could you have billing send up this week's report? I've secured approval from the responsible party's insurance, but I need to send a summary."

"Of course, Mr. Evans. I'll have it ready by the end of today," the nurse promised.

"Very good. You know where to find me."

"Yes, sir. We do."

The weight of Grandpa Evans's concern was clear in his steady, business-like tone. He managed the medical details, ensuring Mom received the best care possible. Until that moment, I hadn't even considered it a responsibility someone needed to shoulder. Shows how naïve I was.

As Grandpa walked away from the nurse's station, his steps were heavy, his shoulders bowed under a weight that seemed to age him more each day. Lines etched his face, every crease telling of countless sleepless nights and relentless worry. His once-bright eyes that used to hold fire now held a faraway look, shadowed by the strain of these past months. Under the dim hospital lights, his thinning silver hair glinted, and it struck me how much he seemed to have aged in such a short time.

With a trembling hand, he reached up and loosened his shirt collar, fidgeting as though trying to release the invisible chains of tension coiled around him. Pausing outside Mom's room, he released a long, weary sigh, his expression distant and burdened.

I abandoned the idea of a snack from the vending machine and jogged over, calling out, "Grandpa, wait up."

Grandpa turned, startled, before his expression smoothed into his familiar calm. He masked his fatigue well; if I hadn't glimpsed it just moments before, I would never have known the full depth of his struggles. I felt fortunate to have caught that unguarded moment, to see the silent weight he carried for us.

"Hey there, kiddo, what are you up to?" I was happy my family had dropped the *Buddy*, resorting to their latest nickname for me, *kiddo*. It seemed to change every few days, but I was alright with that.

"Not much, just stretching my legs," I replied with a small smile.

"Right there with you. I sure could use a good chiropractor right about now." Grandpa arched his back, giving a slight twist to ease his knots.

Without another word, I pulled him into a bear hug, a good, long, tight one.

"What's that for?" he asked, his voice muffled against my shoulder.

I held him a beat longer, savoring the familiar warmth and strength that radiated from him. His arms wrapped around me, just as they always had, strong and steady.

Through the lump in my throat, I whispered, "For everything, Grandpa. For taking care of Mom, for being here for me. For carrying all of this without a single complaint."

He looked at me, a flicker of surprise softening the lines of his furrowed brow, and his hold tightened. For a moment, I saw past the strong facade and into the vulnerability he seldom revealed.

"Noah, it's what family does. You, your mom, Jacob... you're my world. I'd do anything, give anything, to make sure you're safe and happy." Grandpa Evans's voice was thick with a tenderness that surprised me.

A surge of gratitude filled me, chasing away any lingering worries. I held him, letting his strength anchor me. All the anxieties that had gnawed at me since the accident seemed to dissipate, replaced by a profound sense of peace.

I pulled back, studying his face, the silver in his hair, the deep lines around his eyes and across his forehead. Each mark was a testament to his strength, resilience, and unwavering love for us. His love knew no bounds, and I cherished it beyond measure.

"I know, Grandpa, but not everyone would do what you're doing. You've taken on so much, and I see it, even when you try to hide it. You're the rock holding our family together, always finding a way. I don't know where we'd be without you." My voice was steady with conviction.

A flicker of pride lit his eyes, a faint smile tugging at the corners of his lips, his response quiet yet strong, a testament to his character.

"Noah, you've got it wrong. It's your strength, resilience, and love that inspire me every day. You've shown more maturity than I ever expected. I couldn't be prouder. We're in this together, and we'll get through whatever comes our way."

In that moment, I felt the depth of our bond, a bond forged at birth through love and strengthened through shared adversity. With my grandfather at my side, I felt invincible, ready to face any challenge.

Over the following week, I saw my grandfather in a new light. I watched him speaking with doctors, weighing treatment options, and grappling with the rising medical costs. The furrows deepening on his brow during calls with insurance companies revealed a side of him I'd only heard about, like the businessman he'd been before retiring. He took on the battle with insurance and the financial burdens, shielding my mother and me from the worries that came with it.

I also watched my grandmother as she comforted him, sitting beside him, listening, and offering quiet words of encouragement. She always seemed to know what my mother, or I needed, and she was there before we could even ask. She fussed over Grandpa Wilde, making sure he felt included, knowing how hard it must be for him. He had lost his wife and now his oldest son. One afternoon, I overheard her soft words to him: "I understand why you wanted Jared to help. No parent should have to bury their child. I couldn't." Her steadfast support was a calming strength that anchored our family.

The nurses bustled in and out, checking Mom's vitals, administering medications. Doctors visited frequently, offering encouragement and explaining her progress. Amid all the movement and tension, a glimmer of hope emerged each day as her color returned and her strength increased.

I still updated Jacob regularly, but now he'd left the Manila MTC and was in his first area, bound by the mission rules that allowed only quick thumbs-up or thumbs-down responses. Still, each week I counted down the days to p-day, when I'd get to talk to him.

When we connected, we always started with news about Mom, then listened as he shared his own experiences. His first area, San Mariano, sounded like an adventure of its own.

My favorite part of the call was Jacob's description of their transportation. He rode in colorful Jeepneys and clung to the back of speeding Trikes for dear life. The heat was already more intense than the height of our valley summers, and the humidity hadn't even reached its peak. During his first weekend in the area, they had a baptism, and he sent pictures of the family he'd helped bring into the church. He was thrilled about their eternal journey. He also told us all about his companion, who was rapidly becoming both mentor and friend. His stories about the warmth and kindness of the Filipino people made the experience sound unforgettable, and I was grateful he'd stayed on his mission and was having these life-changing adventures.

The next week, Jacob shared that he and his companion had two new IPs—interested persons. He told us about Tatay Mark and Nanay Maria, whom he affectionately called M&M. How cute is that?

As the days stretched into weeks, I marked time by Mom's progress between Jacob's calls. My focus was unwavering. Outside, spring was in full bloom, but it felt distant and inconsequential compared to the battle Mom was still fighting. Every small sign of improvement in her condition fueled my determination. Finally, the day we had all been waiting for arrived.

We gathered around Mom's hospital bed, awaiting the doctor's arrival. The room was thick with anticipation, mixed with a hint of apprehension. Hope shone on every face as we held our breaths.

The doctor entered, his white coat billowing behind him, radiating calm assurance and a serene understanding of our shared struggle. My hand tightened around Mom's, and I watched his face as he spoke.

"Morning, everyone," he began in his doctorly voice. "I have the best news possible. Leah has made remarkable progress over the past two months. Based on her recent test results, it's safe for her to leave the hospital and go home."

A collective sigh of relief swept through us, mixed with whispered prayers of gratitude. "Yes!" I cheered and did a little happy dance next to Mom's bed. My mother's homecoming felt like a victory, a small beacon of light in the darkness we'd been living through.

The doctor's tone shifted as he continued, "Leah will need extensive physical therapy. It may take over a year for her to regain a semblance of mobility and strength. She likely won't be as strong or able to endure as much as she once did."

His words sank in, and I felt a pang of sadness, but I steadied myself before anyone noticed. The journey ahead seemed daunting, yet I refused to let despair overshadow my gratitude. I was determined to only think of the future with positivity: *Look how far we've come already. We'll take each day as it comes. The hardest part is behind us. Together, we can endure anything.* I turned to Grandpa Wilde and smiled, grateful for his steadfast presence and strength in Dad's absence.

Grandpa Evans's eyes met mine, and an unspoken understanding passed between us. Despite the doctor's cautious prognosis, we both knew we'd face whatever challenges lay ahead together. A fierce resolve etched itself into Grandpa's face, a determination to care for my mother and ensure she received the best possible treatment and support. I admired him and hoped, one day, to be as steadfast as he was.

"Thank you, Doctor. We appreciate your care and guidance. We'll do everything we can to support Leah's recovery." Grandpa's voice was steady and filled with gratitude.

The doctor nodded, acknowledging Grandpa's commitment. "With your dedication, Leah will make tremendous strides. All she needs is the right resources and consistency. I am sure with your family's support, her progress will be significant."

After he left, we gathered close around Mom's bed. A strong sense of unity enveloped us, forming a circle of love and determination around her. The days ahead would be full of challenges, with trials we couldn't yet imagine, but in that moment, we celebrated the miracles we had already witnessed.

"Hear that, Mom? You're going home!"

I gripped her hand tight, a silent promise to support and uplift each other through the coming highs and lows. The unwavering strength of our family bond would carry us through.

CHAPTER FIFTEEN

MAY DAY HAD NEVER felt like an actual holiday before. But today, it forever marked the most joyous moment of my life, the day we finally left behind the hospital's sterile walls to take Mom home.

As we walked out to the cars, my mind drifted to the trip to Seattle with Grandpa Wilde a month and a half ago. I remembered his unwavering love and gentle care, not only for my physical needs but for my heart, too. Back then, we'd taken a longer route to avoid the accident site, but today, there'd be no detours. Today, we'd take the shortest route home, passing by where it all happened.

As we prepared to leave, Grandpa Wilde, ever watchful, took me aside. A cloud of emotions seemed to settle over me, and he noticed right away. He rested a reassuring hand on my shoulder, grounding me amid the sea of feelings churning inside. "Noah, before we go home, I want to talk to you."

I turned to face him and met his gaze. I saw a depth of understanding, sorrow, and love that both steadied and comforted me. I nodded, allowing him to continue.

"Today will be challenging for all of us, especially you and your mother. We're going to pass by the accident site. It may stir up difficult memories. And that's okay; however you feel, whatever comes up, it's normal. There's no right or wrong way to grieve."

I swallowed, a lump rising in my throat as unshed tears welled up. It seemed Grandpa Wilde could read my thoughts, understanding the storm of fear, longing, and sadness raging inside of me.

"You're not alone in this. We're all in it together, as a family. If you need support, I'm right here. We've all lost someone dear to us, and we're all still healing." Grandpa's words were like a steady, comforting embrace offering a sense of solace and grounding amid uncertainty. In that moment, I could feel the strength of our bond: the way grief and love wove us together.

"I'm scared, Grandpa. The pain still lingers, even though the nightmares stopped after Mom woke up. What if passing the accident site brings them back?"

He pulled me into a warm embrace, his arms wrapping around me with understanding. "It's natural to feel scared, but fear doesn't define you. You have the courage within you to face this."

I held onto him, drawing strength from his presence. When we pulled apart, he looked deep into my eyes, his voice steady with conviction. "Noah, I have faith in you. Your father would be proud of the young man you've become. This won't be easy, but you can face this road, both the one we'll drive, and the one life has given you. And I'm here, every step of the way."

Tears spilled down my cheeks, a mixture of grief and gratitude. I took a deep breath, a newfound determination anchoring me.

"Thank you for being here and for guiding me. I'll face it with courage. I'll honor Dad's memory."

He smiled, his face bright with pride. "That's my grandson. Now, do you want to ride with me or your mom?"

"I'd like to ride with Mom, if that's alright."

His smile grew wider, his eyes gentle. "It's more than alright. We can be together even if we're not in the same car. Hop in Grandpa Evans's car."

As I climbed in, the weight of the journey ahead pressed on me, though it no longer felt insurmountable. With my grandfather's unwavering support as my guide, I realized I had the strength to face the road before us.

When the engine roared to life, I took my place in the backseat beside Grandma Evans. My gaze drifted to the front, where Mom sat beside Grandpa, her frail frame a testament to the strength that had carried her back from the brink. Vicious scars traced her features, marks left by the accident that had forever altered our lives. At that moment, our return home felt like a hard-won victory.

I gripped the edge of my seat, my knuckles white and pale, as I studied her face. Once so vibrant, her expression now bore the traces of hardship and loss. Her heart had weathered more sorrow than ever before, and yet, here she was, determined to remain on Earth with me and Jacob against all odds. I was in awe of her resilience.

Grandpa's hands held the wheel steady as he guided us along familiar roads. Despite the hum of the engine, a heavy silence enveloped us, carrying the weight of all we'd endured. I glanced back to see Grandpa Wilde trailing behind in Mom's car, a solitary figure in the distance. His presence was a reminder of the empty void my father had left behind.

With every passing mile, we drew closer to the accident site. We had already passed Liberty and were on the downhill stretch into the Cascade Valley. The scenery blurred outside, tinged with memories of that day. Each turn, each landmark whispered of tragedy, reminding us of the courage this journey demanded.

I watched the familiar landscape flash by, each curve and twist of the road fixed in memory, while my mother's gaze remained forward, her eyes clouded. I wanted to reach out, to offer comfort, yet the words stayed lodged in my throat. Our bond, forged through shared pain, felt like a language beyond words.

Grandpa Evans didn't know the exact site of the accident. Neither did Mom nor I. We only remembered the general area, somewhere along this road's winding curves.

I jumped when I heard Mom's shaky voice cut through the silence. "I think ... I think that last curve was where it happened. Just at the end of the guardrail. The weather was so bad, visibility so low, but I'm almost certain."

Tension thickened in the car, a cloud of unspoken fears and grief enveloping us as we passed the place that had changed everything.

"We were so close to home." Her voice was just a whisper as she wiped tears from her cheeks and shifted in her seat. I reached forward and touched her shoulder. She entwined her fingers with mine. Her shoulders shook with silent sobs as she attempted to hold in her pain. I squeezed her fingers, attempting to give her every ounce of strength I could spare.

Grandpa tightened his grip on the steering wheel, his silence heavy with grief masked by stoic resolve. Grandma sat beside me, her hands clenched in her lap, a single tear tracing down her cheek as she looked away. Only the soft hum of the tires on the road broke the quiet in the car. Words felt inadequate, unable to capture the emotions filling the space between us. We traveled on, bound by both sorrow and resilience, each of us bearing the visible and hidden scars that served as reminders of the battles we had fought and triumphed over, wearing our actual badges of survival on our scar-laced bodies.

As we neared the threshold of our home, a mix of relief and trepidation settled over me. Grandpa Wilde pulled up beside us, his silent presence a comforting anchor. The garage door creaked open, and he guided Mom's car inside, stopping near Dad's workbench where his last unfinished project lay, untouched. When her gaze fell on the shelf, he would never hang for her, Mom gasped, her heartache flaring fresh and sharp.

I jumped out of my seat to open Mom's door, offering my hand to steady her as she rose. "Hold on, Noah. I have to get steady," she said, her grip tight on my hand, her face creased with pain.

It had been twelve long weeks since the horrific accident took Dad from us, leaving us broken and adrift. Now, my task was to help bring Mom back to a place that, though altered by loss, still held the echoes of his presence. Our home had always been our family's sanctuary; now, it had to be a place where we could heal, piece by piece.

Once she was steady, we took tentative steps toward the house. Walking through the door felt like crossing onto sacred ground, a place forever changed by absence. When we entered, the sunlight slanted through a crack in the curtains, casting a gentle glow over Dad's chair in the corner. I opened the curtains wider, letting in more light, hoping it would warm the space, perhaps even soothe the ache in her heart.

Mom's gaze scanned the room. Her face was a map of emotions, sorrow in her furrowed brow, nostalgia in the faint tug at her lips, and longing in her eyes. She reached a trembling hand toward Dad's recliner, and I held my breath, hoping she might find solace there.

"Take me to Dad's chair," she murmured. Her voice was so soft that it was almost lost in the quiet room.

Dad's chair was the one place I had avoided, the empty seat that felt like a memorial. Only once had someone sat there: Grandpa, on that first day we returned. But I guided her to it, then fetched Dad's blanket, draping it over her lap, hoping it would bring her a hint of the warmth he'd always provided.

She seemed to find peace, clutching the blanket as though it held some essence of him. I suggested we go to their bedroom, a place filled with memories where they had shared countless moments. But she recoiled, her eyes clouded with fear and sorrow, as if entering that room might make his absence feel even more permanent. She shook her head, her voice a whisper. "Noah, I can't, not yet. Please understand."

And I did. I felt the weight of her grief, the enormity of her loss. Gently, I told her it was alright, that she could take all the time she needed.

Now that Mom was home, my foremost goal was to help us reclaim some semblance of normalcy, whatever that new normal might be. The weeks spent at the hospital had been grueling and exhausting, and all I yearned for was to walk my father's land, embrace the familiar trees, and be in my childhood sanctuary. I loved it here and missed it when I was away.

I cracked open the back door and slipped outside into the endless rows of apple, cherry, and apricot trees, careful not to wake Mom. With each step deeper into the orchard, the sweet scent of blossoms and the gentle rustle of leaves enveloped me. As I wandered further down a cherry row, nearing the heart of the orchard, I gazed up at the sky. Brilliant blue peeked through the branches, providing a stunning backdrop to the delicate white blossoms. I took a deep breath and inhaled the sweet smells from the surrounding trees. I felt a renewed appreciation for the land my father had cherished so much. It was a part of me.

I reached out and touched a branch, drawn to a light pink blossom that beckoned for my caress. But instead of the velvety smoothness I expected to feel, the blossom crumbled in my fingers, falling like a whisper into my palm. Panic surged in my chest. Leaning closer, I examined the blooms, horror settling in. I recognized the signs: every other blossom was withered and dying. A late frost.

My chest tightened, my throat burned, and tears threatened to spill. A late frost meant devastation, a death sentence for the crop. I sank to my knees, as I had seen my father do countless times before.

Before me stretched the orchard, a vast sea of trees adorned with fragile blooms. Kneeling on the damp ground, I felt the mantle of responsibility settle on my shoulders. This orchard was not just a source of income, it was a legacy, a heritage passed down through generations of Wildes. Now it was mine to protect, a cherished inheritance for Jacob and me. Closing my eyes, I steadied my racing heart, the image of my father's weathered hands clasped in prayer filling my mind. He had instilled in me the importance of faith, of believing in something greater than ourselves.

With a trembling voice, I whispered my plea to the heavens, beseeching mercy for our crop. My hopes and fears poured into those whispered words, carried away by the gentle breeze. The uncertainty of the future loomed large, yet kneeling in the orchard, connecting with my Savior and my father's spirit, offered a flicker of solace. Trusting in something beyond my control helped ease the weight pressing on my chest.

When I opened my eyes, the memory of my father's lease settled my mind and calmed my troubled heart. All was well. God had me in His hands, and I could place my trust and faith in Him. I would continue to pray for the crops, but I resolved to add a heartfelt thank you for protecting our home and livelihood. In His infinite wisdom, three years prior, He had sent multiple frosts that nearly broke us, but now, perhaps, they had saved us.

Fueled by renewed determination, I continued my solitary walk, devoted to honoring the land that had always provided me with comfort and safety. I acknowledged and appreciated the sacrifices made by my father, grandfather, and all the generations of Wildes that had led me to this moment.

Grandma and Grandpa Evans remained a constant in our home those first day's home. Their presence was a constant reminder of love and support. Yet, it felt as if they were floating just above us, hovering with concern, their worry palpable. I could see Grandma's anxiety etched into her features as she heated the already prepared freezer meals, her mind preoccupied with thoughts of Mom's well-being. She would stir the pots with a distant look, always stealing furtive glances toward the living room, where Mom was resting. Grandpa hovered too, positioning himself nearby, ready to spring into action at the first sign of need, his watchful eyes never straying far from us. They organized what didn't need to be organized. They cleaned what was already clean and fussed over every detail, their intentions noble and their love explicit. But despite their unwavering vigilance, Mom and I were managing just fine. We were navigating this new reality together, finding our own rhythm amidst the chaos. Their hovering, while rooted in love, felt like a weight. I appreciated their presence and understood the depths of their concern, but I also longed for a bit of breathing room, a chance to reassure them that, while I cherished their love, I didn't need their constant watchful eyes to carry us through.

Grandpa Wilde was there too, but remained out of everyone's way, staying in Jacob's room, reading or watching movies on his phone.

Despite their reluctance to leave, I felt it was time for them to go home, even if just for a few days. I assured them I had everything under control, even if my heart wavered. Their time away had been extensive, and I could see Grandma longed for the comfort of her familiar routines. "Grandpa Wilde will still be here with me," I reminded them, trying to ease their concerns.

They consented, though I could see the hesitance in their eyes as they acknowledged the value of attending to a few matters of their own. Grandma's delight at hearing how Aunt Vee had kept all the houseplants alive provided some comfort. They trusted Aunt Vee, who had managed things admirably in their absence, but it wasn't the same; some things they just had to do on their own.

That night, when Grandpa Evans called to check in, he admitted it was nice to be home, but I could hear the underlying guilt in his voice. I assured him all was well in Wilde-ville, which seemed to set his mind at ease, but he promised to call twice a day, a promise that quickly turned into five calls, each one a reminder of their love and worry.

Our home became a retreat for healing. I assumed the caretaker role, tending to my mother's every need while motivating her to take gradual steps forward. Grandpa Wilde gave us space but remained close, helping whenever I asked, which was becoming rarer.

Together, Mom and I tackled the challenges of recovery. Physical therapy sessions became a bi-weekly event in Wenatchee, and a daily ritual at home as Mom, determined and resilient, pushed herself to regain her strength. I stood by her side, offering encouragement and a helping hand whenever needed. We celebrated every small victory, a longer walk down the hallway, a firmer grip on the therapy ball. But it wasn't just the physical hurdles we faced. Emotionally, the journey was just as demanding, if not more so. Frustration and tears filled moments of overwhelming heartache when doubts crept in. In those moments, I became Mom's rock, reminding her of the countless prayers sent heavenward on her behalf. Together, we clung to the promises of God, finding solace in His unfailing love.

With each passing day, it became clearer that we could handle things on our own. Grandpa Wilde's presence, though appreciated, was no longer needed. I felt the need to broach the subject of him going home as well. I sensed that despite his desire to be there for us, he needed to reclaim his own life as well.

"Grandpa." I approached him three weeks after Grandma and Grandpa Evans returned home, their calls settling into the promised two a day.

"What's up, Noah?" he replied, a hint of concern lingering in his voice.

"I hope you know how much I have appreciated you being here with me these past few months. I couldn't have done this without you."

"There's no place on Earth I would rather be than here with you."

His admission made me hesitate, almost abandoning what I had started. I felt the weight of his sacrifice. He had put his own life on hold for us, and it tugged at my heartstrings.

"Thanks, Grandpa, but I bet you are ready to go home. You've been here so long. I have things under control now. You can go home if you want to. I can call you, Grandpa Evans, or others from the ward if I need help."

Grandpa looked me over, his eyes searching mine. I was determined not to waver under his scrutiny.

"Are you sure, Noah? I don't mind staying a little longer. I've even considered the possibility of moving back here. I can if you need me to."

The thought of Grandpa Wilde moving here hadn't crossed my mind until now. This was, after all, his home first. Dad took over the orchard, and we moved our family into the orchard house near the time of my birth, but it was originally Grandpa and Grandma Wilde's home. Grandpa Wilde had been the orchardist for decades before Dad. He retired early to care for Grandma during her rounds of cancer treatments, wanting to spend as much time as possible with her.

"I never thought about that," I admitted. He didn't respond right away; he just watched me for a moment while I contemplated. "No, I think I want to try just us first, but I like knowing it's an option if I need it. My utmost desire is to restore normalcy to our lives, whatever our new normal will be. My top priority for Mom is establishing a new routine."

Grandpa gave me a curt and knowing nod, respect shimmering in his gaze.

"You're a good boy, Noah. You know that, don't you?"

"Thanks, Grandpa."

He stood and went to Jacob's room, where he had been staying. I heard him call the airline and book a flight to Utah. During my childhood, he and Grandma Wilde had lived in a charming house on the outskirts of Leavenworth. After Grandma's passing, he moved to live with Uncle Jared in Utah. He seemed to enjoy Utah, forging strong bonds with Aunt Megan's family, who lived close to them.

Later that week, I hugged my grandfather goodbye, his warmth enveloping me in a cocoon of safety as I helped him load his luggage into Brother Thurston's car. I had offered to drive him to the airport, but he didn't want me to leave Mom alone and didn't want to force her out of the house.

I had assumed that sending Grandpa Wilde home would be as simple as saying goodbye to Grandma and Grandpa Evans, who lived a short distance away in Wenatchee; however, as he departed, waving goodbye over his shoulder, it felt as if I was bidding farewell to my father all over again. The emotional weight of the moment lingered, and I grappled with the bittersweet realization that I was learning to stand on my own.

The child within me longed to sprint after the car, screaming for it to stop. I was even tempted to ask Grandpa to stay, but it was only a fleeting fancy. He wasn't Dad, and no matter how much I loved him, he didn't belong here in the house with us. Not forever.

Mom grew a little stronger each day, her spirit finding resilience in the face of darkness. The day after Grandpa Wilde left, a flicker of determination ignited within her, prompting her to confront the closed door of her bedroom.

I held her hand as we stood outside, a silent understanding passing between us. "Do you want to go in alone? I can wait here or go in with you," I offered.

"I'd like it if you came in with me. You've been such a tremendous support. I can't imagine facing it without you."

With a deep breath, she turned the doorknob and stepped inside, her heart heavy yet resolute. The room held memories etched into the very fabric of our lives, a testament to a love that would never fade between Mom and Dad. As she surveyed the space, she wept, but it was unlike any tears she had shed before. A deep sorrow was now engraved upon her soul. Mom had known loss, but not a loss as profound as this.

I watched from near the door, pride swelling in my chest as she entered. Once a sanctuary of love and warmth, the room was now an altar of memories. The bed, untouched since the day of the accident, bore witness to their shared dreams and whispered promises. My mother crept closer, her fingers grazing the edges of the bedspread. I saw her hands tremble, betraying the tumultuous storm raging within her.

Mom sat on the edge of the bed, her eyes fixed upon my father's pillow. The indents where his head had long rested still held his scent. It was a silent conversation between her and the lingering presence of my father. I stood there, a mere observer, as she leaned toward the pillow and let her fingers trace the familiar contours, as if trying to etch another part of him into her memory.

Moving with aching grace, she turned her attention to the closet. The clothes still held his scent, hanging like relics of a life well-lived. I watched as she reached out, her fingers brushing the soft fabric of his favorite shirts and jackets. She closed her eyes, perhaps imagining Dad standing there, asking for help to choose a shirt. I could almost hear their laughter echoing in the air, a bittersweet reminder of happier times. The memory tugged at my heart, and I could only imagine the toll it was taking on Mom.

Throughout it all, I remained silent, understanding that these moments belonged solely to my mother. Though I felt immense pain from losing my father, I couldn't comprehend the depth of Mom's grief. Yet, I was proud to witness her indomitable strength shining through with every breath and tear she shed.

The bathroom, a place of daily rituals and shared moments, held its own reminders of my father. His toothbrush lay across the sink, next to his razor, as if he had just gone to work for the day and would soon be home. My mother's hands hesitated above them, her gaze fixed upon her reflection in the mirror. I stood close behind her, my reflection mingled with hers, the bond between mother and son growing stronger. In that moment, our shared sorrow forever intertwined us, adding unbreakable strands to our mother-son relationship as we navigated this path of grief together.

Slowly, almost reverently, Mom picked up Dad's cologne. Its familiar scent mingled with the memories that saturated the room. She closed her eyes and inhaled. That was it. Mom's emotions boiled to the surface and erupted.

"Noah," she cried out.

Opening my arms, Mom collapsed into them, sobbing. I held her as tight as I could, wrapping her in the same embrace I had seen Dad give her countless times. A comforting cocoon that enveloped her, holding her so tight she could barely breathe. I pressed her ear against my chest so she could hear the steady rhythm of my heartbeat, its soothing cadence calming her storm of emotions.

"It's okay, Mom. I'm here. You did great."

"I miss him so much. How can I still be here? My heart seems torn in two."

Together, we took our first step on the healing journey of forging a new path forward. I knew the pain would never vanish, but as long as we faced it together, our faith and love would carry us through. As my mother's tears soaked my shirt, I realized our strength lay in our unity. Together, we would find the courage to overcome even our darkest moments.

Though Mom had conquered her sadness enough to enter her room, she couldn't bring herself to sleep there. She even opted to share my bathroom at the other end of the house. As the days passed, her visits to her bedroom became more frequent. Each time, I noticed a subtle change in her demeanor, a gradual shift from raw pain to tentative acceptance. She would sit on the edge of the bed for long stretches, tracing her fingers over my father's pillow. Now, her touch conveyed a hint of tenderness rather than sorrow. Twice, I even caught her lying down with her head resting where Dad's had been.

When he returned home, I suspected Grandpa Wilde must have called Sister Thurston. Soon, we were greeted by a steady stream of Relief Society sisters dropping off meals and offering to help "tidy up."

One Thursday evening, early in June, a thunderous knock on the door pulled me from my thoughts.

"I thought you'd make me stand out here all night," Grandma Bean declared when I opened the door. Without waiting for an invitation, she rushed in, juggling a handful of goodies while enveloping me in a warm hug. The plate of cookies and banana bread bounced against my back.

"Cookies and banana bread made just the way you like them." She handed the treats over as I closed the door with my foot.

I carried them into the kitchen, and she waltzed right into the front room, plopping down on the sofa nearest Mom.

How I loved this woman. I had missed her so much. There was no hesitancy in her visit. While other church ladies had acted nervous, tiptoeing around my grief, Grandma Bean sat down and chatted like a loyal family member, as if she had been stopping by every night since the accident.

"The Thurston boy has been mowing my lawn in your absence. He's good, but he sure doesn't have you or Jacob's precision. I like the lines you leave. They make me feel like I live on a fancy golf course."

"Steven's mowing for you? Oh, good! I hoped someone was helping. Sorry I haven't been over. It's been busy here."

"Pish-posh! Come sit with us. I didn't come here for your apologies. I miss you. Tell me what's been happening and let's see what this old bird can do to help."

I flopped beside her on the couch, propping my right foot on my left knee like I used to do. I was proud I had worked hard to regain my flexibility. My left hip still protested, but I was healing, slowly but surely.

"I think we've got it handled. Just seeing your smiling face is all we need."

Mom nodded in agreement.

"Well, I doubt that. A cranky old lady like me can't do much, and I'm certainly not much to look at, but I do what I can."

I laughed at her cranky old lady comment.

Grandma Bean didn't miss a beat. "I would have come over before, but I knew your Grandpa Wilde was here. This was his home for a long time, and I didn't want to intrude while he managed everything. Now, let's talk about you getting out of here and having some fun. What if I stay with your mom and you head into town to take a break? Go see friends or something."

"I don't know, I..."

"No excuses. I'll even give you gas money since I know you aren't working in town right now." Grandma Bean slipped a folded hundred-dollar bill from her jeans pocket and pressed it into my hand.

I glanced up at Mom, who was trying not to laugh at my predicament. I'd do anything to hear her laughter again. It was the closest she had come to laughing since the accident.

"All right," I said, accepting the money and settling back into my seat.

"Go. Now." She flicked her finger toward the door, and Mom outright laughed.

I happily obliged. After gathering my keys and wallet, I paused at my bedroom door, listening for a moment.

"So, girl, looks like it's just you and me. What do you want to do? Catch a movie? Or we could pull out George's old convertible and drag the Avenue like we used to in the 1950s? I know, let's take George's motorcycle for a spin. I have a sidecar, so we don't have to worry about my balance. We could wrap you up good and tight, fill it with cushions, and cruise Leavenworth." I didn't hear Mom respond. "Oh, I've got it! I know just what we can do. Let's grab Adam's Harley, and I can teach you how to ride it."

"You do beat all. How about we stay in and talk?"

"Well, it's not nearly so fun, but I suppose it's a good idea for two old broads like us. Too bad the old car and motorcycle could both use a good run. I'll have to take them out for a spin one of these first days or have Noah do it for me."

Would wonder never cease? "Convertibles? Motorcycles? Is that what you keep in the shop behind your house? The one no one ever goes in?" I asked as I walked past.

"You betcha! Can't let my kids get their hands on them. Not until I'm dead."

"If you're serious and they need a good run, this *kid* would love to do it for you." I pointed both thumbs at my chest and gave her my cheesiest grin.

While most avoided discussing topics like death and deceased spouses, Grandma Bean brought them up without hesitation. Her natural ease and playfulness enveloped Mom in comfort. I loved her already, but my admiration deepened as I slipped out the door, their laughter echoing after me.

CHAPTER SIXTEEN

I SAT IN MY parked pickup, halfway to the highway, with nowhere in particular to go. Everyone was already out of school for the day, and in less than a week, school would be over for the summer, but I wasn't used to coming into town just to hang out. The only person I usually hung out with was Jacob; I wasn't really a *hang out* kind of guy. I glanced at Shelby's contact information on my phone, my finger hovering over the text button. I chickened out. It wasn't like I could ask her out. She wasn't even sixteen yet. If I called and invited her to do something, I'd end up with an entire gang of Thurston's tagging along.

Instead, I shifted the pickup into drive and headed to Riverbend Farmstand. The bell jingled as I entered, and Ruth looked up from the register. Her hand flew to her heart, and she abandoned her customer to rush over to me. "Oh my, Good Lord in Heaven! Noah! Come here. Oh, my dear boy, it's so good to see you!" She pulled me into a long, tight hug, while the customer looked on, surprised. I'd never hugged Ruth before, but somehow it felt comforting. She was another mother figure who always seemed to know what I needed when I needed it.

"I'll finish up here, and then we can talk," she said, rushing back to the register. Her fingers flew over the keys at an impressive speed.

Once she was done, she called to a stock girl I hadn't noticed restocking candy nearby. "Shelby, will you take care of the register while I talk to Noah?"

Shelby Thurston looked out from around the end cap and smiled. "Sure thing, Ruth! Hey, Noah, it's good to see you!"

"Hey, Shelby! Do you work here now?" I asked, surprised to see her around the corner of the next aisle. She looked different somehow, more at ease than I remembered. Her hair was pulled back in a loose ponytail, and her outfit, a pair of pink cropped pants paired with a delicate white lace top under an apron, was casual yet charming. It suited her perfectly. A small, shy smile tugged at the corners of her lips as she turned to face me, and I realized just how much time had passed since we last saw each other.

"Yep, I started in March while you were in Seattle," she replied.

I nodded, realizing they had hired her to replace me after the accident. A wave of mixed emotions washed over me: acceptance mingled with a tinge of sadness. It felt strange to see someone else in my old spot, as if a part of my life had moved on without me. Still, I managed a small, understanding smile, trying to push back the lingering sense of loss. Mom still needed me.

Ruth jumped in. "You still have a job here whenever you're ready to return, but I needed a little help right away."

"Thanks, I understand," I replied. I loved working at the farmstand, but I still wasn't sure when I'd be able to come back.

In the office, I spent an hour chatting with Ruth, but none of it was about her or the farmstand. She was a true friend, offering me tons of encouragement. Ruth kept tabs on me through Shelby, who received regular updates from her dad, who was in contact with both of my grandpas.

"Noah, hun, I'm so sad to hear about your dad. He was a good man. The whole town's been praying for you. Maybe even the whole county." Ruth turned her chair around and grabbed a pink basket full of envelopes. "Here, this is for you. We'll gather the rest up front at the register before you leave."

"What is it?" I asked.

"Cards, notes, messages, words of encouragement from everyone in the community. Shelby thought of it just after she started working here. I've had it here waiting for you. I planned to bring them out to you, but then I heard you went to see your mom in Seattle. I decided to keep them here until you returned. Everyone, and I mean everyone, has stopped by to ask about you."

"Wow, that's really nice of everyone. That explains the pink. I never saw you as a pink kind of lady, Ruth," I said lightheartedly. Honestly, I was speechless.

I found myself at a loss for words, and surprisingly, so did Ruth. After a moment of awkward silence, I stood up to leave. "Thank you, for the offer to come back to work. I'm not sure when I'll be able to. Mom still needs me at home."

"I know she does. There's no rush. I just want you to know that if you want to come back, your job is here whenever you're ready."

I hugged her again before picking up the basket to leave.

"Bye, Noah," Shelby said, now restocking some cute dish towels near the door.

"Uh, bye," I replied, then paused, and watched her.

"Do you need something?" she asked, her brow slightly furrowed.

"No, I'm just loitering. Grandma Bean is mom-sitting, so I'm free for a little while." I tried to be funny, but it fell flat.

"Oh good! She loves your mom so much. I hope they have fun together," Shelby cooed.

"She was threatening to take Mom out on George's old motorcycle."

Shelby giggled. "I'd pay money to see that."

"Me too," I admitted, grinning. She smiled back, but I didn't know what else to say.

Shelby paused her task. Her face lit up. "I had fun when we watched a movie together. I know you have a lot on your plate taking care of your mom, but if you ever want to do that again, I'm game."

"That sounds like fun. Could you come to my house again? That way, I can keep an eye on Mom while we watch something," I said with a hopeful smile.

"Yes! I'd love to see your mom. I haven't seen her since she came home. I've been praying for her, and for you, every day. We all have."

"Thank you. We can really feel everyone's prayers. What night works for you to watch a movie? How about tomorrow?"

"I work until six, but I can come over afterward."

"That works. Or if Saturday is better for you, we could plan it for then instead."

"I have nothing planned on Saturday. If we do it then, we could watch a couple of movies or just hang out and chat longer," Shelby suggested. "The school year's almost over, but I still have an earlier curfew on weeknights."

"Let's do Saturday, then."

"Sounds like fun!"

"Hey Shelby, don't think I'm being silly for asking, but I know you're not sixteen yet, and I'm not sure about your family's rules. Should I ask Steven to come too?"

She giggled. "Your mom is going to be there, right?"

I nodded. "Yeah, she will be. I almost forgot about that," I added, resisting the urge to smack my forehead at my forgetfulness.

Shelby smiled. "I'll double-check with Mom, but it should be fine. I'll text you tonight to let you know." She turned back to straighten the last few hand towels before moving on to sort the aprons.

I didn't linger in town much longer. After grabbing a burger at the gas station by the highway, I headed home.

Upon my return, I found Mom and Grandma Bean engrossed in a heated debate over which version of *Pride and Prejudice* was superior. Mom stood her ground in the Colin Firth camp, while Grandma Bean argued that Matthew Macfadyen's portrayal was more emotionally expressive and romantic. "His transformation was more pronounced and satisfying," she insisted as I walked through the door. Mom shook her head in disagreement. Ever the purist. "I don't agree. I prefer the traditional, brooding gentleman of the Regency era."

I flopped onto the couch next to Grandma Bean, cutting into their spirited discussion. "Shelby's coming over Saturday to watch a movie and hang out," I announced, eager to shift the focus.

Mom's lips turned up with a knowing smile. It stretched across her face like a Cheshire cat. "That sounds like fun," she said, her tone a bit too sweet.

"So, what?" Grandma Bean chimed in, a smirk creeping onto her face. "Do I need to scoop up your mom and get her out of Dodge so you can have the place to yourself?"

"No, Mom needs to be here. It isn't a date. We're just hanging out and watching a movie as friends," I clarified

Grandma Bean's eyebrows shot up. "That girl likes you. And I think you like her too!" She poked me twice in the chest with her bony finger.

I opened my mouth to protest, but she cut me off with another poke. "Hush up. I know you Wilde boys better than you think, and I can tell when you like a girl. Why, that brother of yours has been mooning over Heather Nielsen for half his life."

I sighed, knowing there was no arguing with Grandma Bean when she was on a roll. "You know about that? He hasn't told anyone," I said, surprised.

Grandma Bean just shrugged, her expression playful. "Like I said, I know you boys. Methinks this is a date."

"It can't be a date. Shelby isn't sixteen yet," I replied, a little flustered.

She gave me a wink and tapped the tip of her nose with her pointer finger. "I get it. You want it to be a date, but it's really not because she's not old enough to date yet."

Mom chuckled from her spot in the corner, clearly enjoying the banter. "Oh, how nice. What time is she coming over?"

"I'm not sure yet. She's going to text me."

As we chatted, the sunlight outside faded, casting a warm, golden glow across the living room. Grandma Bean shifted in her seat, trying to get comfortable. "I'll tell you what, Noah. If you want to impress that girl, you might consider making her some homemade cookies. Nothing says *I like you* like cookies made with love."

"Chocolate chip cookies are Shelby's specialty. She'll probably bring some. I'll have popcorn and sodas ready."

Grandma Bean nodded enthusiastically. "Good thinking! You're right, that girl can bake! I've had her cookies, and they are delicious. She makes me a double chocolate, chocolate chip, that is to die for. You'll have to ask her about those one day."

After a few more minutes of teasing and laughter, Grandma Bean glanced at the clock. "Well, I'd better get going. My flowers are poking through the ground, and I need to get them watered before it gets too dark." With a warm smile, she gathered her things and stood up, giving Mom a quick hug before making her way to the door. "Take care, you two. And Noah, good luck with your not-a-date movie night," she added, her wink full of encouragement.

Popcorn always took longer to pop when I was waiting for someone special. I watched the microwave like it was a toaster, hoping I was getting everything right. Three bags should be enough for Shelby, Mom, and me, right? Just thinking about it made sweat gather on my palms. I wiped them on my jeans and yanked open the fridge, rearranging the sodas once more. Root Beer, Sprite, Fresca, Ginger Ale, each lined up in neat rows, organized just in case Shelby liked choices.

Shelby had been over before, but today felt different. It signified the first time we had planned something together, even if it was just a family movie night. No big deal, I told myself, trying to calm my excitement. We weren't even going on a proper date. She wasn't sixteen yet, and rules were rules, and we followed them. Still, I couldn't shake the excitement buzzing under my skin.

The microwave beeped, and I grabbed the popcorn, pouring it into a giant bowl. The smell of butter filled the entire house. Good. It felt like home should, warm and comforting, just like how Dad used to make it for us during our real family movie nights when the whole family was together. I paused for a moment, remembering him. It was the little things, like how he added extra salt to the popcorn, even though Mom insisted it was too much.

I glanced at the clock and realized I didn't have much time left before Shelby arrived. I checked the living room to make sure everything was in order. Couch pillows were fluffed, and the remote was in its rightful place. Mom had already settled in Dad's chair, wrapped in his worn blanket. Even though she never voiced it, it was now her favorite.

She gave me a small smile as I walked by, her eyes were a little softer than usual, as if she knew that tonight was important to me. "You ready, Noah?" she asked.

"As ready as I'll ever be," I replied. I fidgeted with the corner of the popcorn bowl while we waited. I glanced down the hall at the bathroom door, remembering I still hadn't double-checked it. "I'll be right back."

I rushed to the bathroom for a quick clean-up. No toothpaste gunk in the sink. Towels hung neat and tidy. Done. Shelby probably wouldn't even use it, but I couldn't take any chances.

Just as I walked back into the kitchen, the doorbell rang. My heart did a little flip, and I told myself to calm down. It was just Shelby, the same Shelby I'd known most of my life.

When I opened the door, there she was, standing on the porch with a plate of cookies in her hands. Her smile lit up the whole front yard, and I could smell the chocolate chip goodness before she even stepped inside.

"Hi, Noah," she said, her voice sweet like honey. "I brought cookies. I made them myself."

I grinned, my heart racing. "You know me too well. These are my favorite." I took the plate from her and led her inside.

"Thanks for having me over," she said. Her glance drifted to Mom sitting in the living room. She gave a little wave. "Hi, Sister Wilde."

Mom waved back from her chair, clutching the blanket a little tighter. "Hi, Shelby. It's nice to see you again."

"You too. I'm really glad you're home and getting better," Shelby replied with a polite smile.

"Thanks, sweetheart. It's a long road to recovery, but I'm getting there."

I grabbed the popcorn bowl and Shelby's cookies, carrying them to the living room. I set them on the coffee table and gestured toward the couch. "We can sit here. Moms already got her spot."

Shelby laughed, a laugh that made me feel like I'd just delivered the best joke in the world. "I figured that would be her seat."

As we settled down, I noticed how close we were. Our legs almost touched. My heart kicked into overdrive, and I tried to focus on something, anything else. But then Shelby leaned in for a handful of popcorn and her hair brushed against my arm. It smelled incredible, like peaches and cream. I lost all train of thought.

"So," she said, looking up at me with those big brown eyes, "what movie are we watching?"

Mom chimed in from her chair, "Something family-friendly, right?"

I nodded. "Of course." I scrolled through the options on Vudu. "What about *Singing in the Rain*?"

Shelby's face lit up with a smile. "I love that one. It's wholesome and classic. I just love musicals."

"Perfect," Mom said, giving a small nod of approval.

As the movie started, I relaxed a little. Shelby reached for more popcorn. Her fingers brushed mine in the bowl. My stomach did a weird flip, and I couldn't help but glance at her. She was smiling again, like she knew exactly what she was doing. Suddenly, it didn't feel like just a family movie night anymore.

"This popcorn's delicious. Did you make it?" she asked as she popped another piece into her mouth.

"Yep. Special for tonight. I slaved over the microwave four minutes at a time for a whole twelve minutes," I replied, trying to sound casual, though my voice cracked.

She giggled. "Well, you did good, Noah Wilde."

For the next hour, we watched the movie, but I could barely pay attention. Shelby leaned into me just enough to make my heart race, and I kept catching her looking at me from the corner of my eye. Twice, our hands brushed in the popcorn bowl, sending zings up and down my arm from fingertip to elbow and back again.

When the movie ended, it felt like time had sped up without me realizing it. I glanced at the clock and saw that it was still early.

"Mom, are you going to be alright in here for a little bit? I want to stretch my legs outside."

"Of course," she smiled.

"Shelby, want to come outside with me?"

"Yes!" she exclaimed, jumping up from the couch with a burst of energy.

We headed outside and around to the back of the house, where we had a trampoline, and an old swing set that Jacob and I hadn't used in years. As we neared the trampoline, I took two running steps and leaped into the center, landing on my side and bouncing until the trampoline stilled. Shelby laughed again, standing at the side, still hesitant to climb on.

"Want to join me?" I asked, holding out my hand to pull her up.

"Sure."

Shelby took my hand and climbed up. She bounced a few times before admitting, "You know, I've only been on a trampoline once."

"No way, you can't be serious?"

"It's true. My mom broke her arm on one when she was eleven and hardly lets me and my brothers near them."

My expression sobered, a hint of concern creeping in. "We can do something else if you'd rather. I didn't know it would be a problem."

"No problem! It's not that I'm not allowed, it's just that my mom avoids them. I've never had the chance to play on one."

"Okay, take a minute to get your jumping legs. I'll sit over here so my movements don't mess you up too bad."

I settled on the edge of the trampoline, resting against the soft blue padding, my heart raced with anticipation. I watched as Shelby bounced a little, her movements tentative at first. Her hair danced around her face in soft waves, catching rays of the sun, giving her an almost ethereal glow. When she let out a laugh, it felt like a burst of joy that filled the yard and resonated deep within me.

"Okay, I think I got it," she said. I noticed her confidence was growing as she bounced higher. Her laughter spilled from her lips.

I smiled, my heart warming at the sight of her joy. "You're a natural."

Shelby's grin widened, her expression sparkling with mischief as she attempted an even higher bounce. For a split second, my heart dropped. It looked like she might fall. I leaned forward, ready to catch her, but she steadied herself, laughter bubbling up again. The sound was infectious, and I couldn't help but join in.

She was having so much fun, and I felt a rush of happiness just being here with her, away from everything else, just the two of us, the trampoline, and the gentle whispers of the afternoon breeze.

After a few more exhilarating jumps, she finally rested, plopping down cross-legged in the middle of the trampoline, breathless. "Okay, I'm done. That's a workout!"

I smiled and slid onto the trampoline, lying flat and gazing at the vast expanse of sky above. "Jacob and I used to sleep out here. I love falling asleep under the summer stars, listening to the night come alive."

Shelby stretched out next to me, and for a moment, we were both quiet, enveloped by the soothing sounds of nature. Birds chirped their lullabies, and a gentle wind rustled through the trees, carrying the sweet scent of ripening fruit.

"This was fun," Shelby said, her voice blending into the breeze.

"Yeah," I agreed, glancing over at her. "I'm really glad you came over."

She rolled onto her side and propped her elbow up, resting her head on her palm. She looked at me; her face was close enough that I could see the faint freckles dusting her nose and cheeks. Each one illuminated by the bright sun overhead. My heart raced, and for a fleeting moment, I contemplated leaning in closer. But I held back. This wasn't a date, and I wasn't about to mess up our friendship for a stolen kiss. I have never kissed anyone before, and I didn't want to mess it up, not with Shelby.

"Do you think your mom's going to be okay?" she asked after a beat. Her voice dropped to a softer tone, tinged with concern.

"Yeah," I replied, though uncertainty tinged my words. "She's doing a lot better than she was a few weeks ago. I think... it's good for her to be here at home." I paused, weighing my next words. "But can I tell you something?"

"Anything."

"I'm a little worried," I admitted, my voice shaky. "Mom won't sleep in her bedroom. Every night, she sits in Dad's chair in the living room to sleep. She says it's because her back and hips hurt, or that it's easier to breathe sitting up, but I think it's because she's afraid to sleep in the bedroom she shared with Dad." My throat tightened as I spoke, the weight of my words heavy in the surrounding air. "Shelby, her heart is broken."

"Noah, I'm so sorry. I can't imagine how hard that must be to witness," she replied with compassion.

I swallowed hard, fighting against the lump in my throat. "Yeah, it's tough. I feel like I need to be strong for her, but sometimes I just don't know how."

Shelby shifted closer, and her hand brushed against mine. The warmth of her touch grounded me. "You're stronger than you think. And you don't have to do it all on your own, Noah. It's okay to lean on people."

I looked into her eyes, brimming with understanding. "Sometimes, I just wish I could fix it, you know? Make everything go back to the way it was before."

"I get that." She paused, the silence between us filled with the distant chirping of crickets. "But you don't have to fix everything. No matter how much you want it, or I want it for you, you can't go back. Just being there for her, that's enough. Your mom knows you love her. And if you ever need to talk, I'm here."

The warmth of her words enveloped me like a soft blanket, and I felt the tightness in my chest shift into something lighter. Maybe, just maybe, I wasn't alone in all this.

"Thanks, Shelby," I said quietly, my voice barely above a whisper.

She smiled gently, her hand still resting near mine. For a moment, everything else, every worry, every fear, faded away, and it was just us, lying beneath the summer sky, sharing a silence that spoke louder than any words ever could.

I longed to tell her how much her presence meant to me, how I enjoyed having her here, but the words caught in my throat. At that moment, I realized she was right. I didn't have to carry this burden alone. Instead, I just smiled and let my fingers brush against hers. The smallest of touches.

"You ready to go back in?" I asked, acting like I hadn't just set my skin on fire with that simple contact.

"Yeah," she replied, but she lingered for a moment, giving my hand a soft squeeze before sitting up. "But don't forget, I'm here for you. Always."

I nodded, aware of a shift inside me: a tiny crack in the armor I had built around my heart.

We watched a second movie while eating one of Shelby's mom's freezer meals for dinner. I let her pick her favorite one, and that's the one we ate. We didn't pay as close attention to the second movie, all three of us opting to talk about the little things we had missed in our absence from church. The Young Women had new leaders. The primary sang for both Mother's and Father's Day.

And Steven gave his first talk in Sacrament Meeting. Shelby was very proud of her brother.

Ten minutes after the second movie ended, headlights flashed in the driveway, shattering the bubble we'd been in. Shelby peeked out the upper window of our front door and saw her mom's minivan. "It's my mom," she said, her voice laced with disappointment.

"Yeah, I guess it's time to go."

"Thanks for tonight, Noah. I had tons of fun."

"Me too," I said, and I meant it.

"Bye, Sister Wilde, thanks for letting me come over and crash your family's movie day."

"Anytime, Shelby."

She smiled once more before slipping out the door and running to the car. I stood there, watching her leave. Sister Thurston waved at me. I waved back as their minivan disappeared down the drive.

As they vanished from sight, I shoved my hands into my pockets, taking a deep breath to calm the racing in my chest. Shelby Thurston was next to perfect, in my opinion.

With a small smile tugging at my lips, I turned and headed back inside.

"You okay, Noah?" Mom asked, her eyes studied me with a knowing look.

"Yeah, I'm good," I replied, sinking onto the couch, with a newfound lightness I hadn't felt in weeks.

And for the first time in a long time, I was.

CHAPTER SEVENTEEN

I snuck across the house to Mom's bedroom in the middle of July and cracked the door. I peered inside to check on her, making sure I could escape if she needed privacy. I didn't see her, so I leaned my head inside. The morning rays of the golden sun flickered through the gap in her curtains, which she hadn't drawn since before the accident.

I found Mom standing in front of her bathroom mirror. There was a subtle change in her reflection. She appeared more serene, her eyes filled with a quiet strength that spoke of resilience. Dad's toothbrush and razor remained on the counter, but their presence no longer made her hesitate when reaching for her own. She touched them and acknowledged his memory in her ongoing life.

Satisfied that she was well, I retreated.

That afternoon, after mowing the lawn, I searched for Mom again but couldn't find her. I called her name when I entered the house, but there was no answer. Finally, I found her again in the bathroom, gazing at her reflection in the mirror. She hadn't heard me approach and worry washed over me. *Was she not as content as*

I had first hoped? I leaned against her bedroom doorframe, a few feet away, watching as she held Dad's cologne once more.

This time, there was a different energy about her. She opened the bottle, filling the room with its familiar scent. After spraying a bit, she lifted her wrist to her nose. A bittersweet smile appeared on her face, and I saw a glimmer of newfound strength. I realized she was embracing not only the memory of my father, but also her own journey of healing and growth.

I snuck out of the room before she could see me.

Ten minutes later, she emerged, wearing one of Dad's favorite shirts. Holding the collar to her nose, she breathed in its scent.

"Looks good on you!" I smiled at her emotional progress, though my heart broke a little more.

"Yes, I think so too." She looked at me, her demeanor brimming with a mix of nostalgia and newfound hope. "Do you want one too?"

I nodded, and she beckoned me to follow her to her closet.

"Pick one," she said, her voice warm with encouragement.

As I ran my hands over Dad's shirts, memories of the last time I'd seen him wearing each came crashing through my mind in waves. I could almost hear his laughter and see the way he would always roll the sleeves to get comfortable. "This one." I pulled a rich brown button-up from the clothing bar, the fabric soft and warm against my fingers. I remembered the last time Dad wore this one. He had stopped by Riverbend Farmstand while I was at work to pass along a message from Mom. I was with a customer when he arrived, so he waited. When I finally finished and got the chance to talk to him, he complimented me on a job well done. The pride I felt from impressing Dad made me feel like I was floating off the ground.

"That's a good choice," Mom said, taking it from me and removing it from the hanger. She paused, her eyes misting over as she examined the shirt, perhaps recalling how it used to fit Dad just right. "You look so much like Dad," she added, her voice thick with emotion. Before her feelings could overwhelm her, she shook off the heartache and held the shirt against my chest, a protective gesture. "This will make you look so handsome."

"Thanks, Mom," I said. I tried to match her smile, but felt a bittersweet pang in my chest. Then, reaching for a vibrant blue shirt, I continued, "Save this one for Jacob. It's his favorite. He even borrowed it once for a date." The memory brought a faint smile to my face, a time when things felt normal, when we could still share stories and laughter as brothers.

"I remember that. He looked so proud wearing Dad's shirt that night." Mom said. A flicker of nostalgia lit up her visage as she tucked the blue shirt into the back of the closet to keep it safe for Jacob until he returned.

As time went by, Mom and our home transformed. The visible pain that had haunted her since returning gradually faded like the remnants of a storm. Though her scarring was severe, both physical and emotional, most of her wounds had healed by mid-summer, both inside and out. I noticed her laughter return in spurts; the sound spilling out like sunlight through a cloud. She regained mobility and confidence, and it was time to move beyond her light physical therapy sessions.

It was time for her to embrace the woman she had always been and could be again. I saw her begin to change. She directed me to help her hang some pictures. She measured, and I set nails to hang new and old framed photos, each a reminder of happier times. We began cooking together again, her laughter mingling with the scents of dinner, filling the house with warmth and life, especially when I did something wrong.

In those small moments, it felt like she was becoming more than just Mom. She was regaining her true self. I could see some of her spunk returning.

With every grueling exercise and repetition, Mom pushed herself to regain her strength and independence. Sweat mingled with tears as it trickled down her brow at the hardest physical therapy session to date. A testament to her perseverance in the face of pain. Day by day, her muscles grew stronger, and her determination fiercer. Mom's spirits soared like a bird breaking free from a cage. She discovered a newfound resilience and courage that emerged from the shadows of her doubt and despair, a courage that had long been dormant, a flicker of strength she hadn't known she had or needed.

During her therapy sessions, the physical therapist's gentle guidance and unwavering belief in her progress became the solid foundation upon which Mom rebuilt her shattered body. But it wasn't just her body that was healing, her spirit was revitalizing and strengthening in ways I could relate to from my own growth in that garden. The parallel of our healing became a silent bond between us, one that stitched together the frayed edges of our lives.

As her old self emerged, so too did a sense of vitality that had been absent for far too long. One Saturday morning, as I sat on the couch enjoying a bowl of cereal—now a staple in our kitchen—and binge-watched the latest *Studio C* comedy sketches, Mom sauntered into the living room with a newfound energy that radiated from her.

"We need to rearrange the furniture," she declared, her bearing determined.

Her plan infused the living room with her fresh touch while still honoring the memories of my father. The once somber recliner, which had stood as a monument to sorrow, now served as a place of reflection and strength. It was adorned with a vibrant cushion bearing the message "Love Eternal... Eternal Love," mirroring the engravings inside their wedding bands, a beautiful reminder of their bond that had transcended even the toughest of times.

That day, Mom also declared that we had been away from church for too long. "Whether I can endure sitting on those hard benches or not, tomorrow we're going back." The statement hung in the air like a promise, a commitment to reclaiming not only her strength but also the sense of community and faith that had once been a cornerstone of our lives.

As we walked into the church building in Leavenworth, a mix of nerves and anticipation washed over me. It had been five long months since we last attended, and that absence felt heavy on my shoulders. Today was a significant step for both Mom and me. Returning to our Sunday routine and reconnecting with our ward family felt monumental, like stepping back into the warmth of a long-lost embrace.

I held the door for Mom, who moved slower than the last time we entered through the doors. Her strength returned a little more each day, but the process was gradual, one we both wished we could rush, yet knew we must respect the pace of healing.

A flood of familiar faces greeted us the moment we walked through the chapel doors. People who had prayed for us, supported us, and brought us meals during our time of need surrounded us. I could see their genuine joy on their faces as they embraced Mom, eager to welcome her back into the fold.

But as the hugs piled on, I couldn't help but notice the pain etched on Mom's face. Her arms, shoulders, and neck were still sensitive, a lingering effect of her accident and grueling physical therapy sessions. Each well-intentioned embrace caused her discomfort, evidenced by the slight winces that betrayed her struggle.

With a sense of protectiveness, I stepped forward, reminding those who swarmed her with a firm yet polite caution. "Please, be careful. Mom's not fully recovered yet. I know you mean well, but your hugs are hurting her. She needs a little more time before you touch her."

Unnerved or surprised at my request, each person took a step back. Once their shock registered, understanding and concern flickered across their faces. They nodded, acknowledging my words, and adjusted their greetings to suit Mom's needs. I felt a sense of relief wash over me, grateful that they understood.

My attention shifted when I spotted Shelby Thurston seated in a pew nearby. She wrestled with her younger brothers, who were quite the handful. Shelby was about to turn sixteen later this week, and I found myself in a battle of nerves about when to ask her on a date. I resolved to do it soon, the day after her birthday, perhaps. That would be perfect.

Unbeknownst to me, Shelby spotted me and left her rowdy brothers behind to come over and say hi.

"Noah! It's so good to see you!"

The moment her sweet and radiant smile appeared in front of me, it brightened my day. I felt my cheeks heat, recalling the *Tinker*

Bell Kiss she had given me in the hospital and the way I felt during our movie nights.

"It's great to see you too, Shelby," I replied, my voice laced with boyish anxiety. Was this how it felt to have the girl I was crushing on notice me back?

"Your mom is looking good. In just the last three weeks, she has come a long way." She nodded toward my mom, who stood nearby, engaged in conversation with another sister in the ward.

"She sure is. Mom is getting stronger every day. She started the second phase of her physical therapy and is doing well. The sessions are tough, leaving her sore the following day, but she perseveres. I'm really proud of her."

"Is there anything I can do to help? My mom and I could make some more meals and cookies. Or we could come help around the house, especially on her therapy days."

"Don't worry about that. I help cook and keep the house clean, so she doesn't have to stress about it. But cookies are always welcome, and Sister Bean tells me to ask about a double chocolate, chocolate chip cookie."

Shelby's smile brightened at the mention of cookies. "She loves those. It's a recipe my Grandma Thurston always makes. I will bring them next time."

"I can't wait to try them."

"Noah, I don't know if you can make it or not. I understand if you can't because of your mom, but my birthday is this week, and I'm having a party on Friday. I'd love for you to come."

"Uh, yeah, I'd like to come. Mom hasn't stayed home alone yet, but she's both physically and emotionally strong enough to. If she doesn't want to stay alone, I could ask Sister Bean to come visit. Mom loves it when she stops by."

"Who said my name?" Sister Bean perked up from behind a middle-aged couple standing a few feet away. "Noah, is that you?"

Sister Bean left the couple mid-conversation and came over. She wrapped her little arms around my waist and squeezed as tight as she could. "I heard you say my name. What do you need? Whatever it is, my answer is yes."

Both Shelby and I laughed.

"Sister Bean, it's my sixteenth birthday, and I'm having a party. I asked Noah to come."

"You did, did you?" Sister Bean looked Shelby up and down, eyes sparkling with mischief. Addressing me, she said, "So, you need me to come over and entertain that mom of yours, right?"

I nodded, grateful for her support.

"I'll be there. You go have a good time."

"Yay! I'm so excited," Shelby exclaimed. She bounced on the balls of her feet and patted her hands together in a silent, church appropriate clap. She was adorable, her ponytail swishing against her neck like a happy metronome.

As our conversation lulled, Shelby excused herself to return to her pew and settle her little brothers. She was a pro at calming them down. She confiscated the hymnals they flapped like birds and shushed their caw-cawing noises. I chuckled at the relief etched on the faces of those who sat in front of the Thurston family.

Mom approached, fatigue evident in her bearing. I felt a pang of guilt for neglecting her, even if only momentarily. She took my arm, and I guided her to the nearest empty pew across the aisle and one behind the Thurston family. Sister Bean joined us.

Shelby threw a little wave over her shoulder, which I returned with a grin.

"Looks like Shelby's legit after Friday night, right?"

"Legit?" I laughed at her hip language.

"You know, she's officially sixteen, so you can ask her on a *real* date."

I blushed, grinning like a fool as I nodded.

Sister Bean slapped my leg and waggled her eyebrows. Just as she was about to say more, the congregation quieted, and the bishop approached the pulpit to start the sacrament meeting. She held her tongue, and I sighed with relief.

"Mom, will you be alright while I run an errand?" I asked Friday morning.

"Of course, I'd be fine tonight without a babysitter too, but since you already scheduled one for me, I guess I'll have to make do. Where are you going?"

A heat crept up my neck and spread across my cheeks. "I need to run to Target in Wenatchee."

"Target? What do you need there?"

I fiddled with my wallet and keys, trying to act nonchalantly. "I need to pick up a gift for Shelby's birthday."

"Sounds good. I'll see you when you get back." She didn't say another word, but her smile spoke a thousand. The color on my neck and cheeks deepened into a dark crimson blush.

"Do you want me to get you anything?"

"No, I'm fine. Go find the perfect gift. Remember, Shelby's favorite color is pink."

"I know, Mom. I'm pretty sure everyone in the valley knows her favorite color is pink." I rushed out the door to my pickup, eager to escape Mom's mischievous smile.

My heart fluttered with nervous excitement, knowing that tonight I'd finally be free to ask Shelby on a date. After parking my truck, I pushed my Aviator sunglasses up the bridge of my nose and stepped out, determination fueling my steps. Walking into Target, I had one mission: to find the perfect birthday present for Shelby.

I wandered through the aisles, looping the store twice, but nothing seemed quite right. A wave of worry washed over me, as I feared I wouldn't find anything special enough, until I finally stumbled across the jewelry section. Somehow, I'd overlooked it on both laps. Jewelry, perfect!

As I scanned the display cases, my gaze landed on a delicate rose gold necklace shaped like a rose, with a light pink gemstone that caught the light beautifully. It was simple yet elegant, just like Shelby. I could picture her reaction, the way her eyes would light up, and it even reminded me of the enchanted rose from *Beauty and the Beast*. A smile spread across my face as I picked it up, imagining her joy. I clutched the necklace box tight in my hand as I made my way to the greeting card aisle. A small pink gift bag caught my eye, and I snatched it up. The jewelry box fit perfectly.

Next on my quest was finding the ideal card to complement the necklace. I roamed the aisles, searching for one that would capture Shelby's sweetness and the connection we shared. After some diligent searching, I stumbled upon a lovely little pocket card adorned with pink flowers. It was perfect. I traced my finger over the delicate design, imagining how much Shelby would love it.

With the purchase made, I tucked the necklace into the small pink gift bag, stuffing it with tissue paper to hide the box. The bag was no bigger than the palm of my hand, just the right size for the jewelry box to slip in snugly.

Back in my truck, I rummaged through the console until I found a pen, determined to write a heartfelt message. But as soon as I tried, the words just wouldn't come. I sat there, staring at the blank card, the pressure increasing. For a moment, I considered driving home to ask Mom for help. But then, as I took a deep breath, the right words finally came to me. They flowed onto the card, capturing my admiration for Shelby and my hopes for a future date with her. When I finished, I sealed the envelope with a kiss that only I would ever know about, then tucked it inside the gift bag with her necklace.

Shelby's party was bound to go late. It was summer, and the movie she'd planned to watch on a projector outside couldn't even start until after sunset. I left her gift on the passenger seat of my pickup and headed inside, deciding I'd wait for a private moment to give it to her, away from prying eyes.

As I walked into the Thurston house that evening, the tantalizing aroma of hot pizza and the sound of laughter hit me all at once. It was a mouthwatering welcome that made my stomach rumble with anticipation. I hadn't eaten pizza in forever. Shelby's party buzzed with life, a mix of friends and family spread out through the house and spilling into the backyard. When I spotted Shelby across the lawn, her smile shone like the summer evening sun. Her joy was contagious as she greeted each guest. And then, as if she could sense me, her gaze found mine. A smile lit up her face, and my heart kicked up a notch.

Every time I tried to approach Shelby, someone seemed to pop up between us. Frustration built with each failed attempt. Just as I was contemplating a new strategy, a cluster of girls surrounded her, leaving me with no chance. It felt impossible to get near her, so I resigned myself to waiting.

"Hey there, Noah. How are you?" Shelby's dad, Brother Thurston, said, catching me off guard. He glanced in the direction of my gaze, straight at his daughter and her friends. A knowing smile played across his lips. "Why don't you go over there and talk to her?"

"No way, not with that group of girls hovering around her. I'd be eaten alive."

Brother Thurston let out a deep, booming laugh, loud enough to draw the attention of a few nearby guests, including Shelby and her gaggle of girls.

"You're wise beyond your years. When I was your age, I was foolish enough to walk right into a similar group. And you're right, I nearly got eaten alive. Give it another half-hour; things will settle down once we start the movie." He patted my shoulder and walked off before I could respond.

I nodded, appreciating his advice, but it didn't make the waiting any easier. A few other people came over to chat, asking about Jacob or Mom. I answered their questions, trying to pay attention and be polite, but my mind was consumed with thoughts of Shelby. Finally, I spotted Steven hanging out in his usual low-key spot at the edge of the yard and made my escape over to him. We chilled there together, keeping things casual, until I noticed Shelby's dad setting up the white projector screen, the signal I'd been waiting for.

I excused myself and slipped out of the backyard, heading to my truck to grab Shelby's gift. I tucked the little pink bag under my arm, hoping no one would notice it, as I made my way back into the party.

By the time I returned, the projector had flickered to life, casting its warm glow across the yard as darkness crept in. The backyard had transformed into a cozy outdoor theater, with blankets and pillows spread across the lawn and guests lounging in chairs along the edges. Laughter and animated conversation filled the air, mingling with the buzz of excitement as the movie was about to begin. My heart pounded as I found a spot near the edge of the teenage crowd, clutching the gift bag, hoping for a moment when Shelby and I could finally talk.

I watched Shelby as she chatted with a few people. She drifted from one group to another, her laughter bright against the backdrop of the film's intro. I realized she'd have to choose a spot soon since the movie had already started.

I reclined and folded my arms behind my head, crossing my legs at my ankles. I did my best to appear calm. Gazing at the sky, I searched for the first stars to break through the twilight, all the while hoping Shelby might decide to sit near me. Just as the thought crossed my mind, she appeared, kneeling on the blanket beside me.

"Are you saving this spot for anyone?" she asked, her voice soft and inviting.

"You," I replied, trying to keep my tone steady despite the flutter in my chest. Her countenance sparkled in the moonlight, and for a moment, I forgot how to breathe.

She settled as the movie began, leaning close enough that I could feel the warmth radiating from her. A few minutes later, she whispered, "Noah, I'm glad you came tonight."

"Me too," I said. I leaned even closer so she could hear me over the hum of the film.

The movie continued, and our conversation faded into the background. Around us, others chatted or wandered off, and by the time we reached the movie's halfway point, the crowd had thinned out. But I couldn't focus on anything but the nerves knotting my stomach. My mind raced, and my hands felt clammy, too jittery to find the right words.

When ten minutes remained in the movie, I finally gathered the courage and slid the small gift bag onto Shelby's lap. It was now or never. My heart pounded as I prayed she'd like it.

Shelby's eyes widened in surprise, and she bolted upright. She pulled the little card from the bag and opened it. I watched every flicker of her expression as she read the message, I'd poured my heart into. A smile tugged at the corners of her lips, and a soft glow lit up her cheeks in the dim light of the projector. She met my gaze, her eyes shimmering with emotion, and nodded, a wordless *yes* to my invitation for a date. Her answer made my stomach flip-flop.

She reached into the bag and pulled out the jewelry box. She opened the lid, revealing the delicate rose gold necklace nestled inside.

"Oh, Noah, it's beautiful," Shelby cooed as she held the necklace toward the house lights to admire it better. Then she took it out of the box. "Will you help me put it on?"

"Sure," I replied, trying to keep my voice steady as I took the necklace with shaky fingers. I'd never put a necklace on anyone before, not even Mom. The realization sent a wave of anxiety through me. What if I messed it up?

I inspected the chain, searching for the clasp. My fingers fumbled with the tiny mechanism, struggling to pinch it open. After what felt like an eternity, I finally got the clasp open, but the chain slipped from my fingers and the pendant fell. I caught it just in time. Shelby glanced back at me, and I wondered if she thought I was inept. I couldn't believe how much I was struggling with something so simple.

With a deep breath, I calmed down and wrapped the delicate chain around Shelby's slender neck. By some miracle, I secured it in place without taking too long or dropping it again.

She clasped the pendant at her throat and looked up at me. Her smile was soft and radiant as she declared, "I love it. It's the most beautiful necklace I've ever seen."

Pride swelled in my chest as we lay back on the blanket, returning our attention to the final few minutes of the movie.

Lying side by side under the starlit sky, our arms brushed against each other again, and the world faded away. We exchanged shy glances and secret smiles, the kind that lingered long after our eyes met.

As the credits rolled, I helped Shelby fold the blankets. Our fingers brushed against each other, sending a rush of warmth through me. My heart thudded in my chest, each touch igniting sparks that danced along my nerves.

It was twenty minutes to midnight when I finally fished my keys out of my pocket. I only had a few minutes to get home before curfew.

"I'll walk you out?" Shelby offered after I stacked the folded blanket on top of the others her parents had gathered.

"Thanks for coming, Noah," Brother Thurston called out as he walked past.

"Thanks for inviting me!" I called back, my voice trailing behind him as he entered the house. I turned to Shelby's mom with a smile. "You too, Sister Thurston."

"You're welcome anytime." Then she noticed the glint of Shelby's new necklace. "Shelby, who gave you the necklace? It's lovely, sweetheart."

Shelby placed a hand on my arm, stopping me in my tracks. "Noah gave it to me. I'll be right back to help. I'm going to walk him to his pickup."

Sister Thurston nodded, her attention returning to folding the blankets and stacking the pillows.

As Shelby and I walked to my truck, the night air felt cooler, and the silence between us felt different, charged with something new. I wanted to say something, but my thoughts tangled up. We reached my pickup, and I fumbled with my keys, stalling for just a little more time with her.

"I had a lot of fun tonight," I said, my nerves creeping into my voice.

"Me too." Shelby smiled and tucked a strand of hair behind her ear. Her other hand fingered the necklace resting around her neck.

I looked at her standing there; the moonlight catching the soft edges of her face, and before I could overthink it, the words tumbled out. "Shelby, do you want to go out with me tomorrow?"

She blinked twice. "You mean... like, on a date?"

"Yeah." I rubbed the back of my neck, nerves crashing over me like a wave. "I know it's kind of short notice, but now that you're sixteen, I thought we could grab dinner and see a movie at the theater... if you want to."

"I'd love to. Noah, I have to go on double dates. Do you think you can find someone else to double with us on such short notice?" Her voice was soft and a little uncertain.

"I have the double date rule as well. I think David or Aaron could find a date at the last minute."

"I know Stephanie's free tomorrow."

"Great idea. I'll mention her to whichever guy can go. Tomorrow, then! I can pick you up around four. Will that work for you?"

"Four sounds perfect. It's a date!" she said, her eyes sparkling under the streetlight.

I couldn't hide my grin if I tried. "Yes, a date. Great. I'll see you tomorrow, then."

As I opened my truck door, I turned back, wanting to say something more, anything to hold onto the moment. "Goodnight, Shelby."

"Goodnight, Noah," she replied, and for a heartbeat, it felt like the world had narrowed to just the two of us.

I hesitated, then took two big steps forward. I leaned down to her height and placed a quick, gentle *Tinker Bell Kiss* on her cheek. "Happy birthday," I whispered, before rushing back to my truck. With Shelby still standing there, a bit wide-eyed, I started the engine and drove off.

I pressed the speed limit going home. Adrenaline surged as I tried to make it before curfew. I ran into the house, closing the front door with just seconds to spare.

CHAPTER EIGHTEEN

IT TOOK SOME EFFORT Saturday morning, but I eventually found a friend who could scrounge up a date fast enough to double with Shelby and me that night. I texted Shelby to tell her that Aaron and Stephanie were meeting us at the restaurant. Now all I had to do was make sure I didn't look like a complete idiot.

I wore Dad's shirt. I'd always liked the way it looked on him, like he had somewhere important to be, some place he belonged. I hoped it would make me look a little more put-together than I felt. I retrieved it from the closet and ran my fingers over the soft fabric. I slipped it on, buttoning it carefully.

I was rolling the long sleeves into place above my elbows, just like Dad always did, when Mom knocked on the doorframe. She took one look at me and tilted her head, a small smile breaking through her usual tired expression.

"You look handsome, Noah. Dad would be proud."

"Thanks, Mom," I mumbled, my cheeks flushing. I didn't know what else to say to that, so I just looked down and straightened the collar.

I grabbed my wallet and keys from the dresser, double-checked to make sure the $100 bill Grandma Bean had slipped me awhile back was still tucked safely inside. She'd called it *gas money*, but I figured my first date with Shelby was the perfect use for it. With one last look in the mirror, I smoothed down Dad's shirt, tucked my wallet into my pocket, and took a steadying breath. Mom was still watching from the doorway, and she gave me an encouraging nod as I headed down the stairs and out the front door.

When I finally pulled up to Shelby's house, the hum of the engine seemed loud in the quiet evening air. My hands gripped the steering wheel, white-knuckled, as I tried to wrestle down the nerves that had been bubbling inside me ever since she'd agreed to go out with me. I stared at her front door, took a deep breath that didn't do anything to calm my racing heart, and told myself to get a grip.

"Just knock," I muttered under my breath, forcing myself out of the car. Each step toward her door felt like a countdown. My heart raced faster with every step.

I knocked, the sound echoing through the porch like a drumbeat in the stillness.

A moment later, the door swung open, and there she was, Shelby Thurston. Her hair was pulled back into a high ponytail, the pink ribbon dancing in the soft evening breeze. Her eyes sparkled under the porch light, a mix of excitement and warmth. She wore blue jeans that hugged her frame just right, a pink blouse tied at her waist, and matching sandals that seemed to glow. At that moment, she was perfect.

"Hey," I managed, trying to sound cool, but my voice cracked slightly.

"Hey yourself," she smiled, a hint of mischief in her eyes. "Ready?"

I nodded, stepping aside and though it was hot outside, she grabbed her just-in-case sweater from the hook behind the door. The door clicked shut behind her, sealing off the world and leaving just the two of us.

"So," I started, walking beside her down the steps, the gravel crunching under our feet. "I hope you like sushi."

Her grin widened. "Yeah, it's one of my favorite types of food."

"Great! Let's grab dinner at *Sumo*. It's my family's go-to sushi place. Aaron and Stephanie are meeting us there."

I opened her door, and she slid into the passenger seat and buckled her seatbelt, her excitement palpable. "How fun! Stephanie is one of my best friends. I love *Sumo*, I think my family has tried almost everything on the menu."

"Perfect, you'll have to choose, then. My mom has this tendency to always order her same old favorites. It takes a lot of family dinners there to try everything when I can only manage one or two rolls on each trip. Can you believe there are over 50 types of sushi? It's crazy how many flavors they have."

"My dad counted them once," she said, her eyes gleaming. "There are 46 different sushi rolls alone."

"I was totally guessing!" I laughed, relieved to see her enthusiasm matching my own.

The drive was quick, and as we pulled into the parking lot of Sumo, the familiar aroma of soy sauce and fresh fish greeted us, wrapping around me like a warm blanket. Once inside, we found a cozy booth by the window, the soft glow of the overhead lights casting a welcoming ambiance. As we settled in, Shelby immediately picked up the menu, scanning the options with excitement.

"So, what's your go-to?" I asked, genuinely curious as we waited for the others.

She studied the menu for a moment, her brow furrowed in concentration before a grin broke out on her face. "I love the *Wenatchee Roll*. It's superb. Have you tried it?"

"Of course! We live in the Wenatchee Valley. It'd be sacrilegious not to."

"What about the *Love of the Sea Roll*?" she asked, tilting her head slightly.

I shook my head. "I haven't had that one."

"We should try it then. Wait! Do you have any nut allergies or anything?"

"No, why?"

"It has peanuts in it. My cousin would die if she ate it," Shelby said, her expression turning serious as she peered over the top of the menu. It was understandable why she took food allergies seriously, and I appreciated her concern.

"Lucky for me, I can eat anything. No allergies here. What about you?"

"None for me either," she said, glancing up with a playful smile that sent a flutter through me before she returned to her menu.

Just then, Aaron and Stephanie joined us. They slid into the booth across from us and Shelby handed over one of our menus for them to look at since the server hadn't arrived with two more.

"Have you two eaten here before?" Shelby asked, her eyes bright with excitement.

Aaron and Stephanie shook their heads. "Nope, first time for both of us," Aaron admitted.

Shelby's face lit up as she took on the role of hostess. "Alright, well, you're in for a treat! This place has the best sushi, and I've practically tried everything on the menu." She scanned the options like a pro, then shared her favorites.

Aaron and Stephanie exchanged glances, intrigued. "You sound like you should work here," Stephanie said with a laugh.

"Maybe I missed my calling!" Shelby joked, then nudged me with a smile. "What about you, Noah? Tell them what you like."

"Honestly, I haven't tried nearly as many as Shelby has, but I think the Wenatchee Roll is my favorite. It just resonates, you know?"

While Aaron and Stephanie inspected the menu to choose their selections, Shelby asked me, "How many should we get?"

"I could easily eat six or more all by myself," I bragged, puffing out my chest slightly.

"I bet you can!" she giggled, and my heart squeezed at the sound. "So, we should order one of everything!"

"Totally, but let me check my wallet first." I pretended to pull out my wallet, opening my hands like I was counting imaginary bills. "Let's make it four rolls for tonight."

Her laughter filled the space, and I couldn't help but smile. I loved making her laugh.

Just then, our server approached, and I let Shelby take the lead. I watched, impressed, as she confidently ordered the *Wenatchee Roll*, *Love of the Sea Roll*, *Pirate Roll*, and *Seahawks Roll*. Before he walked away, I added, "Oh, and miso soup. It's a family tradition, after all."

Aaron ordered for himself and Stephanie, opting for the *Cowboy Roll*, the *Ninja Roll* and a classic *California Roll*, and then we all settled into easy conversation as we waited for our food to arrive.

The background hum of the restaurant created a cozy bubble around us, and soon enough, talk turned to family, friends, and school.

"So, how's your mom doing? I can't even imagine going through what your family did," Stephanie asked gently, her eyes soft with concern.

I appreciated her asking; sometimes, it felt like people didn't know whether they should bring it up. "She's doing better," I said, nodding slowly. "It's been rough, but she's pushing through. Physical therapy's been hard on her, but... you know my mom, she's not one to back down."

"That's good to hear. She's got some serious strength," Aaron said.

"Yes, she really does. And honestly, so many people have helped us. Shelby and her mom put together tons of freezer meals and brought them over. They have helped us so much. It's been a lifesaver not having to worry about dinners."

Shelby waved a hand, brushing it off with a modest smile. "It was nothing. We just wanted to help."

"Still," I insisted, meeting her eyes, "it's made a huge difference. Mom doesn't feel like she's a burden, and we're eating healthy meals."

Shelby's cheeks flushed a little, but she just smiled and shrugged. "Well, I'm glad we could do something."

Stephanie leaned in, curious. "And how's your older brother? Remind me, which mission is he in again?"

I perked up at the chance to talk about Jacob. "He's serving in the *Cauayan Philippines Mission*. It's on Luzon, the northern big island."

"Whoa," Aaron said, impressed. "That's a world away. He must be having some incredible experiences."

"Yeah, he really is. It's been life-changing for him, I think. We talk to him every Sunday evening. It's Monday in the Philippines which is his p-day. He tells us all about the people he meets and how different it is there. He even ate balut, which, uh… I'll let you look up if you're curious."

Everyone laughed, Aaron pulling a face. "I'm sure he's braver than me. I'd stick to the basics."

Stephanie smiled, looking thoughtful. "That's awesome. Missions aren't easy, but it sounds like he's doing great."

"Definitely! He's always been the adventurous one, so this is right up his alley. Plus, it's been good for Mom to hear about his experiences. It keeps her mind off things, you know?"

"Sounds like you're all handling it pretty well," Shelby said, looking at me with admiration that made my chest tighten a little.

"Thanks," I replied, giving her a quick smile. "We're trying, anyway."

As our sushi arrived, I had to admit Shelby had great taste. The *Love of the Sea Roll* was incredible: spicy, with a hint of something that made me crave more. I watched her as she took her first bite, her face lighting up in delight. Our conversation continued to flow easily, covering everything from school to stories about mutual friends, each topic rolling into the next like we'd done this a hundred times before.

After dinner, I drove us to the movie theater, Aaron and Stephanie following. The excitement of the evening buzzed between us. We bought tickets and headed straight for the concession stand. "Popcorn?" I asked, grinning.

"Obviously," she laughed. "And candy? I like Whoppers and Starburst."

"Whoppers, Starburst, and frozen Junior Mints," I told the girl running the concessions, the familiar routine bringing back memories of past movie nights with Mom, Dad, and Jacob.

Shelby raised an eyebrow, a teasing smile playing on her lips. "Frozen Junior Mints?"

I gasped dramatically. "You've never had them?"

"Nope. Are they good?"

I grinned, a playful glint in my eye. "You'll see. These are Jacob's absolute favorite candy in the entire world."

We settled into our seats, the girls taking center, sitting between me and Aaron. The theater was dark and cool, with the scent of buttery popcorn wafting through the air. As the previews rolled, we shared the popcorn, the sound of kernels crunching mingling with the low hum of the crowd. I handed her the box of Junior Mints.

She hesitated for a moment, eyeing the candy before popping one into her mouth. Her eyes widened in surprise. "Okay, these are amazing."

"Told you," I whispered, trying to hide my satisfaction at her reaction.

We watched the rest of the movie, passing the boxes of candy and popcorn back and forth, laughter and whispers punctuating our shared enjoyment. As the credits rolled, I felt a pang of regret; I wished the night wouldn't end. But it did, and it was time to take Shelby home.

"That was such a great movie, wasn't it?" Shelby cooed as we walked towards the vehicles in the parking lot.

"It sure was. Thanks for inviting us out," Stephanie answered.

"Our pleasure," Aaron said.

We said goodbye to Aaron and Stephanie, and I held the door for Shelby to get into my pickup while Aaron held the door of his Subaru for Stephanie.

The drive back to Shelby's house was quiet, a comfortable silence, the kind that speaks volumes without uttering a word. We were both a little tired, but content. As I pulled up in front of her house and turned off the engine, my heart raced at the thought of this night ending.

She smiled, her eyes sparkling in the dim light from the streetlight as she unbuckled her seatbelt. In that brief, unguarded moment, I felt something shift. I wanted this to be more than just one night. I wanted it to be the start of something real. But that thought was terrifying and impossible. I wasn't ready for a steady girlfriend, not yet. I still had to work past my own nerves and get comfortable dating. I had my mission ahead of me, and in my mind, the plan was simple: date around a little until my mission, then maybe settle down and get serious with someone in college. I couldn't change that plan for Shelby—not only because of the family dating rules, but because I didn't want to mess this up. Shelby wasn't just another girl. She was remarkable, a breath of fresh air who made my ordinary life feel full of color.

But as I nodded in response to her smile, an awkwardness crept in, wrapping around me like an unwelcome blanket. *Should I say something? Or just get out and walk her to the door?* My thoughts were a tangled mess, and I hoped she didn't pick up on my internal chaos.

Suddenly, I leaped from the pickup, adrenaline propelling me forward as I rushed to her side. I flung open her door with a flourish, a smile breaking across my face despite the nervous energy swirling within me. I had opened her door all evening, and now she sat patiently, waiting for me instead of jumping out on her own like she had at our first stop for dinner.

"After you," I said, my voice steadier than I felt. As she stepped out, I couldn't help but admire her, the way her hair caught the light, the way she moved with a grace that made everything feel right in that moment.

I walked her to her front door, my heart racing as I said, "I had a good time. I hope you did too."

"I did. Thanks, Noah." I swear her smile brightened the dim porch light.

"I'm glad," I said, rocking from the balls of my feet to my heels, each shift amplifying my nerves. I felt like a sinking ship, floundering with no clear way off the Thurston's porch.

"Goodnight, Noah," she said, giving me a little wave as she opened the door to her house.

"Goodnight, Shelby," I managed. I should have said more, but I kept coming up blank.

She disappeared inside, and for a moment, I stood on the porch, letting the awkwardness settle like dust before making my escape. I dashed to my pickup, adrenaline still buzzing, and headed home. Despite my clumsiness, at the end, the night had been a success. A smile tugged at the corner of my mouth as I replayed our laughter and connection.

I didn't bother trying to enter the house quietly, as I knew Mom would still be awake. When I opened the door and walked in, her gentle smile greeted me, curiosity glimmering in her eyes like stars in the night.

"Noah, how was your date? I want to hear all about it. Did you have a good time?"

My heart swelled with happiness, knowing Mom cared about my night, regardless of whatever else was going on in hers.

"Mom, it was amazing! Shelby and I really hit it off. We laughed, talked, and connected on so many levels. It was truly a night to remember."

Her eyes sparkled with genuine interest as she leaned forward, hanging on my every word. "Tell me more, Noah! What did you do? What did you talk about? Did you have any funny moments?"

I settled onto the couch, the familiar comfort of home wrapping around me as I relished the chance to share the details of my evening with her. "Well, we ate at *Sumo*. Here, I brought you a few pieces of sushi." I handed over the to-go box, and her eyes lit up as she opened it.

"All our favorite rolls! Thanks!" she exclaimed, her joy infectious.

As she examined the sushi, I felt a warmth spread through me, a sense of belonging that made this night even more special. It wasn't just about my date; it was about sharing these moments with the people I loved.

I made my way to the kitchen, grabbing a fork since we didn't have chopsticks at our house. I returned and handed it to her.

"Then we went to the movies. We shared popcorn and candy. Did you know she's never had frozen Junior Mints?"

"Weird! I thought everyone ate their Junior Mints frozen," Mom said between bites of sushi, her brows lifting in surprise.

"I know, right? Our conversations flowed easily. We talked about Jacob, schoolwork, favorite movies, and food. It felt so easy and natural, Mom."

A smile of pride spread across Mom's face as she listened, her eyes sparkling with joy. "Noah, I'm so glad to hear that. It sounds like the perfect date. You deserve all the happiness in the world."

Her words warmed my heart, filling me with gratitude for her unwavering support. "Thanks, Mom. It was a great night. Shelby is just an amazing person."

She reached out, giving my hand a loving squeeze. I nodded, overwhelmed by a profound sense of love and appreciation for Mom's understanding and encouragement. As the night grew late, Mom yawned, her eyes glimmering with contentment. "Noah, it's late. I should get some rest. You must be tired, too."

I stood up from my seat and went to her. Then I leaned over to give her a gentle *Tinker Belle Kiss* on the cheek. "You're right, Mom. It's been an eventful day. Goodnight, and thank you for everything."

She smiled, her face softening with affection. "Goodnight, Noah. Sleep well, and remember, I'm always here for you, no matter what."

"I know, Mom. I love you too. Do you need me to get you anything before I go to bed?"

There was a moment of indecision on her face, and I felt a flutter of concern. I wasn't sure what was happening until she said, "Actually, Noah. I want to sleep in my room tonight. I love this chair, but it's time. I can breathe easy now, even when I sleep. My hips and back don't ache like they did before. I've just been prolonging the inevitable."

My heart swelled with pride for Mom. She was healing in leaps and bounds. Today had been a great day. She had carried the weight of grief for months, and now she was taking a significant step toward healing. "Mom, that's incredible. Let me help you."

She closed the footrest and pulled Dad's blanket off her lap. I tossed it onto the couch, took her hand, and helped her stand. As we made our way to her bedroom, I lingered by the door, asking if she needed anything.

"Why don't you come in and say prayers with me? It's been a while since we had a *family* prayer." Her voice wavered slightly over the word.

"I'd love to, Mom."

Since Mom couldn't kneel yet, I helped her settle into bed, carefully arranging her pillows and tidying the blankets. I kneeled beside her bed, holding her hand with my eyes closed and head bowed.

Silence enveloped us, a sacred space where words weren't necessary.

When I opened my eyes to check on her, I noticed tears streaming down her face.

"Mom, what's wrong? Is it too much being in here? Do you want to go back to the living room?" I tugged on the blankets I had just straightened, anxiety rising within me.

"No, no, nothing's wrong. I'm fine. It's just that your dad always chose who said the prayer. He was the priesthood holder and head of our family. With Jacob gone, it's up to you now, Noah."

The weight of her words settled heavily on my shoulders. The realization hit me hard, awakening a mix of emotions within me. Awe and humility washed over me as I comprehended the significance of the priesthood and its role in our home.

Pondering my responsibility, I took a deep breath, welcoming this newfound role. I held the Aaronic Priesthood, and in the absence of my father and brother, who bore the fullness of the Melchizedek Priesthood, it was my duty and privilege to lead our family prayer. As the only man in the house holding the priesthood, the task fell upon me to seek divine intervention and blessings on our behalf. It was an honor that filled me with resolve.

"Tonight, I'd like to say the prayer," I said. My voice was steady despite the weight of my emotions.

Mom nodded in agreement, her expression radiating trust and faith. I closed my eyes and prayed, pouring my heart into the words. I sought guidance, strength, and protection for each remaining family member, crying out to the Lord for my father.

During the prayer, I felt a sense of unity and purpose, a connection that transcended our grief, bringing us closer together as we moved forward in healing.

"Oh God, our Eternal Father in Heaven, we bow our heads before You, two souls intertwined by grief, Mom and me. We seek solace and strength through Your divine guidance. Our hearts are heavy with the weight of loss over Dad and our separation from Jacob, yet we are filled with deep trust in Your guiding hand. We believe all things work together for our good because of You."

I couldn't help the tears and choking sobs that escaped. Mom's grip tightened on my hand in shared sorrow.

"Lord, please help Dad feel our love for him. Send him to watch over us. We know now that he has shed his mortal coil and continues his journey in Your eternal presence, an angel among You. The ache of his absence has etched a permanent mark upon our souls, leaving us longing for his comforting presence, yet willing to trust in Thy plan. Please send Thy Comforter to help us heal.

"Father, we thank You for the gift of Dad's life, for the love and cherished memories we hold close to our hearts. Though the pain of his death lingers, we are grateful for the time we shared with him, the lessons he taught us, and the love he gave us.

"We also come to You with hearts overflowing with love for Jacob as he serves Thee in the Philippines. As we navigate the vast distance that separates us, we pray for his safety and well-being. Surround him with Your divine presence and guide his steps. Lord, I wish I could hug my brother. This time is challenging for Mom and me, and I can't imagine what it is like for him to be so far away. Wrap Thy arms around him and whisper peace to his soul. Help him feel our love, and Dad's.

"Father, I am grateful for Jacob's willingness to serve and share the message of Your gospel with those who seek truth and salvation. Bless him with strength and wisdom as he navigates the challenges and blessings of missionary work. Put the people who need Thy gospel in his path and help him recognize them. Please watch over him with every step he takes. Protect him from physical harm, sickness, and distractions that may divert him from his sacred purpose. Strengthen his resolve to stand firm in his faith, to be a beacon of light in a world that sometimes appears shrouded in darkness and doubt. Surround him with kind and understanding companions and leaders who will uplift him. Help Jacob find joy in the small victories, recognize the impact of his service, and remain steadfast in his dedication to You and Your work.

"Father, we humbly ask for Your divine guidance on our healing journey. Grant us the strength to rise above our pain as we regain our health. Help us find comfort in the memories we hold dear and discover new purpose now that our family has changed. Assist us in leaning on one another to support and uplift each other. Amid our trials, may we not lose sight of the countless blessings surrounding us. Open our eyes to the beauty, love, and opportunities that still exist. Help us always recognize our miracles.

"Father, we offer this prayer with broken hearts and contrite spirits. We seek Your unwavering love and grace. Our trust in Your divine plan stems from the knowledge that You will guide us through the darkest nights and lead us into the bright sunshine of a new day. We humbly pray in the name of Your Son, our Savior, Jesus Christ. Amen."

As I uttered the last words, a sense of peace enveloped me. I had stepped into a role that carried immense responsibility, performing it to the best of my ability. It was an opportunity to draw closer to God and serve my mother.

When I opened my eyes, I saw Mom's awe-struck, tear-stained face, her countenance reflecting a mix of pride and wonder as she stared at me. "Where in the world did you learn to pray like that?"

Her question lingered. I shrugged. "It's been a long few months. I've spent a lot of time on my knees, but not all my prayers felt as good as that one. There was a time when I was angry at God. Do you remember the day after you woke up and couldn't breathe? They rushed you into surgery." Mom nodded, her expression somber.

"That day, I ran out of the hospital and ended up in a Japanese garden. Grandpa Wilde followed me. Mom, I was furious. My faith felt shattered, and I didn't know what to believe anymore. It felt like God was taking everyone from me and leaving me behind, alone.

"Grandpa spoke to me. He was kind and caring, never pushing me, just encouraging me not to give up on my faith. When he left, I prayed. Mom, I poured my heart out to God. I was angry, hurt, and utterly broken. I can't even describe the depth of my sadness."

I paused, taking a deep breath, needing a moment to collect myself. Mom didn't interrupt; she just waited, her presence reassuring.

Looking into her loving eyes, I closed mine briefly and revealed, "Mom, the Savior spoke to me. It wasn't just a sense of peace or the Holy Ghost testifying; I heard His voice. I can't find the words to describe it, but it was beautiful, overwhelming and much-needed when I was ready to give up. If you had died, I honestly don't know what I would have done. I was at the edge, ready to give up."

Mom was the first and only person I would ever tell about this experience. She didn't question me or probe for details. There was no doubt whether she believed me. She understood.

"Oh, my dear sweet boy," she said, pulling me into her arms, tears spilling onto my head where she pressed her cheek. "I love you, Noah."

I sat up and straightened her blankets, smoothing out the wrinkles and fluffed one of her pillows. It didn't need it, but I did it anyway. It was my way of caring for her, making sure everything was just right.

"You go get some sleep now."

I gave Mom a quick *Tinker Bell Kiss* and headed to my room, carrying the warmth of her love and support with me. That night had transformed us, not just me, but her as well, and our mother-son relationship. We were uncovering the beauty of shared experiences, of caring and being there for each other.

As I lay in bed, ready to drift off into a peaceful slumber, I whispered one more prayer of gratitude, a prayer that included a special thank you to God for keeping my beautiful and perfect mother here on Earth with me a little longer and for the wonderful time I had getting to know Shelby Thurston a little better.

CHAPTER NINETEEN

On a beautiful, sunlit Wednesday, my heart took flight, as free as a bird escaping its cage. It soared, filling the air with its own imagined melodies of joy. This ethereal transformation happened because, after so long, Mom's true, unrestrained laughter returned to our home. Since the accident, she had laughed a few times, but it was never the same. These weren't the warm, familiar laughs that used to fill our house, the ones I cherished. Instead, she gave stifled, hollow laughs I couldn't shake off as anything but *pity laughs*. Sounds made of obligation rather than pure joy.

Her real laugh, the one I grew up with and remembered from my childhood, felt like sunlight breaking through months of storm clouds. It was a sweet balm to my troubled soul. I hadn't realized how much I missed it until it took me by surprise, spilling out like pure sunshine. In my excitement, I bolted toward the sound, not watching where I was going, and crashed into the wall, painfully stubbing my toe.

I doubled over, clutching my foot, hopping on one leg, trying to hold back the sharp sting of pain.

"Oh dear, that must have hurt!" Mom's laughter faded into concern, her brows furrowing.

I waved off the pain, grinning through the ache, determined to bring her laugh back. I would do anything to keep that sound alive in our home, even if it meant enduring a bruised toe in silence.

"What's so funny?" I asked, attempting to sound casual as I poured myself a glass of apple juice, my heart racing with hope.

Her smile lingered, a rare warmth lighting her face. "Oh, just a silly meme Aunt Megan sent."

Curiosity flared in me like a match struck in the dark. Whatever had made her laugh like that was a treasure. A digital miracle. A meme that held magical powers over my Mom's amusement. I would frame it if I had to, plaster it all over the house if it meant keeping her laughter around.

"Can I see it?" I asked, my eagerness breaking through my attempt to sound calm.

With a glint of amusement in her eyes, Mom handed me her phone. On the screen was a picture of a chubby toddler, legs pumping furiously as he ran, arms flailing in pure, unrestrained delight. The caption read, "When I hear someone say they're going to the bookstore. I'm coming! I'm coming! I'm coming."

It wasn't just the meme, I realized then it was the simple, silly joy of it that brought her back to life for a moment. And there, with my toe throbbing and my heart swelling, I made myself a promise. Whatever it took, I would find more moments like this to keep her laughter alive in our home.

"That's absolutely adorable," I said, unable to suppress a grin.

"That's just how Jacob looked as a baby. I miss that boy. How do I send this to him? He'll get a kick out of it," Mom mused, a hint of longing in her voice.

"I'm sure he will. Here, I'll do it," I offered, seizing the chance to help.

Taking her phone, I saved the meme, pinning it to her gallery's top, so she'd see it often, and sent it to Jacob on Messenger. When I handed her phone back, Mom's eyes sparkled with gratitude as she reached out, clasping my hand. In that silent moment, words became unnecessary. Time seemed to pause, and in the quiet between us, we shared a rare joy. Right there, in our familiar kitchen, I was reminded how love and laughter could bridge any distance.

Unable to resist, I typed a private message to Jacob, explaining how that simple meme had sparked Mom's first genuine laugh in months. My fingers flew over the screen, carried by excitement and the relief of hearing that sound again. It was a triumph after endless days, weeks, and months of worry, pain, and uncertainty.

I hit send, watching the message disappear into the digital ether, hoping that when Jacob read it, he'd feel even a hint of the joy I felt in that moment.

With renewed spirits, we went about our day, but I felt lighter, buoyed by the memory of Mom's laughter. That little meme, as simple as it was, had reignited something in her, and it would forever be etched in my heart. I could picture Jacob all the way in the Philippines, opening his Messenger, seeing the meme, and reading my note. I could almost see the smile spreading across his face.

In the days that followed, I scoured the internet for every funny book meme, every chubby baby meme, even a few classic cat memes for good measure. Dad had always loved those, and while Mom hadn't been as taken with them before, she appreciated them now simply because he had. I sent her anything that might make her smile: texts, emails, Messenger posts, always hoping for another chuckle, maybe even another laugh. And she did smile, sometimes rolling her eyes, sometimes laughing out loud. But each time, her face lit up with that warmth that made every effort worth it.

I shared Aunt Megan's *little miracle meme* with the whole family. Uncle Jared suggested starting a group chat, and soon, our chat thread was alive with everyone's updates. Aunt Megan sent photos of each recipe she tried from a new cookbook, sharing updates nearly every day. Mom and I even tried a couple ourselves. It was fun knowing our family in Utah was eating the same meals. And, of course, we shared memes, silly, heartwarming, anything that kept the conversation flowing. The thread became more than a chat. It felt like a lifeline, a thread of love binding us together across the miles. It was an unspoken promise to stay close.

I cherished that connection, maybe more than anyone else. Though I'd never admitted it, I'd been afraid we might drift away from Dad's side of the family after he passed. Sometimes, I even fell asleep with that fear heavy on my mind, wondering if we'd lose that piece of him along with him.

One Sunday evening, after church, I scrolled through my phone and found the latest meme from Jacob. It was evening here, but already the next morning for him on his p-day. He hadn't called yet, but his message said he'd be reaching out soon, now that he had Messenger up and running. I laughed, loving how he always found the best scripture memes, keeping us all smiling from halfway across the world.

"Hey, Mom," I called from the living room.

She peeked out of her bedroom, calling back, "What's up?"

"Have you checked Messenger? Jacob's already awake. He sent a funny meme."

"No, I haven't yet." Her curiosity piqued, she stepped closer. "Pull it up. Let me see."

I handed her my phone, still displaying Jacob's message. She read aloud, "'Why were the Lamanites' legs sore? Because of all the knee fights.'" She paused, her expression shifting, and then burst into laughter. "Oh, my goodness, that is hilarious!"

Mom leaned back, pressing a hand to her chest as girlish giggles spilled out, each one warmer and more genuine than the last. Her laughter filled the room, warm and contagious, and I felt grateful for the power of joy, its unique way of healing and bringing us closer. In that moment, I longed to share everything with Jacob, to let him know how much his little messages meant to us and the difference they were making. My fingers hovered over the screen, ready to type it all out to him.

Just then, Mom's phone chimed, and a notification popped up on my phone screen. Startled, I looked down and saw his name flashing on Messenger.

"Jacob's calling!" I gasped, hardly believing my luck at his timing. I tapped the video call button, and Mom tapped hers also and leaned closer, her face lighting up with excitement as we waited for him to appear.

Jacob's face filled the screen, his smile as wide as ever. "Mom! Noah! It's so good to see you guys!"

Mom reached out, almost instinctively, as if she could pull him through the screen for a hug. "Oh, Jacob, honey, it's so good to see your face. How are you? You look great!"

He chuckled, adjusting his earbuds. "I'm doing well! Actually, I have some news. I got transferred! I'm in the southern part of the mission now. It's a beautiful rural area in Quirino Province. There are fields and mountains everywhere."

"Wow, that sounds incredible," I said, imagining the lush landscapes he was seeing every day. "What's it like?"

"It's really peaceful and green. We've been meeting tons of people and teaching loads of lessons, which is amazing. But... honestly, it's been a bit frustrating too. Despite all the conversations and connections, no one is coming to church," Jacob admitted, a hint of disappointment crossing his face.

Mom's expression softened, and she nodded knowingly. "That sounds tough, Jacob. I know it can feel discouraging when the effort you're putting in doesn't show the results you're hoping for."

"Exactly! I mean, they're kind, and they listen. They even seem interested. But when Sunday rolls around, it's like there's no follow-through." He sighed, running a hand through his hair. "I'm trying not to get discouraged, but it's hard."

Mom reached forward, her voice filled with warmth and encouragement. "Jacob, remember, the Lord sees the effort you're making, even if it doesn't show up in ways you expect. Noah and I will do a special fast for you, and we'll pray that the people's hearts will be softened. Sometimes, it's all about showing them love and service. The best way to reach them might just be by being there for them."

"Serve them," I added, nodding. "Offer to do things for them. If they see how much you care, maybe their hearts will open. It might take time, but they'll feel it."

Jacob's face relaxed, a bit of the frustration melting away. "Thanks, guys. That really helps. I'll keep at it and focus on the service. Hopefully, it'll make a difference."

"We know it will. Just remember, you're planting seeds. It might take a while, but you're making a difference, even if you can't see it just yet," Mom encouraged.

"Thank you. I needed that reminder. Oh! I have to tell you about something cool we're doing today. We're going to this place called Susong Dalaga Eco Park in Cabarroguis. It's these hills... uh," he faltered, clearly embarrassed. "They're shaped, um, kind of like a woman's—uh, well, you know."

Mom laughed, amused. "Like a woman's chest?"

Jacob's face turned pink, and he nodded, embarrassed. "Yeah, exactly. But it's a popular spot, and they have this panoramic viewpoint up top, so you can see the whole area. There are 180 steps to get up there. We're going as a District."

"Wow, it sounds amazing! Take pictures if you can," I added.

Jacob described one of his recent days in vivid detail: how he and his companion had felt prompted to walk an incredibly long distance through the rural landscape. They followed their instincts, trekking over hills and narrow paths with breathtaking views, only to realize that not a single person was around. After hours of walking, exhaustion set in, and as evening approached, they had to call a member from the ward to come pick them up. It was getting very dark, and they had no light. When the member arrived, he mentioned needing help to give a blessing to a Nanay nearby. As it turned out, they were already close to her home, and Jacob felt that maybe their journey had been guided by something more than they realized.

Now six months into his mission, Jacob was settling into his third area, the beauty of the Philippines continuing to captivate him. Though he wasn't quite fluent in Tagalog, he could communicate fairly well, throwing in Tagalog words as he spoke to us about his experiences. He described how every lesson they taught brought new word challenges, but also a deeper understanding of the language. He shared, with excitement, the names of families they were working with, mindful of their stories as he balanced his own frustrations with the slow progress in bringing them to church. Yet, despite the hurdles, Jacob remained hopeful, believing that each encounter held the potential for change, just as his mission was changing him. The warmth of the Filipino culture surrounded him, and he felt grateful for the love and support he received from home, which strengthened his resolve to serve and connect with the people near him.

Mom told Jacob about the late frost and how it had reduced this year's cherry crop, a reminder of the challenges at home but also of the resilience our family had always shown. She recounted how the contracts were a blessing that eased her mind. I assured Jacob that Mom was making solid progress in physical therapy, and with each session, her steps were growing steadier and faster. Jacob smiled as Mom relayed the love and well-wishes from our grandparents and extended family, each one eager for Mom to send them the weekly Jacob update after our chat with him. Everyone was proud of the work he was doing so far away. These little updates with Jacob grounded me, filling the distance between us with a renewed sense of connection and purpose.

Jacob glanced at his watch, letting out a small sigh. "I'd love to keep talking, but I only have an hour."

Mom nodded, her expression tinged with both pride and sadness. "We understand. Thank you for calling us, Jacob. We'll keep praying and fasting for you. Just remember how much we love you and that we're with you every step of the way."

"Thanks, Mom. Thanks, Noah. I love you guys. And don't worry, I'm going to serve these people with everything I've got."

We exchanged goodbyes, waving and blowing kisses until the screen faded to black. After the call ended, the room felt full, as though Jacob's spirit was still there with us, strengthening us with the same hope and love we'd shared with him.

I moved to the couch and started an email to Jacob, pouring out the story of this past week. I couldn't share Mom's reaction to the meme in person since she had been on the call, so I described it instead, how those silly images had unexpectedly lifted us from the lingering shadows of grief, helping us find our footing again. It felt as though Dad, watching over us, had nudged us to see life's blessings once more, even amid our sorrow.

I told him how those simple jokes had become a turning point, each one chipping away at the heaviness that had hung over us. For so long, Mom had been trapped in sadness, but now a quiet strength was returning to her. Her spirit rekindled bit by bit, as though she'd found the courage to step from grief's shadow and embrace hope and joy once more.

Each day, her resilience grew, a gentle but steady healing that touched everything she did. The light in her eyes grew warmer, her steps lighter, her laughter freer. She engaged with the world again, finding new meaning in each day. I, too, felt a sense of relief, no longer worrying each time I left, knowing grief wouldn't overwhelm her in my absence. She was reclaiming her strength, independence, and hope.

As days became weeks, our home transformed. What was once shrouded in loss now felt illuminated by a growing light, a light of love, laughter, and faith. Warmth returned to fill every corner, reminding us that life could blossom again. And as I sent that email, I hoped Jacob would feel a piece of this joy, a spark of the resilience he'd helped reignite in us.

CHAPTER TWENTY

The calendar on my bedroom wall read late August, just a few days shy of four months since Mom returned home. Life had settled into a comfortable routine, each day flowing into the next. Yet beneath the surface of this blissful normalcy, a heavy burden weighed on my young shoulders, casting a shadow over my newfound stability.

Every day, when I retrieved the mail, a wave of anxiety washed over me. The bills kept piling up, and I felt increasingly overwhelmed, unsure how to navigate the mounting financial pressure. It all started innocently enough with an electric bill that arrived late last month. I snuck it into my room and made a call, but the utility company refused to speak with me since I was a minor and not listed on the account. In a moment of desperation, I even tried to deepen my voice and call back, but that ploy fell flat. Determined to take matters into my own hands, I drove to the PUD and paid the bill in person, telling a little white lie about Mom sending me with her debit card. Surely, that couldn't hurt, right?

Paying bills had become almost routine for me, whether in person, over the phone, or online, but it was a routine tinged with dread. I even considered setting everything up on auto-pay until last week when I checked Mom's bank account and was met with a stark reality: money was going out but nothing was coming in. The balance was so low that we could hardly afford gas or groceries. With a heavy heart, I stashed the rest of the bills in my desk drawer, hoping they might somehow pay themselves.

Every day, sometimes twice, I opened the bank app, to check the balance. I clung to the hope that a miraculous deposit might appear, just enough to cover the overdue bills. The weight of our financial struggles and my own emotional turmoil felt like a ravenous beast, gnawing at my spirit, leaving me empty and desperate. I did not know how to keep us afloat, and I couldn't bring myself to worry Mom. Dad had always been the breadwinner while Mom stayed home to homeschool Jacob and me. Now, I realized I had no plan for how our finances would survive another day.

With a heavy heart, I sank to my knees beside the bed, seeking solace in prayer. I clasped my hands together and shut my eyes, noticing that familiar vulnerability creep in. "Dear Lord," I murmured, "I feel so lost right now. I want to be there for Mom, but I just don't know how. We're out of money, and I can't see a way to support us. I don't want to worry her. She's getting better, but not enough to work. Heavenly Father, what should I do? You know what we need. Please help us. In Jesus' name, Amen."

When I opened my eyes, I still didn't have a plan, but a wave of peace washed over me. It was fleeting, yet it reminded me I wasn't alone in this struggle. God was listening, and somehow, I knew He would guide me through the chaos.

Another week passed, and I continued to support Mom the best I could, but the evidence of our struggles kept piling up in my desk drawer. I collected the mail daily, hiding the bills from her. It wasn't just local bills anymore; medical bills had arrived, too. The burden felt heavier with each envelope I tucked away.

After Grandpa Wilde left, Mom had asked about the household bills twice, but I told her that Grandpa Evans had everything under control. She hadn't inquired again, and I hoped she wouldn't. The thought of bringing her worries back into the light felt unbearable.

I considered calling Ruth to ask if I could start working again. Mom was well enough to be left alone now, but even if I started working again at the farmstand, it wouldn't solve the immediate problem. That position was only part-time, and I realized that even if I could return to work, it wouldn't be enough to cover the mounting bills. I was already too late to pay the current bills, and things were bound to get worse before they got better. With school about to start, the weight of my responsibilities grew heavier. If I wanted to finish my senior year, I couldn't work full-time, especially when I needed to focus on my education and graduation. The thought of balancing a full-time job with my studies and helping Mom continue her physical therapy felt impossible, and I couldn't help but wonder how I could keep everything afloat. Unsure of what else to do, I dialed Grandpa Evans, my heart racing as I explained our situation.

"Hasn't your dad's life insurance money arrived?" he asked, his voice laced with concern.

"No," I replied, trying to keep my tone steady. Though the deposit hadn't come through yet, the thought that relief might be just around the corner gave me a small measure of peace.

"What day is it?" he muttered, and I could hear him working through the dates. "Let's see, the accident was in February. It's the end of August now, nearly a full seven months." His voice sharpened with urgency. "It should have arrived a couple of weeks ago. Let me make a few calls and get back to you. Noah, if there's ever a next time, don't wait so long before you call me. You can't let anything go past its due date. Do you understand?"

I mumbled my agreement, a mix of relief and embarrassment washing over me for not asking for grandpa's help sooner.

An hour later, Grandpa called back, frustration plain in his voice. "The nerve of those people. They said they never received your dad's death certificate. It took me forty-five minutes to prove I had sent it five months ago. You should see a deposit within three days. I want everything paid the moment the deposit is made, and if for some reason it doesn't show up, you call me, and I'll catch up all the bills."

"Thanks, Grandpa," I said, grateful for his help.

"Noah, listen carefully. You need to understand that your and Jacob's portions of the life insurance policy will be placed in trusts for each of you. You'll have access to them when you turn twenty-one. The sums aren't huge, as your mother was the primary beneficiary, but you each get some. You should have enough to cover your mission and college, and depending on how extensive your education is, perhaps there will even be a little to give you a head start in life. Your mom will receive a monthly annuity for twenty years. I thought this would be better than a lump sum. The amount is more than enough to cover her monthly bills at the orchard, so she should be able to save some money over the next couple of years until you or Jacob take over, and she finds a place elsewhere."

"Move? Mom can't move. This is her house," I protested, the thought striking a nerve.

"Noah, it's not, really. Your dad's will and the business stipulations mandate the orchard remain within the Wilde family. Under those terms, Jacob now owns the orchard, the house, and the land until you turn eighteen, at which point you'll receive your share. Technically, your mom is an Evans, so she doesn't have a claim on Wilde Growers."

"I hate it, but I know you're right. We all understand how it works, even Mom."

"Correct. Not just your mom, but your grandma and I understand it too. I'm making my decisions based on that and choosing what will be best for Leah."

"Grandpa, Jacob and I would never abandon Mom."

"I know you won't, but Noah, you'll have your own wives and families someday. Your mom will need her own space."

"No, Grandpa, she'll live with one of us. I'll talk to my future wife about Mom living with us, and I won't marry her if she has a problem with it. I'm certain Jacob will agree."

Grandpa chuckled, a hint of amusement in his voice. "Alright, you do that. But in the meantime, I'll plan for your mom to eventually have her own place nearby."

"If you think that's best," I replied, trying to sound more confident than I felt, though a knot of anxiety tightened in my stomach.

"I do. Now, let's talk about the orchard. Your Grandpa Wilde spoke with the orchard conglomerate. As I understand it, the lease runs through the end of this year until the start of the next season, but then it'll need to be renewed. They have the option not to renew, but Allen says they've turned a profit every year so far, so he's confident they will even with the late frost this year. He's handling all the orchard business on Jacob's and your behalf. Jacob won't be back from his mission before the documents need signing, but Allen has power of attorney until Jacob returns or you turn eighteen."

"I understand. I'm a year shy of being able to sign it myself."

"That's right," Grandpa said. "But we've got you covered. You and your mom don't have anything to worry about, as long as you don't let something like the electric bill slip through the cracks."

"Gotcha. Thanks, Grandpa," I replied, with a mix of gratitude and the heaviness of responsibility I now carried.

"There's one more thing I need to tell you," Grandpa said, his voice steady but tinged with concern. "The insurance companies are still piecing everything together and bickering among themselves. When they finally settle, there should be a substantial sum for you and your mom. But Noah, it could take a year or even two before they resolve this mess. And believe me, it is a mess. The only thing they can agree on so far is that the accident wasn't your dad's fault."

"Dad's fault? Of course it's not! It was the white car's fault! They hit the back tire of the big rig in front of us and jackknifed it!" I shot back, my frustration bubbling to the surface.

"That's the general consensus," Grandpa replied, his tone calm.

"I saw it happen. I even remember what I said when it happened. Do you think it would help if I gave a statement?" My heart raced with the urge to help in any way I could.

"There's enough evidence already, and I want to keep you out of this if I can. Understand, the insurance companies are at each other's throats. The wreck involving your family occurred over a mile from where the white car first hit the truck's tire. Your family were the only ones injured, and your father is being hailed as a hero. He slowed the big truck behind him, giving everyone behind it time to react. There were five more cars following the second semi-truck, carrying seventeen people, from infants to folks in their seventies. Everyone says your dad would have stopped your truck from colliding with the jackknifed one if it hadn't been for the second semi-truck rear-ending you so many times."

"I mean, technically, that's true. Dad had us almost stopped twice. We could have avoided the accident if we hadn't been struck from behind by that massive truck. Good old Black could have stopped anyone else but that beast. If the roads hadn't been so slick, I bet Dad could have stopped him too," I said, my frustration welling up.

Grandpa sighed, gathering his thoughts before continuing. "The white car's insurance is fighting to separate their incident from the larger one. They want to claim their driver's collision was a separate event involving only the white car. If they win, the fault shifts to the driver of the semi-truck that hit you. That driver has already admitted to the sequence of events after the white car's accident, but he refuses to accept full responsibility. Since the accident, he's been on paid leave, unable to drive until this is sorted out. Technically, the driver of the white car is also barred from driving, but it doesn't affect their livelihood like it does for the truck driver. If he's found at fault, he'll lose his job, have to pay back half of his paid leave, and it gets even worse from there. Your parents' insurance has already filed claims for vehicular homicide for your dad, critical injury for your mom, and serious injury for you. Everyone's lawyered up and ready to fight this to the end. Noah, I couldn't do it all, so I hired a lawyer to work with your family's insurance. He is looking after yours and your mom's best interest."

"Grandpa, none of this is fair," I said, the weight of the situation bearing down on my chest.

"No, it's not. But that's the reality we're dealing with."

"That poor man," I murmured, thinking of the truck driver caught in this crossfire. "And Grandpa, thanks for taking care of us. I couldn't have done any of this."

"You're welcome. Listen, none of the insurance companies want to be the one to pay," Grandpa explained. "All five witness drivers and the police confirm that your dad's actions kept the other vehicles from getting caught up in the chaos. With the low visibility and the steep grade, those drivers wouldn't have had enough time to slow down without the extra time your dad bought them by trying to slow the second semi-truck. He saved so many lives that day, yet none of that seems to matter in the context of the lawsuit. Four of the five drivers are testifying in court, and every written statement in the police report matches up. The fifth driver is a minor, and her parents want to keep her out of the proceedings as much as possible. I agree with that decision. With enough witnesses willing to testify, we'll be fine without her in court. She's just a few months older than you, poor girl. Her family is from Cle Elum, and she was getting some winter driving experience with her dad and three siblings. They were going to her aunt's house, but that's neither here nor there."

Grandpa gathered his thoughts before continuing, "No one but the lead truck and the truck following you saw the white car hit because of the snow wall, but they all witnessed it veer off the road and land in the ditch. When the snow wall broke up with the jackknifed truck, speeds slowed dramatically. Plus, you were coming out of a turn, so everyone behind had an unobstructed view. They all watched the accident unfold over an absurd length of time, but none of them could do anything to stop it. I've been in court, and the testimonies are incredibly emotional and detailed. No matter how many times I hear them, or which driver speaks, I still get choked up. Grandma came with me once, but she had to leave halfway through and hasn't returned since."

"I understand. The events still haunt my dreams, occasionally," I admitted.

Grandpa's voice softened. "How are you holding up otherwise? How's your mom doing?"

I spent the next ten minutes updating him on our progress. I explained how Mom and I were managing and the small ways we were rebuilding our lives. When we finally ended the call, I felt a strange mix of relief and deep sorrow for the truck driver. This entire ordeal could ruin his life. Silently, I prayed that the truth would come out. If only the driver of the white car, who in my mind was at fault, would just own up to it. Maybe the truck driver's life wouldn't be shattered.

As I finished my prayer, a troubling thought crept into my heart: *Who was driving the white car? What would placing the blame on them do to their life?* The realization hit me hard, catching my breath in my throat. I hadn't considered that before. To ease my troubled mind, I whispered another prayer, placing everything in God's hands. I resolved to trust that the fault would land where it needed to, for the best outcome for everyone involved, even those who seemed most hurt by it. God has a way of turning tragedies into miracles, and I had to believe He was doing that here.

When I finished my prayer and opened my eyes, a profound calm settled over me.

THE FOLLOWING SUNDAY, BISHOP visited us after church. He was a man of gentle strength and unwavering kindness. He carried the weight of his responsibilities with grace and patience. When he arrived, he took a seat on our well-worn couch in the cozy living room, the sweet aroma of Mom's fresh apricot cobbler wafting through the air, a reminder of the comfort we still found in small pleasures.

"Sister Wilde, I've been thinking about your family and wanted to discuss something important," he began. His voice was steady yet tender.

Mom and I exchanged uncertain glances, a mix of curiosity and apprehension flooding the space between us.

"When your brother-in-law was here in February, he mentioned that your family wanted to hold a memorial service for Adam. He said it would happen once you and Noah were well enough to attend. Is that still your wish? If so, I think we should do it before winter. Would you like some help organizing it?"

I turned to Mom, her eyes shimmering. She took my hand, her grip steady and reassuring, grounding me.

"Thank you, Bishop. We truly appreciate your offer, but we've decided not to hold a memorial. Noah and I have made our peace. We visited Adam's grave on our own, and I'd prefer not to reopen those wounds," Mom replied, her voice soft but firm.

Bishop nodded, his smile reflecting understanding and compassion. "Of course, Sister Wilde. Is there anything else you need? How is Jacob doing in the Philippines?"

Mentioning my older brother brought a surge of pride and hope into the room. Jacob was thriving as a missionary, sharing his love of Christ, and making a difference in a faraway place. Mom's face lit up as she spoke about Jacob, her voice growing brighter and more animated with each recounting of his letters and experiences. She painted vivid pictures of his adventures, her spirit visibly lifting.

As the conversation shifted, I shared my plans for the upcoming school year. I talked about my online homeschool classes and my seminary schedule, explaining the subjects I'd be studying and my intention to return to my job at the beginning of September. Ruth, my boss, had made it crystal clear she couldn't wait to have me back, insisting that the holiday season would be only half as successful without me there to charm the customers.

With each shared detail, I felt a sense of renewal blossom within me, a reminder that even amid heartache, life still held opportunities for growth and joy.

CHAPTER TWENTY-ONE

THE DAILY GRIND OF seminary, school, and eventually work settled into a new rhythm, a cadence that felt both comforting and monotonous. When I turned seventeen, my senior year officially began. I poured my energy into my faith, my studies, and building up my bank account so I could afford frequent dates. My dating life was the one aspect of my routine that seemed to change constantly, and I relished that unpredictability. Each date brought new experiences, laughter, and the occasional awkward moment that made for great stories later when I told Mom. I dated my way up one side of the valley and down the other, never going out with the same girl twice. Girls from Leavenworth, Cashmere, and Wenatchee filled my Friday and Saturday nights, their laughter blending with the cool and crisp fall air. Yet, no matter how enjoyable those dates were, something always felt amiss. My thoughts inevitably drifted back to one girl, Shelby Thurston.

Every Sunday when I saw her, a familiar tension knotted in my stomach, and I had to bite my tongue to keep from asking her out again. I wanted to, but I found myself thinking about the long-term, about eternity. If I asked Shelby out too often during our teenage years and things went awry, I feared I wouldn't have a chance with her after my mission. So, I held back, waiting for both of us to grow up a bit more.

Even though we weren't going on more dates, our friendship blossomed naturally. Since my family's accident, we'd grown incredibly close, finding solace in a few late-night phone calls and whispered conversations at church, seminary, youth activities, and Riverbend Farmstand, where we both worked. I knew she cared about me, and I felt the same way. Honestly, I don't think I would have been strong enough to get through that first Christmas without Dad and Jacob if it hadn't been for her unwavering support. Shelby was my anchor, the light that guided me through the shadows, and without her, I'm not sure I could have emerged intact. Once we survived that hollow Christmas, everything else seemed a little easier to manage. We even navigated the one-year anniversary of the accident and Jacob's mission milestone without a major breakdown. Or so I thought, until I realized the next holiday would be even harder: Valentine's Day, a day dedicated to love.

A few days before Valentine's Day, a year after the accident, Mom faced a physical setback that plunged her into a deep depression. It started with small things, a missed appointment, a skipped meal, but quickly escalated into a pervasive fog that enveloped her. We might have bounced back quickly if it had been just a physical ailment, but mental struggles are never that simple. Each day, I watched helplessly as she spiraled further into despair, her laughter fading like the sunlight behind a thick curtain. I felt myself slipping back toward the darkness of that awful day when everything changed, every shadow reminding me of the weight of our loss.

The evening after her complete breakdown was the hardest. After I finally managed to settle her, I found myself alone in my room, the walls closing in around me. I cried until my throat felt raw, my heart aching with a mix of grief and anger. I mentally screamed an angry prayer to God, demanding answers that never came. "Why, God? Why can't we just be happy again?" I spoke into the void, tears streaming down my cheeks. When I remembered my experience at the hospital, I repented and placed everything in my Savior's hands. A feeling of peace washed over me.

For the sake of our well-being, I swallowed my pride and dialed Grandma and Grandpa Evans for help. Their warmth felt like a lifeline, and they arrived at the house less than an hour later, their presence filling the cold, empty spaces that loneliness had occupied. As soon as they stepped through the door, I collapsed into Grandma's arms, sobbing hot, painful tears of grief and defeat.

"There, there, sweetheart," she murmured, her voice a gentle balm. "You're not alone in this. We'll get through it together." She settled onto the couch, pulling my head into her lap as if I were still a child. Her fingers gently stroked my hair as I lost all sense of time as she sang sweet primary songs from my youth. The world outside faded away, leaving only the soothing rhythm of Grandma's fingers against my scalp.

Meanwhile, Grandpa took charge, stepping in with the strength I desperately needed, and I let him guide us through the chaos. "Let's make this a safe space for her," he said, his voice steady, filled with authority and compassion. He began organizing her bedroom, disposing of the remnants of neglect, such as empty dishes, scattered clothes, as if removing the physical clutter would help banish the emotional chaos that had taken root. "We need to create an environment where your mom feels loved and supported," he explained. Then he glanced up at me with a reassuring nod. "It starts with us."

Over the next few days, my grandparents worked tirelessly to help us navigate the darkness. They filled the house with laughter, memories, and simple routines. Grandma brought out her favorite recipes, filling the kitchen with the warm scent of baking bread, while Grandpa played old music, the sweet sounds of familiar songs echoing through the rooms. "Remember this one?" he chuckled, glancing at me. "Your mom used to dance around the kitchen to it. Let's crank it a bit." As soon as the volume hit 100, Grandpa started tapping his feet and waving his hands in what I suspected was supposed to be a dance. He may have business acumen, but dancing wasn't his forte.

Two days later, when Grandpa Wilde walked in, I broke down all over again. *How did Grandpa Evans know to bring him? How did he sense our desperate need for the strength of our beloved Wilde patriarch?* It was as if he could read the unspoken thoughts swirling in our minds, feelings we hadn't even realized we had held. The moment he entered, a shift occurred; the air seemed lighter, filled with the comforting weight of history and resilience.

"Let's go walk the trees," he said, his voice a gravelly whisper that carried the weight of wisdom. To him, "walking the trees" meant roaming through the beloved grounds of the orchard, checking on the health of the trees and determining what the ground needed. He always walked the trees when he was the orchardist, and now we were doing it, even in the frigid winter air. I nodded, grateful for the distraction. As we stepped outside, the crisp air hit my face like a gentle slap, invigorating yet grounding. "Sometimes, it's the small steps that lead us out of the dark," he said, glancing sideways at me.

In that moment of despair, we craved reminders of Dad and Jacob, and no one conjured their memories more vividly than Grandpa Wilde. "You know, your dad would always tell me that the best thing we can do in tough times is to lean on each other. He believed in family, and we're here for you. All your family is here for you whenever you need us. I mean it. Anytime."

That was the closest I came to giving up and admitting defeat. I wondered if I could truly take care of Mom and hold our fractured lives together. But the stubbornness rooted deep within me kept pushing me forward, urging me not to surrender. With my grandparents' love and guidance, we persevered.

Together, we pulled Mom back from the edge of her pain and suffering. Slowly, we chipped away at the walls her depression had built around her, reminding her of the warmth of our love. With every shared meal, every laugh, every story of the past, we led her away from the brink of heartache and despair. We learned to breathe again, breaking through the dark days, one small victory at a time.

Just before Shelby's seventeenth birthday, she confronted me about something I'd suspected was coming for a while. "Why haven't you asked me out again? You've been on plenty of dates with other girls since ours, and I know how your family's dating rules work," she asked, her voice a mix of curiosity and hurt.

I took a deep breath, steeling myself for the conversation I had been dreading. "Shelby, you're not the type of girl I want to date." Her face fell, and I could see the hurt wash over her like a shadow. She pulled away, but I grabbed her near her elbow, holding her in place. "Wait! I said that badly. Before you go, let me explain," I begged. Panic rose when I noticed Shelby's tears pooling. "You're the type of girl I want to marry. I need to get all my awkward dating fails out of the way with girls I don't care about, so that after my mission, I can dazzle you with dating perfection."

She swallowed hard, but then she gave me a small, tentative smile, nodding as she twisted her lips into the most adorable pout I'd ever seen.

"When are you going on your mission? You turn eighteen in less than two months. You haven't mentioned submitting your papers yet," she asked, a hint of concern lacing her words.

"I'm not leaving right away. In my old world, I would have already submitted my mission papers and maybe even received my call by now. I'd be packing my bags, getting ready to head off to some far-off place. But I've decided to wait until Jacob gets back before I leave. He still has five more months before he comes home. My plan is to submit my papers next spring."

"I think that's smart. Then Jacob can be here for your mom," she said, her expression softening.

"Shelby, I'm glad you understand. Mom is so important to me, and after last winter's breakdown, I can't risk leaving her alone. I don't know what my leaving would do to her. If Jacob is here, he can take my place and make sure she's okay."

Her eyes softened further as my words sank in. The tension in her shoulders eased, and she squeezed my hand, grounding me in that moment. "So, I'm the kind of girl you want to marry?" she repeated, a small, genuine smile spreading across her face, igniting a warmth in my chest.

"Yeah, Shelby, you are," I said, as my nerves calmed down a bit. "I want to get all the clumsy first-date stuff out of the way, so that with you, I'll have a clue what I'm doing. I want it to be... right."

Her smile grew, and she let out a soft laugh, the sound like music to my ears. "You really think that much about the future, huh?"

"With you, I do," I admitted, a warmth spreading in my chest. "I'm thinking about what comes next and what's best for both of us. If I rush things now and screw it up, I'll regret it forever."

She looked down, blushing, then met my gaze with newfound determination. "You know, Noah, I think that's... sweet. Actually, it's more than sweet. It's kind of perfect. I've always thought that when you care about someone, you want to do what's best for them, even if it means waiting. I've seen the way you've been there for your mom, and I know you'd be that way with me, too. I guess, in a way, I'm glad I'm not just another one of those Friday night dates."

I let out a relieved breath and rolled the tension from my shoulders. "I'm glad you get it. I've never thought of you as just another date. You've always been more to me than that."

She leaned in closer, and her smile turned playful. "So, are you telling me I'm worth waiting for?"

"Yeah, Shelby, you're worth waiting for," I replied with a grin.

She laughed again, the sound light and full of hope. "Good. Because I think you're worth waiting for too, Noah. I'll be here when you get back from your mission. I know you don't even have your call yet, so this might be jumping the gun, but can I write to you while you're on your mission?"

"I'd like that." I couldn't help but smile at that, and for a moment, the weight of everything, the past year, my changed mission plans, the uncertainty of the future, lifted. "Yes, Shelby, I think I'd like that a lot."

As we stood there, I felt a flicker of hope igniting within me. Maybe this waiting wouldn't just be an exercise of patience, maybe it would also be the beginning of something beautiful.

As the weeks passed, excitement for Jacob's return in less than two months grew alongside the shifting landscape. Just when it seemed the anticipation could not swell any further, the mail brought unexpected news that would alter our holiday season. The insurance settlement arrived just before Christmas, a bittersweet reminder of the life we'd lost and the one we were slowly rebuilding.

Mom opened the large manila envelope stuffed with papers, her hands trembling and her heart pounding as she scanned the contents. The figures danced before her eyes, each one a testament to my father's legacy. The wrongful death settlement for Dad amounted to a staggering $1.5 million. It felt surreal, a sum that could never bring him back but represented the countless lives he had saved through his courageous actions. It was a reminder of the hero he had been.

Mom's critical injury claim came to a substantial $750,000, which covered all future medical costs and reimbursed her past expenses that the insurance had not paid directly. She had spent long days in hospitals and therapy sessions, slowly reclaiming her strength. Given her condition, it was likely she would need periodic treatments for the rest of her life to maintain her mobility.

Then came my settlement, which totaled $500,000 for my severe injuries. I had been hurt physically and emotionally in ways that words could not fully express. The money would help provide for my future, but I'd give up every cent to have just one more day with my dad, to hear his laughter or feel his reassuring presence.

As we sat around the table that evening, the news of the settlements hung in the air, heavy yet hopeful. Mom wiped away tears, a mix of grief and gratitude, as she explained, "It won't bring your father back, but it's a step toward rebuilding our lives. I want to set aside some for Jacob, too. He may not have received a settlement beyond his small portion of the life insurance policy, but I want both of you to have something that can help you in the future."

I sat in silence, my gaze distant, processing the weight of the news. I reached out and squeezed Mom's hand, a silent understanding passing between us. We may have received financial support, but the emptiness left by Dad's absence was something no amount of money could ever fill.

In the weeks that followed, the settlement allowed us to make some long-overdue changes. Mom thought about freshening up a few rooms she had wanted to change for over a decade, but never felt she had the means to do it. She pointed out how the paint was peeling and how the kitchen and bathrooms could use new life, her eyes sparkling with the first glimmer of excitement I'd seen in a long time.

"I can't believe how long I've put off these repairs," she said, surveying the kitchen with newfound energy. "It's time for a change. I'll plan now and start the renovations this spring.

Nothing too big since I won't live here forever. It will be yours or Jacob's home someday, depending on how you two decide to settle the orchard ownership when you're older."

I leaned against the doorframe, a teasing smile on my face. "You can live with me forever, Mom. I'll take care of you."

Mom laughed, shaking her head. "Oh, Noah, that would be awful! I'm too stubborn, and I wouldn't want to interfere with your future marriage."

"Future marriage?" I echoed, feigning shock. "I just figured I'd keep you around for your amazing cooking!"

"You're sweet, but really, I have other dreams. I've always thought those little Bavarian-style homes along the Wenatchee River in Leavenworth are so adorable. I want to save a portion of the settlement for a cottage nearby once you boys are married. Can you imagine waking up every morning to that beautiful view?" Her voice sounded wistful.

"I can see it now. You'd have the best garden, too." I smiled at the vision of her in that cozy cottage.

"Absolutely! I'd fill it with flowers and plenty of vegetables. It would be a little sanctuary."

"I love that for you, Mom. I know it will be perfect."

I asked Grandpa Evans to help me invest my settlement wisely, knowing I would need very little for a few years while I served my mission. I wanted to ensure that my future was secure, to carry a piece of my father's legacy with me, even as I forged my own path.

Overall, we dreamed about the future again, holding on to the hope that Jacob's return would usher in a new chapter for our family, a chapter that could be filled with laughter and light, despite the shadows of our past. Each day brought us closer to that moment, and I yearned for the warmth of his embrace, ready to embrace the possibilities that lay ahead.

IT HAD BEEN TWO long years since Jacob left home. Two years ago, the landscape was buried beneath unforgiving snow. This year, the snow was nominal in comparison. Today frost clung to bare branches and there was a chill in the air that seeped into the frozen ground. Two years since the accident that took our father. Two long years without my older brother, my best friend. A lot had changed since then, and the paths we took led us through rough, uneven terrain.

I had slipped plenty of times along the way, stumbling and falling backward as I tried to climb the steep hills life had thrown in my path. But now, things had finally leveled out, and a new sense of hope filled the air as Jacob's return grew near. Anticipation twisted inside me, stirring up a mix of emotions, hope and excitement, tangled up with a thread of uncertainty that pulled tight around my chest.

Anyone could see the change in Mom. Her heart brimmed with anticipation as she counted down the days until Jacob would step onto the familiar soil of our home again. But as that day approached, doubts crept into my mind. I knew Mom would wrap him in her arms and shower him with all the love she'd been holding back, yet I couldn't help but wonder how his arrival might shift the balance we'd worked so hard to find. *Would seeing him again bring back the pain of the day he left? Would it tear open the wounds we'd tried so hard to heal? Or would it be just as sweet as I hoped? A reunion that finally brought us the peace we'd been longing for with his return.*

Before I could sort out my thoughts, the day arrived. We gathered at the airport, a much larger group than the one that had sent him off. I wasn't the only one who'd been worried about today. Nervous energy buzzed through the crowd, mixing with the sounds of the airport, the blaring announcements, the steady hum of luggage wheels, and the murmur of travelers rushing past us. Every minute dragged on, stretching out endlessly, until finally, Jacob stepped out from the sea of faces.

Mom's eyes lit up, bright as fireworks, the moment she spotted him. Happy tears spilled over as she ran toward him, arms wide open and a slight limp that would forever accompany her gait. Jacob saw her and broke into a run, dragging a carry-on behind him, another pack bouncing at his side. Just before she reached him, he dropped his bags and caught her in his arms, spinning her around and around.

Mom sobbed, and Jacob cried too, tears streaming down his face. My own vision blurred when he set her down and placed the softest, sweetest *Tinker Bell Kiss* on the age spot she hated on her right cheek. Watching their reunion, a swell of joy filled my chest, but beneath it lurked that same knot of caution. Memories of the day he left threatened to rise, dragging me back into those old feelings. I pushed them down, refusing to let them ruin this moment.

Instead, I focused on the way Mom's face shone with pure happiness, how her tears of joy washed away the weariness she'd carried for so long. I let myself believe we could keep this peace. Maybe this was our chance to write a new story together, one where the shadows of our past stayed behind us. I let myself hope that, perhaps, we were headed for a new version of a happily ever after.

Jacob held Mom for what felt like forever, his emotions spilling into every second. I couldn't stand back any longer. I stepped forward, wrapping my arms around both of them. Jacob turned and kissed me on the cheek, just like he had with Mom, his embrace now including me and tightening around us. For the first time in what seemed like forever, the three of us stood together, heads pressed close, holding on as if we might never let go.

Time slipped away as we clung to that moment. I don't know how long we stood there, but eventually, another pair of brawny arms joined our embrace.

"Hi, Grandpa!" Jacob exclaimed, looking up in surprise. He hadn't expected anyone other than Mom and me to be there.

But that was just the beginning of his surprise. Not only had Grandpa and Grandma Evans shown up, but our entire Wilde family had made the trip. They'd flown in from Utah, arriving at the airport a couple of hours before Jacob's plane touched down. Grandpa, uncles, aunts, and cousins gathered around us, waiting for their turn to welcome him back with their own hugs.

As we made our way out of the airport, the echoes of laughter followed us like a warm blanket. Jacob shared stories from his mission, his excitement growing with each memory. "I've been in 17 areas and had 21 companions," he said, grinning. "You wouldn't believe the adventures I've had! I even got to visit the Banaue Rice Terraces for my end-of-mission trip. Pictures galore!"

With each story, the air seemed lighter. For the first time in two years, I didn't even notice when we drove past the spot where the accident had happened. The scars of that day would always be there, but right then, in the warmth of Jacob's return, I let myself dream of a future where those shadows didn't darken our path. A future where love and laughter took their place, and the pain of yesterday faded beneath the brightness of tomorrow.

JACOB HAD BEEN HOME for a few weeks now. A sense of normalcy settled back into our lives, but it was a new normal, filled with the promise of fresh beginnings. Less than a month after Jacob came home, he and I talked, and he encouraged me to take a significant step of my own. I submitted my mission papers, anticipation and trepidation for the journey ahead. Just ten days later, the email arrived, a letter from the prophet that carried the weight of my future.

When I opened it at my own party, I could scarcely believe my eyes. I was called to São Paulo South, speaking Portuguese, the exact mission where Dad had served thirty years before. It felt as if God's hand had been in it all along, weaving our lives together in ways I had yet to understand. Tears filled my eyes, and I could almost hear Dad's voice echoing in my mind, urging me to embrace this path. I would walk the very streets my father walked and perhaps even meet people who had known him.

Meanwhile, Jacob took advantage of the BYU-Pathways program, which allowed him to live at home and balance college life with the responsibilities of work and the orchard. He poured himself into his studies and the work that meant so much to our family. That summer, Heather Nielsen returned from her own college experience, ready to earn money for her next year. As Jacob and Heather spent time together, their friendship blossomed into something deeper. I often smiled during my p-day calls when he would tell me how happy they made each other.

When Heather returned to BYU-Idaho that fall, they kept their connection alive, bridging the distance with late-night phone calls and texts that filled the gaps. Their relationship flourished, and at Christmas, when she came home for the break, Jacob surprised everyone with an engagement ring. It felt surreal, knowing that he was taking this step while I was thousands of miles away, serving my mission.

Heather returned to finish the semester and then came back to the valley, taking online courses and planning their wedding, proving to be just as determined as Jacob. They planned a June wedding that promised to be filled with love and joy, although I would miss it. My heart ached at the thought, but I remembered what Dad always said: *"Sacrifice brings blessings."* With ten months left in my mission, I stayed, knowing that the sacrifice of missing my brother's wedding would yield greater blessings for our family.

Mom, with her newfound sense of purpose and joy, had purchased her Bavarian cottage in Leavenworth, fulfilling the dreams she had shared with me. Jacob and Heather's wedding brought everyone together in celebration, reminding us of the beauty that can arise from young love. They made a little video and sent it to me so I could share in their joy. I was so happy that first p-day after their wedding when I got to welcome Heather into our family as my sister-in-law. Her enormous smile and her obvious love for my brother made my heart swell.

As the months passed, the letters from Shelby became my lifeline. Each envelope carried snippets of her life and the world I had left behind. I eagerly anticipated her words, sensing her warmth through every letter, even as I immersed myself in the culture and language of Brazil. It became a source of strength for me, knowing she was waiting, cheering me on from afar.

Finally, the day arrived when I stepped off the plane back home. The familiar sights and sounds washed over me in a comforting wave. I searched the crowd, and there she was, radiant and smiling, standing with my family: Shelby. Time had only deepened my feelings for her, and in that moment, I knew that as soon as I was released, I would make my move. The warmth of her smile wrapped around me like a cherished memory, rekindling every moment we had shared before my mission. It was as if all the distances we had endured vanished in an instant, leaving only a bright future ahead.

Less than a week later, after a whirlwind of emotions and planning, I skipped the formality of dating and proposed to her. The moment felt electric, filled with excitement and nervous energy as I kneeled before her, heart racing. As she said yes, the world seemed to fade away, leaving only our joy. We embraced, laughter spilling from our lips, and in that embrace, I felt the weight of our shared dreams solidify into something tangible. Together, we began planning our wedding, imagining a life filled with love and adventure. Each detail was imbued with meaning, reflecting our unique journey and the bond we had cultivated through years of friendship and yearning.

As I knelt with Shelby at the same altar where my parents had been married, gazing lovingly into her eyes on our wedding day, I felt an overwhelming sense of gratitude for the journey that had brought us to this moment. Our family had endured heartache, but we had also discovered resilience, love, and the promise of brighter days ahead. With each step we took together, I felt my father's presence guiding us, just as he and God had guided me on my mission, reminding me that even through the trials, we could find hope and happiness. In the years that followed, our life unfolded like a vibrant mural, painted with joy and laughter.

Shelby and I welcomed four beautiful children into our lives, each a little miracle that filled our home with energy and love. As we watched them grow, I couldn't help but feel an overwhelming sense of joy knowing they resembled their mama in both spirit and appearance. Their bright smiles, sparkling eyes, and infectious laughter reminded me so much of Shelby, and I was endlessly grateful that they carried her warmth and kindness. I could also see a few Wilde traits in our children. I held great pride knowing I had passed on those traits from my father. Our bustling family was a whirlwind of activity, with laughter echoing through the halls as we navigated the joys and challenges of parenthood together. I pursued a business degree, balancing my studies and managing the orchard contracts alongside Jacob. Together, we forged a path that honored our family's legacy, ensuring that the land we cherished would thrive for generations to come. Jacob and Heather, now parents to six vibrant kids of their own, created an equally joyful household, living at the orchard until their oldest son took over. The bond between our families was strong.

The laughter of grandkids rang like sweet music in my mother's ears, bringing her immense joy as she reveled in her role as a grandmother. Each visit was a celebration of love, and I could see God's handiwork in every moment we shared, each hug, each smile, and each story told around the dinner table. Grandma often told stories about Grandpa, ensuring that every grandchild knew just how much he would have loved them. With each tale, she highlighted the features they shared with him, whether it was a twinkle in their eyes or a quirky sense of humor. Those stories not only connected the past to the present but also fostered a deep sense of belonging and pride in our children. Our life felt blissful and full of miracles, and I knew my father watched over us, a guardian angel guiding us through life's ups and downs. In every triumph and challenge, I felt the warmth of divine love, reassuring me we were never alone, and that our family was exactly where we were meant to be.

Mine and Jacob's children grew up side-by-side, sharing birthdays, holidays, countless adventures, and the deepest family love. I was proud of the next generation of *Wilde Boys* and their sisters.

THE END

Reviews & Books in the Wild

THANK YOU SO MUCH for taking the time to read *Left Behind*. Reviews mean the world to authors and are one of the best ways you can show support. If you enjoyed the story, I would be incredibly grateful if you could leave a review on your favorite platform—it helps connect the book with more readers like you! Thank you for being a part of this journey!

I'd love to see your photos of my books in the wild! Please share and tag me so I can see where my stories are reaching. Every post helps spread the word and makes it easier for others to discover my books. Thank you so much for your support!

Facebook @Emmaline.Hoffmeister
Instagram @Emmaline_Hoffmeister
Pinterest @Emmaline_Hoffmeister
TikTok @Emmaline_Hoffmeister
X @EmmalineAuthor
YouTube @Emmaline_Hoffmeister

About the Author

Emmaline Hoffmeister is the author of eight historical fiction novels and has published nine short stories in various publications worldwide. *Left Behind* marks Emmaline's debut in Christian fiction and her first novel in over a decade.

With degrees in accounting and psychology from Central Washington University and Brigham Young University-Idaho, Emmaline built a 12-year career as a fraud investigator, as well as an accountability, legal compliance, financial, and performance auditor. She later chose to become a stay-at-home mom, focusing on raising her two sons. In 2009, she launched her writing and publishing career.

Emmaline has a heart for adventure and loves to travel with her family. Her novels often feature the places she has lived and traveled, bringing a sense of adventure and authenticity to her stories.

Apple Butter Recipe

A JAR OF HOMEMADE Apple Butter is like a warm embrace from the countryside. Each bite whisks you away to crisp autumn mornings, where the air is cool, the trees blaze with shades of red and gold, and the comforting aroma of simmering apples fills the air. Making Apple Butter is like bottling up the essence of country life—slow, sweet, and deeply satisfying. Whether you slather it on a warm biscuit or enjoy a spoonful straight from the jar (no judgment here!), this rich, spiced spread is the epitome of cozy comfort. So, gather your apples, roll up your sleeves, and let's bring a touch of farm-to-table goodness into your kitchen!

Ingredients:

4 pounds apples (peeled, cored, and sliced)
2 cups white sugar
2 cups brown sugar
1 tablespoon cinnamon
¼ teaspoon ground cloves

Cooking Down the Apples:

Wash, peel, core and slice 4 pounds of apples.

Cook them down with 1/4 cup water in a stock pot, slow cooker, or use a steamer juicer (my preferred method.)

Equipment Preparation:

Prepare your jars by making sure they are clean and hot.

Place a small saucepan on the stove on simmer and insert your lids to soften the seals.

Fill your water bath canner half full with water and place it on the stove on low to begin heating. Do not let it get too hot, just warm it up.

Gather your ladle, jar lifter, lid lifter, chopsticks, clean cloth, and any other needed supplies for canning.

Now that your equipment is ready, it is time to start making apple butter.

Make the Apple Butter:

In a large pot, mix the apples with 2 cups of white sugar, 2 cups of brown sugar, 1 tablespoon of cinnamon, and 1/4 teaspoon of ground cloves.

Simmer until thick.

Fill Jars with the Apple Butter:

Pour or ladle the apple butter into clean, hot, pint-sized jars leaving ¼ inch headspace.

Remove air bubbles and clean the jar rim.

Center the lid on the jar and adjust the band to finger-tip tight. Repeat this process until all of your jars are full.

Process the Jars of Apple Butter:

Process for 10 minutes in a boiling water bath at sea level (adjust time for your elevation).

Remove the jars from the water bath.

Allow them to sit on the counter for 24 hours, then check if they sealed properly. Determine if they sealed properly by checking if the lid center is indented down. If not, place any unsealed jars in the refrigerator and use them right away.

Place the sealed jars in a cool, dry area and use them within the next 3 years. After that, the nutritional value decreases.

Recipe:
https://www.emmalinehoffmeister.blog/apple-butter

Apricot Chipotle Sauce Recipe

Get ready to add a little sweet heat to your life with this irresistible Apricot Chipotle Sauce! Imagine a sun-drenched apricot grove meeting a smoky chipotle pepper at a backyard barbecue—the result is pure magic. This sauce strikes the perfect balance between sweet, smoky, and spicy, with just the right kick to keep your taste buds on their toes. Whether you're slathering it on grilled chicken or adding a bold twist to your tacos, this playful blend will have you dreaming of endless summer days and flavor-packed feasts. Who knew apricots could be so exciting?

Ingredients:

5 cups pitted apricots
1 cup water
¼ cup finely chopped onion
2 large cloves garlic (minced or crushed)
The peel of 1 lemon, grated or zested
1 cup sugar
1 tsp cumin
1 tsp chipotle pepper powder
½ tsp salt
½ tsp coarsely ground white peppercorns
1 ½ cups white wine vinegar

Equipment Preparation:

Prepare your water bath canner by filling it about halfway full with water and place it on the stove on medium heat.

Prepare your jars by making sure they are clean and hot.

Wash whole apricots under cold running water; drain. Cut apricots in half lengthwise. Remove pits. Chop apricots to measure 5 cups.

Peel and finely chop the onion; measure ¼ cup.

Peel garlic and mince.

Make the Apricot Chipotle Sauce:

Add 1 cup water to a saucepan.

Add chopped apricots, onion, lemon zest, and garlic to the saucepan.

Cook over medium-high heat until apricots and onions are tender.

Puree apricot mixture using an immersion blender.

Add all remaining ingredients to the apricot puree.

Bring mixture to a boil over medium-high heat, stirring to prevent sticking.

Fill Jars with the Apricot Chipotle Sauce:

Ladle hot sauce into a prepared jar, leaving ½ inch headspace.

Remove air bubbles and clean the jar rim.

Center the lid on the jar and adjust the band to finger-tip tight. Repeat this process until all of your jars are full.

Process the Jars of Apricot Chipotle Sauce:

Process for 10 minutes in a boiling water bath at sea level (adjust time for your elevation).

Remove the jars from the water bath.

Allow them to sit on the counter for 24 hours, then check if they sealed properly. Determine if they sealed properly by checking if the lid center is indented down. If not, place any unsealed jars in the refrigerator and use them right away.

Place the sealed jars in a cool, dry place and use them within 3 years. After that, the nutritional value decreases.

Recipe:
https://www.emmalinehoffmeister.blog/apricot-chipotle-sauce

Herbed Tomato Jam Recipe

HERBED TOMATO JAM MIGHT just become your new favorite way to capture the essence of a summer harvest in a jar! Tomatoes have a fascinating history—did you know they were once called "love apples" and thought to be poisonous in the 18th century? But this jam is far from dangerous; it's brimming with sweet and savory delight. Imagine the burst of juicy tomatoes, elevated by fresh herbs like basil, oregano, lemon peel, and garlic, creating a symphony of flavors on your taste buds. Whether spread on toast or paired with your favorite cheese, this Herbed Tomato Jam offers a playful twist on traditional preserves, perfect for foodies and anyone who likes to add a touch of pizzaz to their pantry!

Ingredients

3 cups peeled, seeded, chopped tomatoes

4 ½ cups sugar

¼ cup lemon juice

6 tbsp pectin

1 tbsp minced garlic

1 tsp lemon peel

1 tsp basil

1 tsp oregano

½ tsp butter

Equipment Preparation:

Prepare your jars by making sure they are clean and hot.

Place a small saucepan on the stove on simmer and insert your lids to soften the seals.

Fill your water bath canner half full with water and place it on the stove on low to begin heating. Do not let it get too hot, just warm it up.

Gather your ladle, jar lifter, lid lifter, chopsticks, clean cloth, and any other needed supplies for canning.

Making the Herbed Tomato Jam:

Place all ingredients except sugar in a large pot. Bring to a boil.

Add sugar. Return to a rolling boil.

Boil for 1 minute.

Fill Jars with the Herbed Tomato Jam:

Ladle hot jam into a prepared jar, leaving ¼ inch headspace.

Remove air bubbles and clean the jar rim.

Center the lid on the jar and adjust the band to finger-tip tight. Repeat this process until all of your jars are full.

Process the Jars of Herbed Tomato Jam:

Process for 10 minutes in a boiling water bath at sea level (adjust time for your elevation).

Remove the jars from the water bath.

Allow them to sit on the counter for 24 hours, then check if they sealed properly. Determine if they sealed properly by checking if the lid center is indented down. If not, place any unsealed jars in the refrigerator and use them right away.

Place the sealed jars in a cool, dry place and use them within 3 years. After that, the nutritional value decreases.

Recipe:
https://www.emmalinehoffmeister.blog/herbed-tomato-jam

1. King James Version of the Bible – Matthew 25: 40 And the King shall answer and say unto them, Verily I say unto you, Inasmuch as ye have done it unto one of the least of these my brethren, ye have done it unto me.

2. *I AM A CHILD OF GOD Words:* Naomi Ward Randall, 1908–2001. © 1957 IRI. Fourth verse © 1978 IRI | *Music:* Mildred Tanner Pettit, 1895–1977. © 1957 IRI. Arr. by Darwin Wolford, b. 1936. Arr. © 1989 IRI

3. *FAMILIES CAN BE TOGETHER FOREVER Words:* Ruth Muir Gardner, 1927–1999. © 1980 IRI | *Music:* Vanja Y. Watkins, b. 1938. © 1980 IRI

www.ingramcontent.com/pod-product-compliance
Lightning Source LLC
Chambersburg PA
CBHW011552190726
48287CB00010B/2858